THEY CAME
THEY SAW
THEY . . .

Some of them, having set down, stayed where they were. Some, after a time, floated into the air and set about their observations. They cruised back and forth over industrial plants, they circled and recircled cities, they made sweeps of vast stretches of farmlands.

Others sought out forests and settled down to eat. They gobbled up a number of lumber-yards. In the St. Louis area, three of them landed in a parking lot, ate a dozen or so cars, and then took off. They did little actual harm. Most people with whom they came in contact were only marginally inconvenienced; no one was killed. The highway accidents, few of them more than fender-benders, decreased as motorists became accustomed to the sight of the great black boxes floating in the sky, coming at last to pay only slight attention to them.

The Visitors qualified as first-class nuisances . . .

"Clifford D. Simak has produced one of the most engaging novels of alien invasion ever written. Working in the tradition of the best alien contact stories, the author creates believable and likeable human characters who are easy to identify with as they are awestruck, then curious, then charmed by the aliens. Readers of all ages will love this."

—*Library Journal*

THE VISITORS

Clifford D. Simak

A Del Rey Book

BALLANTINE BOOKS • NEW YORK

A somewhat different version of this novel was serialized in *Analog* Magazine.

A Del Rey Book
Published by Ballantine Books

Library of Congress Catalog Card Number: 79-2282

ISBN 0-345-28387-2

Manufactured in the United States of America

First Edition: January 1980

Paperback format
First Edition: November 1980

1. LONE PINE, MINNESOTA

George, the barber, slashed his scissors in the air, snipped their blades together furiously.

"I tell you, Frank, I don't know what goes with you," he said to the man who sat in the barber chair. "I read your article on what the fish and wildlife people did up on the reservation. You didn't seem too upset about it."

"Actually, I'm not," said Frank Norton. "It doesn't mean that much. If people don't want to pay the reservation license, they can go fishing someplace else."

Norton was publisher-editor-advertising manager-circulation manager-general sweeper-out of the Lone Pine *Sentinel*, which had its offices across the street from the barber shop.

"It galls me," said the barber. "It ain't right to give them redskins control over the hunting and fishing rights on the reservation. As if the reservation wasn't a part of the state of Minnesota or even of these here United States. Now a white man can't go fishing on the reservation on the regular state license. He'll have to buy a license from the tribe. And the tribe will be allowed to set up their own rules and regulations. It ain't right, I tell you."

"It shouldn't make much difference to people such as you and I," said Norton. "If we want to go fishing, we have this trout stream right at the edge of town. In the pool below the bridge, there are rainbow of a size to scare you."

"It's the principle of the thing," the barber said. "The fish and wildlife people say the redskins own the land. Their land, hell! It's not their land. We're just letting them live there. When you go to the reservation, they will charge you to fish or hunt; they'll charge you plenty for the license. Probably more than you pay the state. They'll put on their own limits and restrictions. We'll have to live by their laws, laws that we had nothing to do with making. And they'll hassle us. You just watch, they'll hassle us."

"George, you're getting yourself all worked up," said Norton. "I don't think they'll hassle anyone. They'll want people to come up there. They'll do everything they can to attract fishermen. It'll be money in their pockets."

George, the barber, snipped his scissors. "Them goddamn redskins," he said. "Always bellyaching about their rights. And putting on airs. Calling themselves native Americans. Not Indians any more. Oh, Christ, no, now they're native Americans. And saying we took away their land."

Norton chuckled. "Well, when you come right down to it, I would suppose we did take away their land. And no matter how you feel about it, George, they are native Americans. If that is what they want to call themselves, it appears to me that they have a right to. They were here first and we did take away their land."

"We had a right to it," said George. "It was just lying there. They weren't using it. Once in a while, they'd harvest a little wild rice or shoot a duck or kill a beaver for its fur. But they weren't really using the land. They were letting it go to waste. They didn't know how to use it. And we did. So we came and used it. I tell you, Frank, we had a right to take it over and use it. We have the right to use any land that isn't being used. But, even now, we aren't allowed to.

"Take this land over across the river. Big, tall, straight trees that have been standing there since Christ was a pup. Waiting to be used. Somehow, in the early days, the loggers missed them and they're still just standing there, like they been standing almost since creation. Thousands of acres of them, just waiting. Millions of board feet waiting to be sawed. There are lumber companies that want to go in there. They went into court to gain themselves the right to harvest them. But the judge said no. You can't lay an axe to them, he said. They're a primitive wilderness area and they can't be touched. The forest service told the court those thousands of acres of trees are a national heritage and have to be saved for posterity. How come we can get so hung up on heritage and posterity?"

"I don't know," said Norton. "I'm not upset about it. It's nice to stand here and look out over that primitive wilderness, nice to go out for awhile and walk in it. It's peaceful over there across the river. Peaceful and sort of awesome. Sort of nice to have it there."

"I don't give a damn," said the barber. "I tell you it isn't right. We're being pushed around. Pushed around by fuzzy-headed do-gooders and simple-minded bleeding hearts who scream we got to help those poor, downtrodden redskins and we got to save the trees and we can't pollute the air. I don't care what those bleeding hearts may have to say, those redskins have no one but themselves to blame. They're a lazy lot. They ain't got an honest day of work in all of them together. They just lie around and bellyache. They always have their hands out. They're always claiming that we owe them something—no matter how much we give them, they claim we owe them more. I tell you, we don't owe them nothing but a good, swift kick in their lazy butts. They had their chance and they didn't make it. They were too dumb to make it, or too lazy. They had this whole damn country before the white men came and they did nothing with it. For years, we've been taking care of them and the more we do for them, the more they want. Now they're not only asking for things, they're demanding them. That's what everyone is doing—demanding things they haven't got. What right have any of them to be demanding anything? Who do they think they are?

"You mark my word. Before they are through with it, those redskins up on the reservation will be demanding that we give them back all of northern Minnesota, and maybe some of Wisconsin, too. Just like they are doing out in the Black Hills. Say the Black

Hills and the Bighorn region belong to them. Something about some old treaties of a hundred years or more ago. Saying we took the land away from them when we had no right to. Got that bill in Congress and a suit in the courts demanding the Black Hills and the Bighorn. And, more than likely, some silly judge will say they have a right to it and there are eggheads in Congress who are working for them, saying they have a legal right to the land that the white men have spent years and millions of dollars making into something that is worthwhile. All it was when the Indians had it was buffalo range."

The barber flourished his shears. "You just wait and see," he said. "The same thing will happen here."

"The trouble with you, George," said Norton, "is that you are a bigot."

"You can call me any name you want to," said the barber. "We are friends and I won't take offense at it. But I know what is right and what is wrong. And I ain't afraid to speak out about it. When you call a man a bigot, all that you are saying is that he doesn't believe something that you believe in. You've come to the end of your argument and you call him a name instead."

Norton made no answer and the barber ceased his talking and got down to work.

Outside the shop, the two blocks of stores and business places in the town of Lone Pine drowsed in the late afternoon of an early autumn day. A few cars were parked along the street. Three dogs went through elaborate, formal canine recognition rites, three old friends meeting at the northwest corner of an intersection. Stiffy Grant, tattered and disreputable man-about-town, sat on a nail keg outside the town's one hardware store, paying close attention to the smoking of a fairly decent-sized cigar stub that he had rescued from the gutter. Sally, the waitress at the Pine Cafe, slowly swept the sidewalk in front of her place of employment, making the job last, reluctant to leave the warm autumn sunshine and go inside again. At the end of the easternmost block, Kermit Jones, the banker, drove his car into the corner service station.

Jerry Conklin, forestry student working for his doctorate at the University of Minnesota, parked his car at the end of the bridge that spanned the Pine River below the town, took out his cased fly rod, and began assembling it. When he had stopped at the Lone Pine service station several months ago, en route to a forestry camp in the primitive wilderness area, the attendant had told him of the monster trout that lurked in the pool below the bridge. An avid fly fisherman, he had kept this piece of information in his mind ever since it had been given him, but with no chance until now to act upon it. On this day, he had driven a number of miles out of his way from another forestry camp where he had spent several days studying the ecology of a mature and undisturbed white pine forest, so that he could try the pool below the bridge.

He looked at his watch and saw that he could afford no more than thirty minutes at the pool. Kathy had a pair of tickets for the symphony—some guest conductor, whose name he had quite forgotten, would be directing the orchestra and Kathy had been wild, for weeks, to attend the concert. He didn't care too much for that kind of music, but Kathy did and she would be sore as hell if he didn't get back to Minneapolis on time.

In the barber shop, George said to Norton, "You put the papers in the mail this afternoon. It must feel good not to have much to do for another week."

"You are dead wrong there," said Norton. "You don't just snap your fingers and get out a paper, even a weekly paper. There are ads to be made up and sold, job printing to be done, copy to be written and a lot of other things to do to get together next week's paper."

"I've always wondered why you stay here," said George. "A young newspaperman like you, there are a lot of places you could go. You wouldn't have to stay here. The papers down at Minneapolis would find a place for you, snap you up, more than likely, if you just said the word to them."

"I don't know about that," said Norton. "Anyhow, I like it here. My own boss, my own business. Not much money, but enough to get along on. I'd be lost in a city. I have a friend down in Minneapolis. He's city editor of the *Tribune*. Young to be a city editor, but a good one. His name is Johnny Garrison . . ."

"I bet he'd hire you," said George.

"Maybe. I don't know. It would be tough going for a time. You'd have to learn the ropes of big-city newspapering. But, as I was saying, Johnny is city editor there and makes a lot more money than I do. But he's got his worries, too. He can't knock off early in the afternoon and go fishing if he wants to. He can't take it easy one day and make up lost time the next. He has a house with a big mortgage on it. He has an expensive family. He fights miles of city traffic to get to work every day and other miles of it to get home again. He's got a hell of a lot of responsibility. He does a lot more drinking than I do. He probably has to do a lot of things that he doesn't want to do, meet a lot of people he'd just as soon not meet. He works long hours; he carries his responsibilities home with him . . ."

"I suppose there are drawbacks," said the barber, "to every job there is."

A confused fly irritatingly, and with stupid persistence, buzzed against the plate-glass window of the shop front. The bar back of the chair was lined with ornate bottles, very seldom used, window dressing from an earlier time. Above the wall, a .30-.30 rifle hung on pegs against the wall.

At the corner gas station the attendant, inserting the nozzle into the tank of the banker's car, looked upward across his shoulder.

"Christ, Kermit, look at that, will you!"

The banker looked up.

The thing in the sky was big and black and very low. It made no noise. It floated there, sinking slowly toward the ground. It filled half the sky.

"One of them UFOs," the attendant said. "First one I ever saw. God, it's big. I never thought they were that big."

The banker did not answer. He was too frozen to answer. He couldn't move a muscle.

Down the street, Sally, the waitress, screamed. She dropped the broom and ran, blindly, aimlessly, screaming all the while.

Stiffy Grant, startled at the screaming, lurched up from the nail keg and waddled out into the street before he saw the black bigness hanging in the sky. He tilted back so far in looking that he lost his balance, which wasn't as good as it might have been, a result of having finished off what was left in a bottle of rot-gut moonshine made by Abe Parker out somewhere in the bush. Stiffy went over backwards and came to a solid sitting position in the middle of the street. He scrambled frantically to regain his feet and ran. The cigar had fallen from his mouth and he did not retrace his steps to retrieve it. He had forgotten that he had it.

In the barber shop, George quit his haircutting and ran to the window. He saw Sally and Stiffy fleeing in panic. He dropped his scissors and lunged for the wall back of the bar, clawing for the rifle. He worked the lever mechanism to jack a cartridge into the chamber and leaped for the door.

Norton came out of the chair. "What's the matter, George? What's going on?"

The barber did not answer. The door slammed behind him.

Norton wrenched the door open, stepped out on the sidewalk. The barber was running down the street. The attendant from the gas station came running toward him.

"Over there, George," the attendant yelled, pointing to a vacant lot. "It came down near the river."

George plunged across the vacant lot. Norton and the attendant followed him. Kermit Jones, the banker, pelted along behind them, puffing and panting.

Norton came out of the vacant lot onto a low gravel

ridge that lay above the river. Lying across the river at the bridge, covering the bridge, was a great black box—a huge contraption, its length great enough to span the river, one end of it resting on the opposite bank, its rear end on the near bank. It was not quite as broad as it was long and it stood high into the air above the river. At first appearance, it was simply an oblong construction, with no distinguishing features one could see—a box painted the blackest black he had ever seen.

Ahead of him the barber had stopped, was raising the rifle to his shoulder.

"No, George, no!" Norton shouted. "Don't do it!"

The rifle cracked and almost at the instant of its cracking a bolt of brilliant light flashed back from the box that lay across the river. The barber flared for an instant as the bolt of brilliance struck him, then the light was gone and the man, for the moment, stood stark upright, blackened into a grotesque stump of a man, the blackness smoking. The gun in his hands turned cherry red and bent, the barrel dropping like a length of wet spaghetti. Then George, the barber, crumpled to the ground and lay there in a run-together mass that had no resemblance to a man, the black, huddled mass still smoking, little tendrils of foul-smelling smoke streaming out above it.

2. LONE PINE

The water boiled beneath Jerry Conklin's fly. Conklin twitched the rod, but there was nothing there. The trout—and from the size of the boil, it must have been a big one—had sheered off at the last instant of its strike.

Conklin sucked in his breath. The big ones were there, he told himself. The attendant at the station had been right; there were big rainbow lurking in the pool.

The sun was shining brightly through the trees that grew along the river. The dappled water danced with little glints of sunlight shining off the tiny waves on the surface of the pool, set in motion by the rapids that came down the ledges of broken rock just upstream.

Carefully, Conklin retrieved his fly, lifted the rod to cast again, aiming at a spot just beyond where he had missed the strike.

In mid-cast, the sun went out. A sudden shadow engulfed the pool, as if some object had interposed itself between the sun and pool.

Instinctively, Conklin ducked. Something struck the upraised fly rod and he felt the tremor of it transmitted to his hand, heard the sickening splinter of bamboo. My God, he thought, an eighty-dollar rod, the first and only extravagance he had allowed himself.

He looked over his shoulder and saw the square of blackness coming down upon him. The blackness struck the bank behind him and he heard, as if from far off, the crunch of tortured metal as it came down upon his car.

He tried to turn toward the bank and stumbled, going to his knees. He shipped water in his waders. He dropped the rod. Then, without knowing how he did it, not even intending to do it, he was running down the stream along the edge of the pool, slipping and sliding as his feet came down on the small, water-polished stones, at the pool's edge, the shipped water sloshing in his waders.

The far end of the square of blackness, tipping forward, came down on the far river bank. Timbers squealed and howled and there was the rasping of drawn nails and bolts as the bridge came apart. Looking back, he saw timbers and planks floating in the pool.

He had no wonder of what had happened. In the confused turmoil of his mind, in his mad, instinctive rush to get away, there was no room for wonder. It was not until he reached sunlight again that he realized he was safe. The high banks of the river had protected him from harm. The blackness lay across the river, resting on the banks, not blocking the stream.

The pool ended and he strode out into the shallow stretch of fast-running water below it. Glancing up, he saw for the first time the true dimensions of the structure that had fallen. It towered far above him, like a building. Forty feet, he thought—maybe fifty feet—up into the air, more than four times that long.

From some distance off he heard a vicious, flat crack that sounded like a rifle going off and in the same instance a single spot in that great mass of blackness flashed with a blinding brilliance, then winked out.

My god, he thought, the rod busted, the car smashed, and I am stranded here—and Kathy! I better get out of here and phone her.

He turned about and started to scramble up the steep river bank. It was hard going. He was hampered by his waders, but he couldn't take them off, for his shoes were in the car and the car now lay, squashed flat more than likely, beneath the massive thing that had fallen on the bridge.

With a swishing sound, something lashed out of

nowhere and went around his chest—a thin, flexible something like a piece of wire or rope. He lifted his hands in panic to snatch at it, but before his hands could reach it, he was jerked upward. In a blurred instant, he saw the swiftly flowing water of the river under him, the long extent of greenery that lined the river's banks. He opened his mouth to yell, but the constriction of the wire or rope or whatever it might be had driven much of the air out of his lungs and he had no breath to yell.

Then he was in darkness and whatever it was that had jerked him there was gone from about his chest. He was on his hands and knees. The platform on which he found himself was solid—solid, but not hard, as if he had come to rest on top of thick, yielding carpeting.

He stayed on his hands and knees, crouching, trying to fight off the engulfing terror. The bitter taste of gall surged into his mouth and he forced it back. His gut had entwined itself into a hard, round ball and he consciously fought to relax the hardness and the tightness.

At first it had seemed dark, but now he realized there was a faint, uncanny sort of light, a pale blue light that had a spooky tone to it. It was not the best of light; there was a haze in it and he had to squint his eyes to see. But at least this place where he found himself was no longer dark and he was not blind.

He rose to his knees and tried to make out where he was, although that was hard to do, for intermixed with the blue light were flares of other light, flaring and flickering so swiftly that he could not make them out, not quite sure of the color of them or where they might be coming from. The flickerings revealed momentarily strange shapes such as he could not remember ever having seen before and that was strange, he thought, for a shape, no matter what its configuration, was no more than a shape and should not cause confusion. Even between the flashes, there was one shape that he could recognize, rows of circular objects that he had thought at first were eyes, all of them swivelling to stare at him with a phosphorescent glare, like the eyes of animals at night when a beam of light caught them by surprise. He sensed, however, that what he was seeing really weren't eyes, nor were they the source of the faint, blue, persistent light that filled the place. But, eyes or not, they stayed watching him.

The air was dry and hot, but there was, unexplainably, a feeling of dank mustiness in it, a sense of mustiness imparted, perhaps, by the odor that filled the place. A strange odor—not an overpowering smell, not a gagging smell, but uncomfortable in a way he could not determine, as if the smell could somehow penetrate his skin and fasten to him, become a part of him. He tried to characterize the odor and failed. It was not perfume, or yet the smell of rot. It was unlike anything he had ever smelled before.

The air, he told himself, while it was breathable, probably was deficient in oxygen. He found himself gasping, drawing in great rasping breaths of it to satisfy his body's needs.

At first, he had thought he was in a tunnel and why he should have imagined that he did not know, for as he looked further, he could see that he was in some great space that reminded him of a dismal cave. He tried to penetrate the depth of the space, but was unable to, for the blue light was too dim and the flickering of the place made it difficult to see.

Slowly and carefully, he levered himself to his feet, half expecting that his head would bump against a ceiling. But he was able to rise to his full height; there was sufficient head-room.

In the back of his mind a whisper of suspicion came to life and he fought to hold it back, for it was not a suspicion that he wanted to admit. But, gradually, as he stood stark in the blue-lit, flickering place, it forced itself upon him and he felt himself accepting it.

He was, the whisper said, inside the huge black box that had fallen astride the river. The rope or wire or tentacle, or whatever it might have been, had been extruded from it. Seizing him, it had jerked him here, in some manner passing him through the outer wall and depositing him here in its interior.

To one side of him he heard a slight sound that was between a snick and a gulp and when he looked to see what had occasioned it, he realized there was something flopping on the floor. Bending over to peer at the place where the flopping was taking place, he saw that it was a fish, a rainbow from the size and shape of it. It was about sixteen inches long and muscular of body. When he put a hand down to grasp it, it had a hefty feel to it. He got his hand around it, but it slipped away from him and continued flopping on the floor.

Now, he told himself, let's look at all of this realistically. Let's step away from it and have a long, hard look at it. Let's not go jumping to conclusions; let's try to be objective.

Item: A huge blackness had fallen from the sky, landing on the bridge and, from the crunch of metal he had heard, probably crushing his parked car.

Item: He was in a place that could be, more than likely was, the interior of the blackness that had fallen, a place quite unlike anything he had ever seen before.

Item: Not only he, but a fish, had been introduced into this place.

He took the items, one by one, into the computer of his mind, and tried to put them all together. They added up to one thing: He was inside, had somehow been spirited or absorbed inside a visitor from space, a visitor that was picking up and looking over the fauna of the planet upon which it had landed.

First himself and then a fish. And in a little while, perhaps, a rabbit, a squirrel, a coon, a bear, a deer, a bobcat. After a time, he told himself, the place was going to get crowded.

The gleaming circular objects that were watching him could be receptors, watching and recording, extracting data and storing it, making note of him (and the fish as well), picking up every vibration of his brain, every quiver of his psyche, analyzing him, breaking down the kind of organism that he was and classifying him by whatever code that might apply, tucking him away in memory cells, writing him up in chemical equations, seeking an understanding of what he was and what might be his status and his purpose in the ecology of the planet.

Probably it was not only the circular objects that were doing the work. Perhaps the flashing lights and the mechanisms behind the flashing lights were a part of it as well.

He could be wrong, he thought. When he could really come to think of it, he *must* know that he was wrong. Yet it was the one explanation that squared with what had happened. He had seen the blackness fall; he had been snatched up from the river—he remembered the running water under him as he was hoisted in the air, he remembered the long lines of trees that grew along its banks, he remembered seeing the town of Lone Pine, set on its gravel terrace above the river's bed. He remembered all these things and the next that he had known had been the darkness of this cave-like place. Except for the interior of the object that had fallen on the river, there was no other place into which he might have been tucked.

If all of this had happened, if he were not mistaken, then it meant that the object that had fallen across the river was alive, or that it was operated by something that was alive, and not only alive, but intelligent.

He found himself instinctively fighting against what he was thinking, for in the context of human experience, it was utter madness to believe that an intelligence had landed on the Earth and forthwith snapped him up.

He was astonished to find that whatever terror he had felt had drained out of him. In its stead, there was now a coldness, a bleak coldness of the soul that, in a way, was far worse than terror.

Intelligence, he thought—if there was an intelligence here, there must be a way to talk with it, in some manner to work out a system of communication with it.

He tried to speak and the words dried up before his tongue could shape them. He tried again and the words came, but only in a whisper. He tried once more and this time the words came louder, booming in the hollowness of the cave in which he stood.

"Hello," he shouted. "Is there anyone around? Is there someone here?"

He waited and there was no answer, so he spoke again, even louder this time, shouting at the intelligence that must be there. The words echoed and reverberated and then died out. The circular, eye-like objects still kept on watching him. The flickering still continued. But no one, or nothing, answered.

3. MINNEAPOLIS, MINNESOTA

Kathy Foster sat at her typewriter in the *Tribune* newsroom and hammered out the story—such a stupid story and such stupid people. Damn Johnny for sending her out on it. There must have been other assignments he could have sent her on, assignments that did not have the phoney mush content that this one did, nor the sloppy mysticism. The Lovers, they called themselves, and she could still see the sleepy innocence of their eyes, the soft, smooth flow of posturing euphuisms—love is all, love conquers all, love encompasses everything. All you have to do is love someone or something hard enough and long enough and the love would be returned. Love is the greatest force in the universe, more than likely the only significant force, the be-all and the is-all and the end-all of everything there is. And it was not only people, not only life, that would respond. If you loved any kind of matter, any kind of energy, it would return the love and, in consequence of that love, do anything that you wished it to, even to the point of disobeying or disregarding all empirical laws (which, they had told her, may not exist in fact), perform in any manner, do anything, go anywhere, stay anywhere, do anything one wished. But to accomplish this, they had told her solemnly, with the innocence in their eyes gleaming brightly at her, one must strive to understand the life, the matter, the energy, whatever it might be, and to love it so that it became aware of you. That was the trouble now, they said. No one had sufficient understanding, but understanding could be obtained through the force of love. Once the depth of love was great enough to secure the understanding, then man in all truth would be in control of the universe. But this control, they had said, must not be a control for the sake of control alone, but to perfect the understanding and the love of all that went into the makeup of the universe.

That damn university, she told herself, is a hot-bed for the nurturing of such phoney misfits groping for significance where there is no significance, employing the search for nonexistent meaning as a means to escape reality.

She looked at the clock on the wall. Almost four o'clock and Jerry hadn't phoned. He had said that he would phone to tell her he was on his way. If he made her late for the concert, she would have his hide. He knew how she had counted on the concert. For weeks she had dreamed of it. Sure, Jerry didn't like symphonic music but for once he could do what she wanted, even if he squirmed the entire evening. She had done a lot of things, gone to a lot of places that she hadn't wanted to, but had gone because he wanted to. The wrestling matches—for sweet Christ's sake, the wrestling matches!

A strange man, Kathy told herself, strange and at times infuriating, but a sweet guy just the same. He and his everlasting trees! Jerry lived for trees. How in the world, she wondered, could a grown man get so wrapped up in trees? Other people could develop an empathy for flowers, for animals, for birds, but with Jerry it was trees. The guy was silly about his trees. He loved them and seemed to understand them and there were times, she thought, when it seemed he even talked with them.

She jerked out the finished page, threaded in another. She hammered at the keys. The anger boiled within her, the disgust smothered her. When she turned in the story, she'd tell Johnny that she thought it should be spiked—or better yet, thrown into the waste basket, for then no one could rescue it from the spike if the day's copy should run thin and a news hole needed filling.

Across the newsroom, John H. Garrison, city editor,

sat at his desk, staring out across the room. Most of the desks were empty and he ran down the list—Freeman was covering the meeting of the airport commission and it would likely come to nothing, although with all the flurry about the need of extra runways, it was a meeting that the newsroom had to cover; Jay was at Mayo Clinic in Rochester, getting the story on the new cancer procedures that were being developed there; Campbell was still at city hall, piddling his time away at a park board meeting that, like the airport meeting, probably would fizzle out; Jones was out in South Dakota working on the Black Hills-Indian controversy, getting together material for a Sunday feature; Knight was at the Johnson murder trial; Williams was in the suburban town of Wayzata interviewing that old gal who claimed to be 102 years old (although she probably wasn't). Sloane was tied up with the oil spill at Winona. Christ, Garrison wondered, what would he do if a big story suddenly should break? Although that, he knew, was unlikely. It had been a bad day and was not improving.

He said to Jim Gold, the assistant city editor, "What does the budget look like, Jim?"

Gold looked at the sheet of paper in his typewriter. "Thin," he said. "Not much here, Johnny. Not really much at all."

A phone rang. Gold reached out, spoke into the mouthpiece softly.

"It's for you, Johnny," he said. "Line two."

Garrison picked up the phone at his desk, punched a button.

"Garrison," he said.

"Johnny, this is Frank Norton," said the voice at the other end. "Up at Lone Pine, remember?"

"Why, Frank," said Garrison, genuinely pleased, "how great to hear from you. Just the other day I was talking with some of the fellows here about you. Telling them about the great setup you had. Your own boss, the trout fishing at the edge of town. One of these days I'll come up, primed for some of those fish. How about it, Frank?"

"Johnny," said Norton, "I think I may have something for you."

"Frank, you sound excited. What is going on?"

"Just maybe," said Norton, "we may have a visitor from space. I can't be sure ..."

"You have what?" roared Garrison, jerking upright in his chair.

"I can't be sure," said Norton. "Something big came down out of the sky. Landed straddle of the river. Smashed the bridge to hell."

"Is it still there?"

"Still there," said Norton. "Just sitting where it landed, only ten minutes or so ago. It's huge. Big and black. The town is going wild. The place is in an uproar. One man was killed."

"Killed. How was he killed?"

"He shot at the thing. It shot back. Burned him to a cinder. I saw it happen. I saw him standing there and smoking."

"Oh, my god," said Harrison. "What a story, right on top of you."

"Johnny," said Norton, "I can't be certain of what is going on. It happened too short a time ago to know what's going on. I thought you might want to send someone up to get some pictures."

"Hold on, Frank," said Garrison. "I tell you what I'm going to do. I'll get right on it. But first, I want to turn you over to someone here on the desk. You tell him what happened. Tell him everything. When you get through, don't hang up. I'll get hold of a photographer and do some other things."

"Fine, I'll hang on."

Garrison cupped the receiver with his hand, held it out to Gold.

"Frank Norton is on the other end," he said. "He's owner and editor of a weekly paper at Lone Pine. An old friend of mine. We went to school together. He says something fell out of the sky up there. One man's been killed. Fell just fifteen minutes or so ago. You get down what he has to tell you and then ask him to hold for me. I want to talk with him again."

"I'll get it here," said Gold. He picked up his phone. "Mr. Norton," he said, "I'm Jim Gold. I'm assistant city editor . . ."

Garrison swung around in his chair, spoke to Annie Dutton, city desk secretary.

"Annie," he said, "get a hold of the plane charter people. See if they can have a plane standing by for us. To fly to—what the hell town with an airstrip is closest to Lone Pine?"

"Bemidji," said Annie. "That would be the closest."

"All right. Then get hold of a car rental outfit in Bemidji and arrange for a car to be waiting for us. We'll phone them later and tell them when we'll be getting in."

Annie picked up her phone and started dialing.

Garrison stood up and looked over the newsroom, flinching at what he saw.

Finley over in one corner, pecking away at a story— but Finley was the rankest cub, still wet behind the ears. Sanderson, but she was not much better and had the unfailing habit of writing a bit too cutely. Some day, by god, he thought, she would have to mend her ways or be out the door. Jamison, but Jamison took forever. All right on an in-depth story, but too slow and deliberate for a story that was breaking fast.

"Kathy!" he bawled.

Startled, Kathy Foster stopped her typing, got up and started for the city desk, fighting down her anger. Jerry hadn't called as yet and her story, as she wrote it, seemed sillier and sillier. If she had to miss the concert . . .

Gold was on one phone, listening, speaking only now and then, his fingers stabbing at the typewriter, making notes. Annie was busy on another phone. Garrison had sat down again and was dialing.

"This is Garrison," he said into the phone. "We need a good photographer. Who you got back there? Where is Allen? This is an out-of-town assignment. Important. Top priority."

He listened. "Oh, hell," he said. "You mean Allen

isn't there. He's the man for the job we have. Where is he? Can you reach him?"

A wait, then, "Yes, I forgot. I do remember now. Allen's on vacation. All right, then. Send him up."

He hung up the phone and turned to Kathy. "I have something for you," he said.

"Not now," she said. "Not tonight. Not overtime. I'm almost through for the day. And I have tickets for the symphony tonight."

"But, good god, girl, this could be important. The most important assignment you have ever had. Maybe our first space visitor . . ."

"First space visitor?"

"Well, maybe yes, maybe no. We don't know quite yet . . ."

Gold was holding out the phone to him. He took it and spoke into it. "Just a minute, Frank. I'll be right with you."

Annie said, "There'll be a plane waiting, ready to go. There'll be a car at Bemidji."

"Thanks," said Garrison. He asked Gold, "What have you got?"

"Good story, far as it goes," said Gold. "Solid. Lots of facts. Loads of detail. Sounds exciting. Something did fall out of the sky up there."

"Solid enough to go after?"

"I'd say so," said Gold.

Garrison swung around to Kathy. "I hate to ask this of you," he said. "But there's no one else. No one I can reach out and grab quite fast enough. Everyone is working. You and White fly up to Bemidji. There'll be a car there, waiting for you. Play story. I'll guarantee you that. Byline. The works. You ought to be in Lone Pine by six or before. Phone before eight. We can make the first edition that way, with what you have."

"All right," she said. "If you'll buy this pair of tickets. I'll be damned if I'm going to be out the price of these tickets."

"All right," he said, "I'll buy them. I'll work them into my expense account somehow." He dug his wallet out of his pocket. "How much?"

"Thirty bucks."

"That's too much. That's more than you paid for them."

"They're good seats. Anyhow, that's what you'll have to pay for them."

"All right. All right," he said, stripping out bills.

"And if Jerry Conklin calls, be sure someone tells him what happened. He was to be my date tonight. Promise."

"I promise," said Garrison, handing her the money.

He lifted the receiver and said, "Some last minute details, Frank, that needed taking care of. You heard? I'll have someone up there by six o'clock or so. I'll ask them to look you up. But how come? You have a paper of your own. Why give this all to us?"

"Today was my press day," said Norton. "Won't publish again until this time next week. This kind of news doesn't wait. I wanted to give you a jump on it. A couple of state patrol cars came roaring into town just a few minutes ago. Otherwise everything's the same."

"I wonder if you'd mind keeping us filled in," asked Garrison, "until our people get there. Something happens, just give us a call."

"Be glad to," Norton said.

4. WASHINGTON, D.C.

It had been a rough day. The press, at the early afternoon briefing, had been out for blood. Principally, the questions had had to do with the movement by the Native American Association for the return to the federated tribes of the Black Hills of South Dakota and the Montana Bighorn region, although there had been considerable sniping about the energy situation, centered on the administration's proposal to develop a southwestern desert solar energy system and its advocacy of substantial funds for research into a cryogenic transmission system. The press had stormed out considerably indignant at his unsatisfactory answers, but, David Porter told himself, that was not unusual. For the past several months, the press, in general, had been either enraged or disgusted at him. Any day now, he felt sure, there would be a move by some factions of the media to get him canned.

A hush hung over the pressroom office, scarcely broken by the teletype machines ranged against the wall, chuckling among themselves as they continued to spew out the doings of the world. Marcia Langley, his assistant, was gathering up and putting away, getting ready to leave for the day. The telephone console on Marcia's desk was quiet; for the first time in the day no lights were blinking, signalling incoming calls. This was the calm of the news-gathering period. The last afternoon editions had gone to press, the morning editions were being readied for the presses.

Shadows were beginning to creep into the room. Porter put out a hand and turned on his desk lamp. The light revealed the clutter of papers. Looking at them, he groaned. The clock on the wall said it was almost 5:30. He had promised to pick up Alice at 7:30 and that left him little time to get through with his paperwork. There was a new eating place out in Maryland that some of Alice's friends had been recommending, with Alice mentioning it off and on for the past several weeks. Tonight, they planned to go there. He relaxed in his chair and thought about Alice Davenport. Her old man, the senator, and Porter had never gotten along too well, but, so far, the old man had raised no objection to their seeing one another. Which, Porter thought, was rather decent of the old buzzard. Despite her parentage, however, Alice was all right. She was a lot of fun, bright and cheerful, well-informed, a good conversationalist. Except that, at times, she had the unfortunate tendency to engage in long and partisan discussion of her currently favorite social enthusiasm. Right at the moment, it was the Indian claim to the Black Hills and the Bighorn, which she passionately believed should be returned to the federated tribes. A few months earlier, it had been the blacks of South Africa. Which all came, Porter told himself dourly, from too good an education in exactly the wrong disciplines. She didn't always talk about these things and tonight perhaps she wouldn't. In the last few months, they had spent some happy times together, for Alice, when she left off her crusader togs, was a good companion.

It wouldn't take more than half an hour or so, he estimated, if he really applied himself, to get his desk at least haphazardly cleared off. That would give him time to get home, get showered and shaved and change his clothes. For once, he promised himself, he'd pick Alice up on time. But, first, he needed a cup of coffee.

He rose and started across the room.

"Do you know," he asked Marcia, "if there's any coffee left out in the lounge?"

"There should be," she told him. "There might be some sandwiches left but they will be stale."

He grumbled at her. "All I need is a cup of coffee."

He was halfway across the room when one of the

teletype machines came to sudden, insane life. A bell rang loudly and insistently, clamoring for attention.

He turned about and went swiftly back across the room. It was Associated Press, he saw. He came up to the machine, grasped each side of it with his hands. The printer, blurring across the paper, was typing a string of bulletins.

Then: BULLETIN — LARGE OBJECT REPORTED TO HAVE FALLEN FROM THE SKY IN MINNESOTA.

The machine stopped, the printer quivering.

"What is it?" Marcia asked, standing at his shoulder.

"I don't know," said Porter. "Perhaps a meteorite."

He said to the machine, "Come on. Come on. Tell us what it is."

The telephone on his desk shrilled at them.

Marcia took a step or two and picked it up.

"All right, Grace," she said. "I'll tell him."

The teletype came to life: WHAT MAY BE OUR FIRST VISITOR FROM OUTER SPACE LANDED TODAY NEAR THE TOWN OF LONE PINE IN NORTHERN MINNESOTA . . .

At his elbow, Marcia said, "That was Grace on the line. The President wants to see you."

Porter nodded and turned away from the machine. Bells on other machines began to ring, but he walked away, heading for the door and going the few steps down the corridor.

As he came into the outer office, Grace nodded at the door. "You're to go right in," she said.

"What is it, Grace?"

"I don't really know. He's talking to the army chief of staff. Something about a new satellite that has been discovered."

Porter strode across the office, knocked on the inner door, then turned the knob and went in.

President Herbert Taine was hanging up the phone. He motioned Porter to a chair.

"That was Whiteside," he said. "He's got a hair up his ass. Seems some of our tracking stations have sighted something new in orbit. According to the general, something so big it scares you. Not one of ours, he says. Most unlikely, too, to be Soviet. Too big for either of us to put up. Neither of us have the booster power to put up anything as big as the trackers spotted. Whitehead's all upset."

"Something out of space?" asked Porter.

"Whitehead didn't say that. But it was what he was thinking. You could tell he was. He was about to come unstuck. He'll be coming over as soon as he can get here."

"Something fell, or landed, I don't know which, in northern Minnesota," said Porter. "It was just beginning to come in on the teletype when you phoned."

"You think the two of them could be tied up?"

"I don't know. It's too early to know what came down in Minnesota. I just caught part of a bulletin. It might be no more than a big meteorite. Anyhow, apparently, something came down out of the sky."

"Jesus, Dave, we have plenty of trouble without something like this happening," said the President.

Porter nodded. "I quite agree, sir."

"How was today's briefing?"

"They roughed me up. Mostly the Black Hills and the energy situation."

"You doing all right?"

"Sir, I'm doing what I'm paid to do. I am earning my wages."

"Yes," said the President. "I suppose you are. It ain't easy, though."

A knock came on the door, which opened a ways, Grace sticking in her head. "Marcia gave me this," she said, waving a sheet of paper ripped from the teletype.

"Give it to me," said the President. She walked across the room and handed it to him. Quickly he read it and pushed it across the desk to Porter.

"It makes no sense," he complained. "A big black box, it says, sitting on a bridge. A meteorite wouldn't be a black box, would it?"

"Hardly," said Porter. "A meteorite would come in with a hell of a rush. It would dig a monstrous crater."

"So would anything else," said the President. "Anything that fell out of the sky. A decaying satellite . . ."

"That is my understanding," said Porter. "They'd come in fast and dig a crater. If they were big, that is."

"This one sounds like it is big."

The two men faced one another across the desk, staring at one another.

"Do you suppose . . ." the President started to say, then stopped in mid-sentence.

The intercom on the President's desk purred and he flipped up the toggle. "What is it, Grace?" he asked.

"It's General Whiteside, sir."

"O.K.," he said. "Put him on."

He lifted the phone and said, out of the side of his mouth, to Porter, "He's heard about the Minnesota business." He spoke into the phone and then sat listening. From where he sat, Porter could catch the buzz and hum of the torrent of words the man at the other end of the line was pouring into the phone.

Finally, the President said, "All right, then. Let's keep our shirts on. Let me know when you have anything more."

He hung up and turned to Porter. "He's buying it," he said. "Someone in the National Guard phoned him from Minnesota. Says the thing came down and landed, that it didn't crash, that it is still there, that it is the size of a good-sized building, all black, like a big box."

"Strange," said Porter. "Everyone is calling it a big box."

"Dave," asked the President, "what do we do if it should turn out to be a visitor out of space?"

"We play it by ear," said Porter. "We handle it as it comes. We don't go running scared."

"We have to get some facts awful fast."

"That's right. The news wires will give us some of them. We ought to send out an investigating team, fast as we can. Get hold of the FBI in Minneapolis."

"The area should be secured," said the President. "We can't have the public piling in, interfering."

He lifted the toggle. "Grace," he said, "get me the governor out in St. Paul."

He looked at Porter. "What I'm afraid of is panic."

Porter glanced at his watch. "The first evening news programs will be hitting TV in another hour or less. Even now, they'll be flashing bulletins. The news will spread fast. I imagine my phones are ringing now. Asking White House reaction, for Christ's sake. They probably know more about it than we do."

"Is Marcia still out there?"

"She was getting ready to leave, but not now. With this, she'll stay on. The woman's a pro."

"We may need some sort of statement."

"Not yet," said Porter. "Not too fast. No shooting from the hip. We've got to know more about it . . ."

"Something to give the people," said the President. "Some assurance that we are doing what we can."

"They won't start wondering for a while what we are doing. They'll be all agog over the news itself."

"Maybe a briefing."

"Perhaps," Porter said. "If there is enough to go on before the night is over. No one knows about this new object in orbit, I take it. Only Whiteside and the two of us—and, of course, the trackers. But they won't say anything."

"It'll leak out," said the President. "Given a little time, everything leaks out."

"I'd rather we be the ones to tell them," said Porter. "We don't want to give the impression of any cover-up. That's what the UFO believers have been saying all these years, that the UFO information has been covered up."

"I agree with you," the President said. "Maybe you better call a briefing. Go out and start the ball rolling. Then come back in again. I may have people with me, but barge in when you're ready. There should be more information by that time."

5. LONE PINE

The fish was gone. The rabbit had hopped into the darkness and now was hopping back again, hopping slowly and deliberately, its nose aquiver, a much puzzled rabbit, wondering, perhaps, Jerry told himself, what manner of briar patch it might have landed in. The coon was pawing and nuzzling at the floor. The muskrat had disappeared.

Jerry had done some cautious exploring, but never moving so far away as to lose his orientation to the spot on which he had been deposited when he had been jerked into the place. He had found nothing. Approaching some of the strange shapes that had been revealed in the flicker of the lights, the shapes had gone away, receding and flattening into the level floor. He had investigated the circular patches that he first had thought of as eyes. He had thought when he had first seen them that they were positioned in walls, but found that they were located in mid-air. He could pass his hand through them and when he did, it seemed to have no effect upon them. They still remained circular luminosities and they still kept on watching him. He had felt nothing when he touched them. They were neither hot nor cold and imparted no sensation.

The flickering still continued and the pale blue light persisted. It seemed to him that he could see slightly better than he had earlier, probably because his eyes had adjusted to the paleness of the light.

He had tried on several occasions to talk with the strange presence that he felt was there, but there had been no response, not the slightest indication that he had been heard. Except for the sense of being watched, there was no sign that anyone or anything in the place was aware of him. He did not have the feeling that the imagined observer was in any way hostile or malignant. Perhaps curious, but that was all. The alien smell continued, but he had become somewhat accustomed to it and now paid it slight attention.

The terror and the apprehension had largely fallen from him. In its stead came a fatalistic numbness and a wonderment that such an event could happen. How could it be, he asked himself, that he had been so positioned in time and space for this incredible happening to befall him? From time to time, he thought of Kathy and the concert, but this was something, he told himself, that could not be remedied and the thought then was swept away by the concern for his predicament.

It seemed to him that from time to time he could detect some motion in the structure in which he was imprisoned. On a couple of occasions, there had been a lurching and a jerking as if violent movement were taking place. Of none of this, however, could he be positive. It might be, he told himself, no more than certain convolutions or biologic readjustments in the organism.

And that was the crux of it, he thought—was it biologic? There had been nothing to start with, at the time it had fallen from the sky, to indicate it was—and perhaps not even now. It could be, rather, a machine, a pre-programmed, computerized machine able to react approximately to any number of arising situations. But there was about it the sense of the biologic, a feeling, for whatever reason, that it was alive.

While he had no evidence, he was becoming more and more convinced that it was a biologic being, a functioning consciousness that was observing him. A visitor from the stars that, immediately after it had landed, had set about learning what it could of the life indigenous to the planet, snatching up himself, a fish, a rabbit, a coon and a muskrat. From the five of them, he had no doubt, could be gleaned some basic information, perhaps even the beginning of an understanding of the principle upon which life here had evolved.

It was alive, he told himself; this great black box was a living thing. And even while he wondered how he could be so convinced, suddenly he knew, as if a voice had spoken to him, as if a special light of intellect had blinked inside his brain. It was like a tree, he thought. He could feel within it the same aliveness that he found in any tree. And that, he told himself, was ridiculous, for this thing was nothing like a tree. But the thought persisted: this thing inside of which he had been thrust was similar to a tree.

He tried to squeeze the idea out of his thinking, for it was, on the face of it, a silly idea at best. But it hung on, refusing to be banished, and now another idea came out of nowhere to link up with the idea of the tree—the unsummoned thought of home. But what this new idea meant, he did not know. Did it mean that this place was home to him? He rebelled at the thought, for it certainly was not home. It was about as far from home as any place he could imagine.

How, he wondered, had the idea come to him? Could it be that this living alien—if it was living alien—was trying to communicate with him, that it was planting suggestions in his mind, trying to bridge the gap that lay between their two intelligences? If that should be the case, and he could not bring himself to think it was, what then did the alien mean? What connection could there be between a tree and home? What connotation was he expected to derive from the two ideas?

Thinking this, he realized that he was more and more beginning to accept the premise that the big black box was a visitor from outer space and that it was not only alive, but intelligent.

The ground, he reminded himself, had been well laid for such a thought and such acceptance. It had been talked about and written about for years—that some day, an intelligence from outer space might come to visit Earth, with all the attendant speculation of what might happen then, of how the great unwashed, uncomprehending public might react to it. It was not a new idea; for years it had lain skin-deep in the public consciousness.

The rabbit came hopping up to him. Crouched tight against the floor, it stretched out its neck to sniff at the toes of his shoes. The coon, through with its worrying of the floor, went ambling off. The muskrat had not reappeared.

Little brothers, Jerry thought. These things are my little brothers, gathered with me in this place, common denizens of what this alien being regards as an alien planet, gathered here to be studied by it.

Something whipped around him. He was jerked from his feet and slammed against the wall. But he did not hit the wall. The wall opened in a slit and he went through, sailing free of it.

He was falling. In the darkness he could see very little, but below him he could make out a blob of shadow and jerked up his hands to protect his face. He crashed into a tree and the upward-thrusting, but resilient branches slowed his fall. Desperately he reached out with one hand, the other still up to protect his face. Grabbing blindly, his fingers closed around a branch. It bent beneath his weight, slowing his fall; with the other hand, he stabbed out and his fingers found and closed upon a larger branch, which was stout enough to halt his fall.

For a moment he hung there, dangling in the tree, the sharp, welcome scent of pine redolent in his nostrils. A gentle wind was blowing and all around him, he heard the murmur of the conifers.

He hung there, thankful—filled with a surging thankfulness that he had escaped from inside the alien structure. Although escaped, he knew, on second thought, was not quite the word for it. He had been thrown out. They, or it, or whatever it might be, had gotten all it needed from him and had heaved him out. As it probably earlier had thrown out the fish and, in a little while, would heave out the rabbit, coon and muskrat.

His eyes by now had become partially adapted to the darkness and carefully he worked his way along the branch to the body of the tree. Once he reached it, he clutched it with both arms and legs, resting for a moment. Because of the thickness of the branches, he could not see the ground and had no idea how high he might be in the tree. Not high, he told himself, for he could not have been thrown out of the structure more than forty feet or so above the ground and he had fallen for at least a short distance before the tree had intervened to break the fall.

Slowly, he began his descent down the tree. It was not easy work, especially in the dark, for there were many branches sprouting from the trunk and he had to do some maneuvering to make his way down through them. The tree, he judged, was not very large or tall. The bole, he estimated, was no more than a foot in diameter, although, as he descended, it increased in size.

Finally, without warning, his feet touched the ground and his knees buckled under him. Carefully, he felt about with one foot to be certain he had reached the ground. Satisfied that he had, he released his hold on the trunk and fought his way clear of the low-growing, drooping branches.

He stood to one side of the tree and peered all about him, but the darkness was so thick that he could make out very little. He calculated he was some distance to one side of the road down which he'd driven before he parked the car, and was astonished and slightly terrified to find that he had no idea of direction.

He moved around a bit, hoping to find a place where the tree growth was less dense and he would have a chance of seeing better, but he had moved only a few feet before he became entangled in another tree. He tried another direction and the same thing happened. He crouched against the ground, peering upward, in hope that he could catch the dark outline of the thing that had come down from the sky, but was unable to locate it.

From where he was, he told himself, he should be able to glimpse the lights in the town of Lone Pine, but, try as he might, he could not see so much as a single light. He tried to make out some familiar patterns in the stars, but there were no stars—either the sky was overcast or the forest cover was too thick to see through.

Christ, he thought, crouched against the ground, here he was, lost in a woods not more than a mile from a town—a small town, of course, but still a town.

He could, of course, spend the night here until morning light, but the air was already chilly and before morning, it would get much colder. He could start a fire, he told himself, and then realized that he had no matches. He didn't smoke, so never carried matches. And the approaching cold, he told himself, was not the sole consideration. Somehow, as quickly as possible, he had to find a phone. Kathy would be furious. He'd have to explain to her what had held him up.

He remembered one adage for a lost man—travel downhill. Traveling downhill, one would come to water and by following water, soon or late, people would be found. If he traveled downhill, he'd come to the river. By following along its bank, he'd come to the road. Or he could try to cross the river, which might put him in striking distance of Lone Pine. Although that had small attraction, for he did not know the river and trying to cross it could be dangerous. He could run afoul of deep or rapid water.

Or, perhaps, he could find the contraption in which he had been caged. If he could find it, then by turning to his left, he would find the road that led to the bridge. But even so, he could not cross the river, for the bridge was out. Or the contraption might still be sprawled across the river; he had thought he felt it move, but he could not be certain that it had.

He couldn't be too far away from it, he thought. He had been thrown from it and he could not have been too distant from it when he'd crashed into the tree. The structure in which he had been caged, he felt certain, could be no more than thirty feet away.

He started out or tried to start out. He got nowhere. He collided with trees, he became entangled in undergrowth, he tripped over fallen logs. There was no possibility of covering more than a few feet at a time; it was impossible to travel in a straight line. He became confused; he had no idea where he was.

Worn out with his effort, he crouched against a tree trunk, with the drooping branches almost on top of him, almost brushing the ground. God, he thought, it seemed impossible a man could get so thoroughly lost, even in the dark.

After a short rest, he got up and went on, floundering blindly. At times, he asked himself why he just didn't give up, hunker down for the night, waiting for the dawn. But he could never persuade himself. Each new effort that he made might be the lucky one. He might find the alien structure or the road or something else that would tell him where he was.

What he found was a path. He hadn't been expecting to find a path, but it was better than nothing and he decided to stick with it. The path, or trail, would surely lead him somewhere if he could only follow it.

He had not seen the path. He had found it by stumbling on it, tripping on something and falling flat upon his face upon it. It was fairly free of obstructions and he made it out by patting the ground with his hands, tracing out the narrow, hard-packed pathway. Trees and underbrush crowded close on either side of it.

There was only one way to follow it—on his hands and knees, feeling with his hands to keep himself upon it. So, thoroughly lost, not knowing where he was or where he might be going, he inched his way down the trail on his hands and knees.

6. LONE PINE

Frank Norton spoke into the phone, "I don't know where they are, Johnny. They just haven't showed. You said six o'clock and I've been waiting for them here. It might be the traffic jam."

Garrison's voice rasped at him, "What the hell, Frank? Since when have you developed traffic jams up there?"

"Worse than the opening day of fishing season," said Norton. "Everyone's trying to reach here. Traffic is backed up on all the roads leading into town. The state patrol is trying to close us off, but they're having a hard time doing it. As soon as radio and television began flashing bulletins . . ."

"It's too late now to get pictures of the thing that fell," said Garrison. "You say it moved?"

"Quite some time ago," said Norton. "It moved across the bridge and up the road into the forest area. It's dark now. There's no chance to take any pictures. But I did take some before it moved . . ."

"You took pictures!" yelled Garrison. "Why the hell didn't you tell me that before?"

"Johnny, they aren't much. Not the kind of pictures you'd take with the press cameras you have down there. Just a small ordinary tourist camera. I got two rolls of film, but I can't be sure there is anything worth looking at."

"Look, Frank, is there any way you can get those two rolls to us? Would you be willing to sell them?"

"Sell them? They're yours if you want them, Johnny. I'd like some copies of them, that's all."

"Don't be a fool," said Garrison. "Those films are worth money. A lot of money. If you'll let us have them, I'll get you, from this end, all that the traffic will bear. Is there any way you can get them to us? Anyone who would drive them down? I don't want you to bring them yourself. I would like you to stay right there until Kathy and Chet show up."

"There's a kid here who works part time at a gas station. He has a motorcycle. He'd get them to you the fastest, if he doesn't kill himself getting there."

"Can you trust him?"

"Absolutely," Norton said. "I give him work now and then, a few odd jobs every now and then. He's a friend of mine."

"Tell him there's a hundred in it for him if he gets them here before midnight. We'll hold up part of the press run to get the pictures in tomorrow morning's paper."

"I think the kid's at the station right now. I'll get in touch with him. He can find someone else, or I can find someone else, to man the pumps for him. Hell, I'll handle them myself if I have to."

"Are there any other newsmen in town? Any of the TV crews show up as yet?"

"I don't think so. TV crews I'd see. I suppose Duluth will be sending someone, but if they got here, they'd probably look me up. So far, there's been no one. The highway patrol has the roads sealed off fairly well. Not too many people have actually gotten into town. Some of them left their cars at the roadblocks and are walking in. The roads are clogged with cars. That way, a motorcycle is better than a car to get out of town. This kid I told you of will take to ditches, go across country if he has to."

"You'll do it, then."

"Almost immediately. If I can't get the kid, I'll get someone else. One thing, Johnny. How's the country taking it?"

"It's too soon to know," said Garrison. "I have a man out talking to people in the street. Going into bars, standing at theater entrances, catching people wherever he can, asking what they think of it. A man-in-the-street reaction story. Why do you ask?"

"I had a call from Washington. Army chief of staff, he told me. Said his name, but I don't remember it. A general, I do remember that."

"There's been no reaction so far from Washington," said Garrison. "They need time to get their feet under them. You still think it may be something from the stars?"

"It moved," said Norton. "It moved across the river and went a ways into the forest. It could mean it was alive, or at least a very sophisticated machine, or a machine operated by intelligence. People up here have no doubt. So far as they are concerned, it's a visitor from space. You should see it, Johnny. If you saw it, you might believe it, too."

The door to the office came open and a woman came in; following her was a man loaded with camera equipment.

"Just a minute," said Norton. "I think your people are here. They just came in the door."

He said to the woman, "Are you Kathy Foster?"

Kathy nodded. "And the man all loaded down is Chet White."

"Frank," said Garrison.

"Yes?"

"Let me talk with Kathy, please."

"Right," said Norton. "I'll get going with the films."

He handed the phone to Kathy. "Johnny's on the line," he said.

"Did I hear you say films?" asked Chet.

"Yeah. I shot two rolls before the thing moved across the bridge. While it could still be seen."

"It's not there any more!" wailed Chet.

"It moved. Across the bridge, up the road into the woods. It's too dark to see it. No way to get at it."

"You sending those rolls to Johnny?"

"I have a man with a motorcycle. He'll take them for me."

"That's good," said Chet. "A car couldn't get

through. These damn two lane roads of yours. I never saw such a snarl. We walked a couple of miles, I'd judge, to get here. The car's back there somewhere."

"See you later," said Norton, ducking out the door.

On the phone, Kathy was saying to Garrison, "It was awful, Johnny. Everyone is trying to get here. The cops have stopped them. The cars are piling up."

"Well, you're there now," said Garrison. "Hang in there. Get us what you can. Talk to people. Get reactions from them. How is the town taking it? What do they think it is? You know what we want."

"Johnny, did Jerry phone?"

"Jerry?"

"Dammit, Johnny, I told you before I left. Jerry Conklin. My date for tonight. I explained it to you."

"I remember now. I spread the word around. Just a minute."

Faintly over the line, she heard him bellow, "Anyone get a call from a guy by the name of Jerry Conklin? Kathy's date."

Mumbling voices answered him while Kathy waited.

Garrison came back on the line. "No, Kathy. No one got the call."

"Dammit," said Kathy.

"Let me see," said Garrison, swiftly dismissing Jerry Conklin. "It's a quarter of eight now. We'll have to go with what we have on the first press run. Frank's been keeping us filled in. We know about the thing moving across the river. Phone me back in a couple of hours. Sorry about your being tied up on the road. Glad you got there."

"Johnny, what else is happening? Fill me in."

"The governor has about half the state patrol funneling in on Lone Pine. Closing off all the roads. He's put the National Guard on alert and standby. No one as yet has any idea of what is going on. Idea seems to be that this really is a ship from space, but no one can say for sure."

"If Jerry does call, you'll explain to him."

"Sure will," said Garrison.

"I'll phone you," said Kathy. "Wait a minute. I have

a hunch the phone lines into this place will be jammed. Why don't you have someone use the WATS line to get in here by nine thirty or so. Keep trying if they can't get through. You have this number?"

"That's right. Will you have someone who can answer there and hold the line for you?"

"I'll get someone," said Kathy. "How much can I pay them? How's the budget on this operation?"

"As little as you can," said Garrison. "As much as you have to."

"All right, then," said Kathy. "I'll be in touch."

As she hung up the phone, Norton came in the door. "Jimmy is on his way," he said, "with the films. He got one of his pals to take over the station."

"That didn't take long," said Chet.

"I was lucky," said Norton. "Found Jimmy right away and there was this pal of his loafing around the station."

"We'll need one thing more," said Kathy. "Johnny will be calling back nine thirty or so. We'll need someone to hold the line for us until I get back here. The lines may be jammed, hard to get through."

"I think I have the man for you," said Norton. "I saw him just up the street. Old codger, name of Stiffy Grant. He'll do anything to get the price of a drink."

"Reliable?"

"If there's a drink in it."

"How much should I pay him?"

"Couple of bucks."

"Tell him I'll give him five. Impress on him he's not to give up the phone to anyone at all. For no reason, whatsoever."

"You can rely on him. He's got a single track mind. Sober now. He'll understand."

"I don't know what we'd have done without you," said Kathy.

"That's all right," said Norton. "Johnny and I have been friends for a long time. Went to school together."

"There was a car crushed under the thing that fell," said Chet. "Is it still there?"

"Far as I know," said Norton. "Patrolman is guarding it. Orders not to move it until someone shows up."

"Who's going to show up?"

"I don't know," said Norton.

"Let's get going, then," said Kathy. "I want a look at that car. Take some pictures of it."

"Go straight down the street," said Norton. "Follow the road down to the river. Not far. There's a police car with red lights. That's where you'll find it. I'll get hold of Stiffy and put him to work. See you later on."

At the end of the first block, they spotted the flashing red lights of the patrol car. When they reached the car, a patrolman stepped out of the shadows to meet them.

"Newspaper people," Kathy told him. "The Minneapolis *Tribune*."

"Could I see identification, please?"

Kathy took her wallet out of her bag, handed him her press card. He pulled a flashlight from his pocket, directed a beam of light on it.

"Katherine Foster," he said. "I have seen your byline."

"The man with me is Chet White. He's our photographer."

"Okay," said the officer. "Not much to see here. The thing, whatever it is, is across the river."

"How about the car?" asked Chet.

"It's still here."

"How about taking some pictures?"

The patrolman hesitated. Then he said, "I guess that would be all right. Don't touch it, though. The FBI has asked us to leave it as it is."

"What has the FBI to do with it?" asked Kathy.

"Ma'am, I wouldn't know," said the officer. "But that's the word I got. Some of them are headed up here."

They went around the patrol car and walked a short distance down the road. The crushed car lay at the end of the bridge—or rather, at the end of where the bridge had been. The bridge was gone. The car was flattened out, as if it had been put through a rolling mill.

"Is there anyone in it?" asked Kathy.

"We don't think so, Ma'am."

Chet was taking pictures, walking around the flattened machine, the camera's light mechanism winking.

"Any identification?" asked Kathy. "A license plate, perhaps?"

The officer shrugged. "I suppose there is, but not visible. It's a Chevrolet. Several years old. Can't be sure of the model."

"No idea of who was in it? What might have happened to them?"

"Probably someone stopped to fish the pool under the bridge. Supposed to be some big trout in there. People often do that, I am told."

"But if that's the case," said Kathy, "wouldn't you think whoever it was would have showed up by now to tell about his big adventure?"

"That does seem strange," said the patrolman. "He might be in the river, though. The bridge collapsed when it hit. A timber might have hit him."

"Someone must have made an effort to find him."

"I suppose," the patrolman said. "I don't know about that."

"Did you see the thing that fell?" asked Kathy.

"Briefly. Before dark closed in. It had already crossed the river before I got here. It was there across the river. A few hundred feet beyond the river. Just sitting there. And big."

"It still was on the road?"

"On it, but extending over it on each side. Many times wider than the road. It had knocked down a few small trees."

"It's still sitting there, right now?"

"I'm almost certain it is. If it moved, it would knock down more trees. There'd be some noise. It's been quiet over there ever since I arrived."

"What's up ahead? Up the road, I mean?"

"Ma'am, that is a primitive forest area over there

across the river. A stand of primeval pines. Big trees. Some of them hundreds of years old. The thing, whatever it is, is trapped, I tell you. It won't be able to get through the trees. It has no place to go."

"Any signs of life in it?"

"Not that I saw. Just a huge black box. Like a huge, awkward army tank. Except it seemed to have no treads. I can't imagine how it moves."

"And that was your impression of it? A big army tank?"

"Well, no. More like a big black box. A big oblong box that someone had painted the deepest possible black."

"Is there any way we could get across the river?" Kathy asked.

"Not a prayer," the patrolman told her. "There's this deep pool under the bridge and fast water at both ends of it."

"A boat, maybe?"

"You could ask around," the patrolman said. "Probably you could get across the pool in a boat. If you can find a boat."

"Up here," said Chet, "everyone's got a boat."

"I wish you wouldn't try," said the patrolman. "I'd have to check on my radio. Probably I'd be told not to let you go."

"Any other way to get around?"

"Not on the roads. The roads are all closed."

"How about the people over across the river?"

"There aren't any people. That's a primitive forest area over there. Miles of forest. No one lives there."

"Officer," said Kathy, "could I have your name? Could I quote some of what you've told me?"

Proudly, the officer gave her his name. "But go easy on the quotes," he said.

7. WASHINGTON, D.C.

Porter stood and watched the press corps enter the room. They seemed more subdued than usual and there were more of them than he had expected. After all, this was a late hour for a briefing.

They filed in and took seats, quietly waiting.

"I must beg your indulgence for the lateness of the hour," he told them. "Perhaps we should have waited until tomorrow morning, but I thought some of you might want to know what we know. This, however, may not be a great deal more than you know.

"Basically, we only know that an object fell out of the sky near the town of Lone Pine in northern Minnesota. The Pine River flows just north of the town and the object fell so that it bridged the river, one end of it on the near bank, the other on the far bank. Curiously enough, it fell on a bridge that spanned the river. The bridge was demolished and a car parked at the near end of it was crushed. No one, at the time, seems to have been in the car. Just before dark, the object moved across the river and, apparently, is still there.

"I think there is one additional matter to report. Whether this ties up with the object that fell in Minnesota we don't know, but tracking stations have discovered a previously unknown and rather large object in orbit about the Earth."

The New York *Times* asked, "Mr. Secretary, you say large. Can you tell us how large and describe the orbit?"

"Mr. Smith," said Porter, "no determination as to size has been made as yet. The best estimate is that it may measure some miles across. As to orbit, I think it is what is called a synchronous orbit. Its height is about 20,000 miles and its speed such as to match the revolution of the Earth. At the moment, as I understand it, it is hanging somewhere over Iowa."

"Dave," asked the Chicago *Tribune*, "you say the new object has been detected by tracking stations. Does that mean it has just now been discovered after achieving orbit, or was it seen earlier before it established orbit?"

"My impression is that it was discovered, already in an established orbit, within just the last few hours."

"Would we be justified in speculating that it might be a mother ship from which came the object that fell at Lone Pine?"

"That, I think," said Porter, "must be up to you—whether you so speculate or not. At this early stage, I'm not engaging in that sort of speculation. Such speculation would imply that both the object in orbit and the one that fell in Minnesota are from some other area of space. This we don't know as yet."

"From your preliminary estimate of the mass of the object in orbit, however, the size of it would seem to rule out it having been launched from Earth."

"Yes, I would think so, but, as I say, there is as yet no certainty."

The Washington *Post* asked, "You said that the Minnesota object moved. I think you said it fell so as to bridge a river. Then moved across the river."

"Yes, that's correct."

"Can you tell us how it moved? How would you characterize its movement?"

"Joe, you have me at a loss for words. I don't know how it moved. That's all the word we have—that it moved. I would assume that to mean it moved independently, by itself. You must realize that at the time it moved, there were present no qualified observers. All we have is what a number of townspeople said they saw."

"Can you give us any further detailed description of it—better than what we have so far? Better than the big black box description?"

"I'm afraid I can't. We have no new information on that point. So far as we know, no pictures have been taken of it. It fell late in the afternoon. Only a few hours later, darkness closed in."

Associated Press asked, "You continue to say you don't know and I imagine no one really can know at this point—but from all that is known, the evidence seems to point strongly to the fact that it may represent an intelligence out of space. Would you have any comment?"

"I'll try to give you a fair answer," said Porter, "and not fall back on my 'I don't know' routine. The thing did fall on a roadway, so you could argue that it was able to pick a good landing spot. It has moved, apparently by itself, which might argue either that there is an intelligence on board or some sort of sensory-controlled machine. As you all know, when a man fired a rifle at it, it, in effect, fired back and the man was killed. This would argue a defense capability. These are points that most of you must have thought of yourself, that anyone might think of. But having said this much, summarized thus far, I can say nothing more. This is not sufficient evidence to justify any solid conclusions. We'll have to wait and see. We need more evidence."

"You appear to be ruling out an Earth origin for the new object in orbit," said NBC. "Could it be some sort of new experimental craft?"

"I suppose, under the circumstances, that anything could be possible. I'm sorry if I seem to be ruling out anything at all. But our people assure me it is nothing of ours."

"Of someone else's?"

"I would doubt it."

"Then you're saying it's a space visitor."

"You said that, Carl. I didn't."

"Could I intrude for a second time?" asked the New York *Times*.

"Certainly, Mr. Smith."

"Could you outline for us what the government is

doing? Has there been conversation with any other governments? I understand the Lone Pine area has been sealed off. Was that by federal order?"

"So far as I know, there have been no conversations such as you mention. Later there may be, once we know more about the matter. The area was sealed off by the state. The governor has been in contact with the President, but we had nothing to do with securing the area. I assume that some of the federal agencies will be sending in observers, but so far I have not been advised of it."

"Thank you, sir," said the New York *Times*.

"But wouldn't you agree," asked the L.A. *Times*, "that if this object, or both of these objects, the one on the ground and the one in orbit, should turn out to be from outer space, that the matter then becomes a matter of international concern rather than simply national concern?"

"I can't presume to speak for the Secretary of State," said Porter, "but I would think there might be some logic to the form your question takes."

"Let us pursue this assumption a little further," said the Kansas City *Star*. "If it should be established that the object that fell at Lone Pine is actually a spaceship from the stars, or at least from outside our solar system—assuming that this could be the case, then what would be the national attitude? Will any attempt be made to establish some contact, perhaps a limited conversation, with the intelligence that may be aboard it?"

"Our thinking," said Porter, "has not advanced that far. As yet there is no evidence . . ."

"But, if in the next few days such evidence should come about, is there any indication of what our attitude might be then?"

"If you are asking if we intend, willy-nilly, to blow any visitors out of the water, I don't think so. This is not an expressed official attitude; it simply derives from my knowledge of how our government works. It is true that someone did take a shot at the object when it landed. But that was the action of an irresponsible citizen, overwrought, perhaps, by what he saw. I would hope that the rest of us may act as reasonable men."

"And how would you think a reasonable man should act?"

"I think," said Porter, "that a reasonable man might attempt to achieve some sort of reasonable communication. On a very limited basis, more than likely. But once that sort of limited communication was achieved, we could go on to something else. I think that you have forced me to over-extend myself. I have nothing on which I can base an official answer to such a question. The matter has not even been discussed. To my knowledge, at least."

"You realize, of course," said ABC, "that if this should be the case—that here we have contact with another intelligence from somewhere in the galaxy— this might be the most significant event in all of human history?"

"Personally, I do realize this," said Porter. "Again, I am not reflecting official thinking. As I told you, the matter has not been extensively discussed. Our assessment of the situation has not advanced to that point."

"We appreciate that, Dave," said ABC. "We're only asking questions that must occur to many other people."

"Thank you," Porter said.

"To come to more practical matters," said the Baltimore *Sun*. "Can you tell us what the administration's next step might be?"

"I imagine it might be observation. During the next twenty-four hours or so we'll be putting in as many qualified observers as we can. Many of them will probably be scientists drawn from many parts of the country. Not only men who are associated with the government. Other than that, I would think we would be guided by events. I doubt if any one can foretell what may happen next."

"Returning again to the new orbit in space," said the Detroit *News*, "could it be possible that the large mass that has been sighted may be no more than a collection of space junk? We have a lot of stuff up there. Could it somehow have pulled together by some sort of mutual attraction?"

"That's a possible explanation," said Porter. "I know nothing of physics. I can't tell you if that would be possible. The question has not been raised. The space agency might have some thoughts on it."

"Could we send someone up to have a close look at it? Has that been considered?"

"I doubt it has as yet been considered. It's possible that one of the shuttles on the space station might be sent out. Certainly the capability to do so does exist. That is a matter of future consideration."

"If it should be established that we are being visited by someone from the galaxy," said CBS, "would you have some comment on what might be the impact on us . . . on the human race? The realization that there is someone out there."

"The impact, undoubtedly, would be significant," said Porter, "but I'm in no position to comment. A sociologist might have some answers for you."

"Mr. Secretary," said the New York Times, "we thank you for seeing us at such a late hour. You, of course, will keep in touch."

"At all times, Mr. Smith," said Porter.

He watched the press file out. Marcia got up from her desk and came over to stand beside him.

"I think it went rather well," she said.

"This time they weren't out for blood," said Porter. "This business may get political later, but so far it hasn't. It's too new to be political. Give the boys up on the Hill a few days and it will be."

He went to his desk and sat down, watching Marcia get ready to leave and finally go.

The place was quiet. Somewhere, some distance off, a phone was ringing and someone was walking, the footsteps sounding hollow in the distant corridor.

He lifted the phone and dialed. Alice answered.

"I thought you might call," she said. "I was sitting by the phone. How did it go?"

"Not bad. They didn't chew me up."

"Poor Dave," she said.

"It's all right. I asked for it. I take the money."

"You never asked for it."

"Well, maybe not, but I jumped at the chance to take the job."

"Any chance of you running out here? I'd have a drink waiting."

"Afraid not, Alice. I better stay where I can be reached. For a while at least."

"All right, then. Later. Wait a minute. Daddy is signalling frantically. He wants to talk to you."

"Put the senator on. I'm always glad of the opportunity to talk with him."

"Good night, dear. Here's Daddy."

The senator's voice boomed in his ear. "Dave, what's going on down there? TV is full of it, but hell, they don't know what's going on. No one seems to know what's going on. Is there anything to this business of our being visited?"

"We don't know any more about it than the TV people do," said Porter. "One new piece of news. Our trackers have picked up something new in orbit."

Swiftly he told the senator about the new object.

The senator said, "Maybe there's something to it, then. Not like the movies and the TV represent it in their silly shows. No little men so far."

"No little men," said Porter. "We'll have to get used to the idea that, if anyone is there, they might not be men."

"If there is anyone."

"That's right."

"Us Americans jump to conclusions," said the senator. "We have too much imagination and too little sense."

"So far, the country's taken it well. No hysteria. No panic."

"As yet," said the senator, "there's nothing to be hysterical about. In just a little while, there'll be wild stories. Damn fools starting rumors. One thing more, Dave."

"Yes?"

"Is there talk of going international on this?"

"I don't quite understand."

"Are we about to call in other countries? Are we going to share this with them?"

"I don't read you, senator. There's nothing to share as yet."

"But, good Christ, Dave, if there is! If we have aliens landing out in Minnesota, we should grab hold of them. Think of it, a new intelligence, a new technology."

"I see your point," said Porter.

"We, at least, have to have first shot at what we can learn from them," said the senator. "What we could learn from them might turn everything around."

"Have you any idea of how difficult it might be to talk with an alien—if there are aliens in that thing that fell?"

"Sure, I know that. I realize all that. But we have the world's best scientists. We have the brains."

"It's not been discussed here," said Porter.

"You'll drop a word," said the senator. "I'll try to see the President myself, but if you could drop a word . . ."

"I'll drop a word," said Porter. "I don't know how well it will be received."

"A word," said the senator. "That's all I ask. A word before your people down there go charging off in all directions. You want to talk with Alice again?"

"If she wishes."

Alice came back on the line and they talked for a short time and then hung up. Porter swung his chair around and saw that someone was standing in the doorway that led out to the corridor.

"Hello, Jack," he said. "How long have you been standing there? You should have come in and found yourself a seat."

"Just a few minutes," said Jack Clark. Clark was the President's military aide.

"Senator Davenport was on the phone just a minute ago," said Porter.

"What's his interest?"

"Just curiosity," said Porter. "Needed someone to talk with. There are a lot of people tonight who are looking for someone to talk with. I suspect the country may be getting edgy. Nothing to worry about so far, but feeling a bit uncomfortable, doing a lot of wondering, maybe some soul searching."

"And with no evidence as yet that it's any more than some harmless piece of junk falling out of space."

Porter shook his head. "Jack, I think it's more than that. The damn thing moved."

"A machine, maybe."

"Could be," said Porter, "but a machine still is enough to frighten me."

Clark came into the room and sat down in a chair at the corner of the desk.

"How's the President?" asked Porter.

"He went up to bed. I don't imagine he'll get much sleep. He's upset about this. It's the unknownness of it that gets to him. I guess that's what has gotten to the most of us."

"Just now you said it might be no more than a machine. Why is it, Jack, that you are trying to deny it may be an intelligence?"

"Damned if I know. I suppose you're right; that was what I was doing. Somehow I cringe from the idea of an intelligence. There has been so much of a flap the past many years about the UFOs. Almost everyone by this time has made up their minds about them. Everyone, or almost everyone, has some preconceived notions about them."

"But this thing is no UFO, not in the popular sense. None of the characteristics associated with them. No flashing lights, no whining sounds, no spinning around."

"That's beside the point," said Clark. "If there's some evidence the thing's alive or has something alive inside of it, half the country will run screaming in terror, the other half will think the millennium has come. There'll be only a few solid citizens who will take it in stride."

"If it turns out," said Porter, "that an alien intelligence is involved, the federal government, especially the military, will have a lot of explaining to do. For years, charges have been made that the military has played cover-up with the UFOs."

"God," said Clark, "don't you think I've thought of that. It was the first thing I thought of when I heard about it."

"Tell me, true," said Porter. "Has there been a cover-up?"

"How should I know?"

"Who would know? Goddamn it, Jack, if I'm going to be fronting for the administration in this matter, I should know."

"Intelligence, I assume," said Clark. "Maybe the CIA. Maybe the FBI."

"Under the circumstances, would anyone tell me?"

"I doubt it," Clark said.

8. MINNEAPOLIS

Garrison said to Jim Gold, "Has Kathy come on the line yet?"

"No," said Gold. "Stiffy Grant still is holding. He did a lot of talking to start with, but now we've run out of things to say. Gave me a pretty good description of the object. Told me something about the Lone Pine reaction to it. I turned it all over to Jackson. He turned in the story just a while ago."

Gold picked up the phone and spoke into it. "Mr. Grant, are you still there?"

He listened for a moment and then laid down the phone. "He's still there," he said.

Garrison sat down at his desk, picked up the copy of the first edition that a copy aide had left on his typewriter, spread it out to look at the front page.

The headline said: SPACE OBJECT LANDS IN MINNESOTA.

There was nothing but stories concerning the space object on the page—the main story; a sidebar on Lone Pine reaction, supplied by Frank Norton; a story from the governor's office; a statement by the head of the state highway patrol; a piece out of the *Tribune*'s Washington bureau; a speculative story written by Jay Kelly, exploring the possibility of intelligent life throughout the universe and the odds against the Earth being visited by one of the life forms; a map showing the location of Lone Pine.

A good first effort, he told himself. Now if Kathy would only check in and Frank's pictures show up.

He asked Annie, "Any word from the fellow with the film?"

"He phoned ten minutes ago," the secretary told him. "From Anoka. Called when he stopped for gas."

Garrison glanced at the clock on the wall at the end of the newsroom. 10:05. There was still plenty of time to develop the rolls and get a couple of pictures ready for the press.

"Did Kathy's young man call in?" he asked Annie. "When she gets to the phone, she'll want to know."

"Not yet," said Annie. "I looked in Kathy's mail box just a while ago. I thought someone might have taken a call and left her a note. There was nothing there."

"Maybe you better call his home. You have his name?"

"Yes. Jerry Conklin. He's a student at the U. He should be listed in the student directory."

Garrison looked around the room. Unlike the situation earlier, now there were a lot of people at their desks. Most of them, more than likely, should have left by now, their day's work done. Jay, for example, had left early in the day to drive to Rochester to get the cancer story, had come back and written it and then written the piece on speculative life in the universe, and he was still here. As were many of the others, still sticking around, staying in case they should be needed. Good staff, Garrison grunted to himself. But, goddammit, he told himself, they shouldn't be doing this; when their day was done, they should go on home.

"One thing I forgot," he said to his assistant. "We didn't arrange for accommodations for Kathy and Chet. Where will they stay tonight? Is there any place in Lone Pine?"

"A small motel," said Gold. "Annie phoned for rooms."

"Annie thinks of everything."

"When she phoned," said Gold, "the motel told her that Norton had reserved rooms for them."

"Well," said Garrison, "that is taken care of."

Hal Russell, the wire editor, came up to Garrison's desk. "Johnny," he said, "the bureau is sending in another story. The White House just announced that a large, unknown object has been spotted in orbit. There seems to be some thought it may have something to do with the fall at Lone Pine. A mother ship, perhaps."

Garrison put his head in his hands. "Is the night never going to end?" he asked. "We'll have to make room for it. Take the governor's story off page one and shuffle the others around. We'll have to give this one almost equal play with the main story. We'll have to revise the main story lead, get some mention of it in."

"It just started now," said Russell. "It's scheduled at 750 words. We'll be running out of room. We'll have to throw something else out, maybe have a second jump page."

"Look, Hal, there's a lot of crap we can throw out. Run off a copy of it and get it to me when it's finished."

"Sure, Johnny," said Russell.

"I tried Jerry Conklin's phone," said Annie, "and there is no answer. I wonder what could have happened."

"When Kathy gets back, she'll have his ears," said Gold. "I wouldn't want to be the one who stood her up. Even if she wasn't here to be stood up."

Lumbering down an aisle between ranked rows of desks leading to the city desk came the tall, gangling form of Al Lathrop, the managing editor. He had the first edition clutched in his hand and a look of worry on his face. He came to a halt at the city desk and stood there in all his height, looking down at Garrison.

"I don't know," he rumbled. "I'm just a little edgy. We're acting as if this thing at Lone Pine really is something out of space, some sort of visitor out of space."

"But it did come out of space," said Garrison. "It came down out of the sky and landed. We went over all of this at the news huddle . . ."

"But it comes out different than I had envisioned it. The connotation is that it's an intelligence out of space. Some sort of UFO."

"Read it again," Garrison told him. "Read it carefully. Nowhere have we said that. We've said what other people told us. If they believed it was an UFO, or an approximation thereof, we said so. But, otherwise than that . . ."

"This story of Jay's . . ."

"A background piece. Sheer speculation and Jay says so. If there are intelligences in space, what could they be like, what are the chances they'll ever visit us. It's the kind of article that has been written again and again. Published in magazines and newspapers, aired over TV and radio. Jay puts in a qualification every second paragraph. If this should be the case, he writes. If this Lone Pine object is an intelligence out of space, or something else entirely . . ."

"Johnny, we've got to be careful. We could create a panic."

"We're being careful. We've reported objectively. We've not gone an inch beyond . . ."

The phone rang and Annie answered it.

"Well, all right," said Lathrop. "Let's keep on being careful. Let's not go beyond the story."

Annie said to Garrison, "That was the photo lab. The kid just came in with the rolls of film."

Gold was reaching out his phone to him. "Kathy just now came on the line," he said.

Garrison took the phone, said into it, "Just a minute, Kathy."

He cupped the phone with his hand and said to Gold, "Tell the news desk they'll have photos for the next run. A couple on the front page and maybe some inside. Take a look in the photo lab and see what they've got. If they are good, try to get the news desk to pick out a fairly open page for them. There's a lot of junk in the paper that we can clear out to make room for them."

Lathrop, he saw, was going down the aisle between the rows of desks, the paper still clutched in his hand.

Garrison spoke into the phone. "All right, Kathy," he said. "What have you got?"

"First of all," said Kathy, "have you heard from Jerry yet?"

9. LONE PINE

Kathy struggled up from the depths of sleep. Someone was pounding at the door. Behind the drapes, the windows were faintly lighted by a weak and early dawn. She searched, fumbling, for the unaccustomed lamp on the unaccustomed bedside table. The room, even barely glimpsed, held a brutal barrenness. Where the hell am I? she wondered. Then remembered where she was: Lone Pine!

Lone Pine and someone hammering at the door.

She found the lamp switch and turned it. Throwing back the covers, she searched with her feet for the slippers on the floor, found them, scuffed them on. She found her robe, lying across the foot of the bed, and struggled into it.

The pounding still continued.

"All right! All right!" she yelled. "I'll be there."

Pulling the robe close about her, she shuffled to the door, pulled the bolt and opened it.

Frank Norton stood outside.

"Miss Foster," he said, "I hate to bother you at this hour, but something's happening. The thing that fell out of the sky is cutting down trees and eating them."

"Eating trees!"

He nodded. "That's right. It is cutting them down and chewing them up. It's gulping down big trees."

"Please," she said, "will you get Chet up. He's next door. Number three. I'll be right out."

Norton turned away and she closed the door. The room was miserably cold. When she breathed, faint wisps of her breath hung in the air.

Swiftly, gasping with the cold, she got into her

clothes, stood in front of a mirror to run a comb through her hair. She didn't look her best, she knew. She looked a sight; but the hell with it. What would one expect, routed out of bed at this time in the morning.

Norton was crazy, she told herself. The thing across the river couldn't be eating trees. It might be no more than a joke, but Norton didn't seem like someone who would spend much time in joking. But why in the world would the contraption over there be gulping trees?

When she went outside, Chet already had emerged, laden with his camera gear.

"You look good," he said to Kathy, "even at this ungodly hour."

"Go chase yourself," said Kathy.

"I'm sorry," said Norton, "for routing you out even before the sun is up. But I expected you would want to know. I thought about it for all of thirty seconds."

"It's all right," said Kathy. "It goes with the job."

"There are other newspaper people in town," said Norton. "They came in during the night. Dribbling in. Trowbridge from the Minneapolis *Star*, someone from the Kansas City *Star*, a couple of people from the Des Moines *Register* and *Tribune*. All of them brought photographers. I expect there will be others later in the day."

"How are they getting in?" asked Chet. "The roads were blocked."

"The state patrol got them unblocked. Got people turned around and turned back. A few cars left there. I suppose yours is among them. The patrol pushed them over to the shoulder of the road. They're letting in the press and a few others, but keeping the public out."

"Any TV people?" asked Kathy.

"Several crews," said Norton. "They're raising hell. They want to get across the river, but there's no way to get there."

"No boats?"

"They've been looking for boats. Not many people

here have boats. What boats there are are out at lakes in the area. No one uses boats on the river."

There were few people in evidence as they walked down the street. All of them, Kathy told herself, must be down at the end of the ruined bridge watching the thing chew up the trees.

Well before they reached the river, they heard the occasional crash of a falling tree and a growling sound that rose and fell.

"That's the thing chewing up the trees?" asked Kathy.

"That's right," said Norton. "It knocks down a tree and grabs it . . ."

"But those are big trees," objected Chet.

"The thing itself is big," said Norton. "Wait until you see it."

A good-sized crowd was gathered at the shattered bridge. Three TV crews were in position on the roadway. The car that had been flattened by the falling object had disappeared. A state patrol car was parked beside the road and two troopers lounged against it. Neither of them, Kathy noted, was the trooper who had been there the night before.

Across the river lay the object. Kathy sucked in her breath in amazement. Everyone had been telling her how big it was, but, even so, she had not been prepared for the size of it. So big, that while most of the trees in front of it towered over it, it still stood up for half their height or more. Big and black—the blackest thing she had ever seen. But strangely, otherwise unspectacular. No antennae sprouted from it; nothing sprouted from it. None of the gadgets which the TV shows on UFOs delighted in tacking on their flying saucers. Just a gaunt, overgrown black box. And, strangely too, with no menace in it. Nothing except its size to make it a thing to be frightened of.

In front of it, one of the big trees slowly tilted and then came crashing down. In front of the object lay piled-up litter of other downed trees. From the thing came a steady growling of wood being chewed up, ground up, ingested, whatever the thing might be doing to the trees. The tree that had fallen seemed to have acquired a life of its own. It was bobbing and switching back and forth. And, slowly, it was being drawn in toward the front of the machine.

"The damn thing just sucks them in and chews them up," said Norton. "Since it started half an hour or so ago, it has moved almost its length. I'd figure that to be three hundred feet or more."

"What is it doing?" asked Kathy. "Trying to chew a path through the woods?"

"If that's what it's doing," Norton told her, "it has a long way to go. That forest extends for twenty miles or more, all of it heavy growth."

She stood and watched. There wasn't much to see. Just the huge black box knocking down trees and gobbling them up. The frightening thing about it, she thought, was its slow, deliberate movement, its sense of power, its seeming confidence that nothing could prevent it from doing what it was doing.

She walked over to the police car.

"Yes, miss," said one of the troopers. "Anything we can do to help?"

"The car," she said. "The one that was lying crushed at the end of the bridge. It isn't there now."

"A truck came and hauled it away," the trooper said. "The driver had the proper papers to requisition it and we let him take it. We checked by radio and were told it was all right."

"Where did the order come from?"

"Miss," the trooper said, "I can't tell you that."

"The FBI?"

"Miss, I cannot discuss it."

"Well, all right," she said, "perhaps you can't. Can you tell me what is going to happen next?"

"The army engineers will be coming in to build a temporary bridge. We expect them any time. One of those prefabricated bridges, as I understand it."

Chet came walking up. He said to her, "I've taken all I can from here. We ought to get up closer. Trowbridge and me and some of the others have been talking about it. We think we can wade the river. The stream below the pool is fast, but not too deep. Or that's what the locals tell us. If we join hands, form a chain, help one another, we can get across."

One of the troopers said, "You can't cross the river. We have our orders. No one is to cross the river."

Kathy said, "If you are going to cross, count me in. I'm going, too."

"The hell you are," said Chet. "You stay here and guard the equipment that we have to leave behind. I'll just take one camera and some film reloads across."

"Chet White," said Kathy, "I am going. If the others go, I'll go along . . ."

"You'll get your ass soaked. That water's cold."

"I've been soaked before. And cold before."

"The trouble," said Chet, "is them TV jerks. They want to carry a lot of equipment over. They want us to help. That stuff of theirs is heavy."

The trooper who had spoken earlier moved in close to them.

"You can't cross that river," he said. "We have orders."

"Show me them orders," said Chet belligerently.

"We haven't got written orders. Our orders are verbal. Over the radio. No one's to cross that stream."

Trowbridge, of the Minneapolis *Star*, came up. "I heard you," he said to the trooper. "You'll have to use force to stop us. I don't think you'll use force."

The second trooper joined the first. "You goddamned newspaper people," he said, disgusted. He said to his partner, "Get on the radio. Tell them what is going on."

Another man joined them. "I'm Douglas, Kansas City *Star*," he told the trooper. "We'll make note of your order, but we have to get across. It's our job to get across. That's federal land over there. You're state. Lacking a court order . . ."

The trooper said nothing.

Douglas said to Kathy, "You're determined to go with us?"

"You're damned right I am."

"Stick close to me, then. Hang on tight."

"Thank you, sir," said Kathy.

"Here," said Chet, handing Kathy a camera. "Drape this over your neck. I'll help one of these TV jerks with his stuff."

"What will you do with the rest of your stuff?" she asked.

"All of us will pile what we can't take here on the road. The troopers will guard it for us."

"The hell we will," the trooper said.

He turned and walked back to the car, where his partner was talking on the radio.

"You guys were tough with the troopers," Norton said.

"We'll apologize later," said Chet. "Goddammit, we got a job to do."

"There are laws about crossing fire lanes and such."

"This here ain't no fire lane," said Chet. "This here is a river."

"O.K.," said Norton. "I'll cross with you. On the other side of Kathy. Me and the Kansas City *Star* will see she doesn't drown."

One of the troopers came back. "You can cross," he said. "No further objection from us. But on your own responsibility. It's your ass." He said, looking directly at Douglas, "You can also take note of that."

"Thank you, sir," said Douglas. "Most willingly. And thank you."

The line was forming on the river bank. There was some shouting and shoving. Trowbridge hurried down the bank and took command.

"Cut out the horseplay," he shouted. "Get in line, grab hold of the man next to you. Take it easy. Take a deep breath. That water's cold. It will freeze your balls."

He suddenly became aware of Kathy.

"I'm sorry, Kathy."

"Don't think a thing of it," said Kathy. "You can't say a thing I haven't heard before."

The line edged into the water.

"Jesus," sang out a TV man, who was in the lead, "this water is like ice."

"Easy," someone said. "Take it easy, men."

They inched across. In the deepest part of the stream, the water came to a tall man's waist.

Kathy, as she hit the water, gritted her teeth. But as she inched along with the others, one hand engulfed in the big fist of Douglas, the other held, vise-like, in Norton's hand, she forgot the cold and concentrated on making her way across.

The head of the line reached the opposite bank, clustered there to help the others.

Teeth chattering, Kathy climbed the river bank, Chet's camera swinging, bumping against her.

Chet reached back a hand to help her up the last few feet, took the camera from her.

"Run around a bit," he told her. "Jog around. Keep moving. You'll be warmer that way. You look like a drowned rat."

"So do you," she said. "So do all the rest of us."

Some of the others were running up the slight incline that sloped down to the river. She ran along with them. To their left, the object from the sky loomed tall above them, like a great black wall reaching into the sky. The crashes of the falling trees and the deep, rising and falling rumble of the object chewing them up was louder than it had been across the river.

Photographers scattered, their cameras aimed.

Here, close to it, the object was more impressive than seen from farther off. Here the true dimensions of it became apparent. Too, the imperturbability of it— the great black box lurching slowly along, paying no attention, or at least giving the impression of paying no attention, to the humans who swarmed about it. As if it might be unaware of them, or being aware of them, ignored them. As if we didn't exist, thought Kathy, as if we were not worth paying attention to, little scurrying life forms that were beneath its notice.

She gravitated toward the rear end of the object and tried to make out how it moved. There were no treads, no wheels, nothing to propel it. As a matter of fact, it seemed to have no moving parts and, come to think of it, no part of it seemed to touch the ground. She considered crouching down and putting her hand between the ground and the great black mass to see if there actually were some ground clearance, but, at the last minute, her courage failed her. You could lose a hand with a stunt like that, she told herself.

The box, she saw, was not actually a box. The side that she could see went straight up, but the rear end (and maybe the front end, too, she told herself) curved outward slightly, that area of it closest to the ground flaring out slightly. For some reason she could not quite reconcile, the whole thing reminded her of a turtle in its shell.

She walked in back of it and stubbed her toe, pitching forward, but catching herself before she fell. She looked to see what she had stubbed her toe on. Whatever it was, was white and smooth and close to the ground. Squatting down, she brushed away the forest duff that covered it. It was, she saw, a newly cut tree stump, sheared off smoothly, only a couple of inches above the ground.

Stunned, she rubbed the palm of her hand across the smoothness of the stump. Little drops of resin were oozing out of it and smeared her palm. The object, she realized, was not knocking down the trees, as she had thought. It was cutting them close against the ground and pushing them, with its great weight, so they fell in front of it.

And that meant, she told herself, that this harvesting of the trees was not a simple matter of forcibly crashing its way through them. It meant that the object was designed to do this very thing. And, as she did, the back end of the turtle-like shell twitched and then rolled up—like an automatic garage door responding to a signal.

It slid up five or six feet and three large white objects were expelled from it. Along with the three white objects came a sudden gush of chewed-up bark and pine needles, resembling the mulch spewed out by a lawn mower.

Then the back of the object slid down again.

Chutes? Kathy wondered. Had she seen chutes out of which the baled white masses and the mulch had been expelled? She could not be sure she had.

She walked up cautiously to one of the bales, put out a hand, then pulled it back, suddenly frightened, reluctant to touch the bale. She swore luridly at herself for her timidity and put out her hand again. The white material was tightly packed, compressed, but not bound by wires or by anything at all. She dug her fingers into it and the substance resisted the digging. She managed to pull loose a small fragment of the material.

It was, she saw, almost exactly like cotton. Funny thing, she thought, a bale of cotton emerging from this monster that was eating trees.

From across the river came a metallic squealing, and looking to find out what had caused it, she saw that a large truck equipped with a crane had backed up to the other end of the bridge. The crane was lifting an oblong structure of wood off the truck bed. Beneath the structure the crane had lifted were others, stacked upon the truck. It must be, she told herself, the army engineers with their prefabricated bridge. Maybe, she thought, we will not have to wade again across the river, wondering as she thought it how long it might require to put the bridge together. She hoped that it would not take long, for it would be a comfort not to have to plunge again into the chilling cold of the river.

She heard the pound of feet behind her and, turning, saw that Chet was charging towards her, followed by the other photographers and newsmen.

"What have we got here?" Chet panted. "Where did those bales come from?"

"The thing just spewed them out," she said.

Chet was squaring off, his camera to his face, the others rushing in behind him. The TV crews frantically went about setting up their equipment, some of them using hand-held mini-cams, while the others manipulated tripods and electronic gear.

Slowly, Kathy backed away. There was nothing more that she could do—and it was a damn shame, she told herself. This was a break for the afternoon papers. It would be in the evening papers and on the evening TV news shows before the *Tribune* went to press. That was the way it sometimes went, she told herself philosophically. You won a few, you lost a few. There was not much that could be done about it.

What did it all mean, she wondered—this box-like monster eating trees and then, from the other end of it, expelling bales of stuff that looked like cotton, along with bushels of junk that probably was the by-product of its eating of the trees. It made sense, she told herself, that bales had been processed from the trees that had been ingested, but what could that white stuff be? She should know, she thought, searching frantically for a knowledge that she knew must be tucked somewhere in her memory, tucked away in those college days when she had struggled valiantly with biology, but not too successfully. Science, she recalled, science and math had been her two worst subjects and she never had done too well in either of them.

A word came floating up. Cellulose. Could that be it? Trees, she remembered vaguely, were made up, in a large part, of cellulose. Perhaps all plants had some cellulose in them. But how much? Enough to make it worth the effort to chew up trees and extract the cellulose? Did cellulose look like cotton? And if this stuff really should be celluose, what the hell did that big back box want of cellulose?

All the time that she had been thinking this, she had been backing up, step by slow step, head tilted back to stare up at the bigness of the thing, trying to get a better perspective of it, the better to measure its size and massiveness.

A tree stopped her. She had backed into it. Lowering her head to look around, she saw that she had backed into the fringe of the forest through which the big blackness was cutting a swath.

A low voice came from behind her. "Kathy," it said. "Kathy, is that you?"

The moment she heard the voice she recognized it, knowing who it was who spoke. She turned quickly, heart pounding.

"Jerry," she said. "Jerry, what are you doing here?"

And there the damn fool stood, grinning at her, enjoying the fact that he had sneaked up on her and frightened her. He was wearing waders and there were scratches on his face and jagged tears in the woolen shirt he wore.

"Jerry," she said again, not crediting what she saw.

He put a finger to his lips, cautioning her. "Not too loud," he said.

She flew at him and his arms came tight around her.

"Careful," he said. "Careful. Let's move back a ways." Propelling her deeper into the tangled cover even as he said it.

She lifted her eyes to him and could feel the tears running down her cheeks. "But, Jerry, why careful? I'm so glad to see you. I was sent up here by the city desk and I left word for you . . ."

"Careful," he said, "because I can't be seen."

"I don't understand," she protested. "Why can't you be seen? Why are you here at all?"

"I parked the car and went fishing in the pool. Then this thing came down and smashed the car . . ."

"So that was your car?"

"You saw the car? I suppose it was smashed."

"It was flattened. They hauled it away."

"Who hauled it away?"

"I don't know. It was hauled away, is all. Maybe the FBI."

"Damn!" he said.

"Why damn?"

"That was one of the things I was afraid of. They'll find the license plates. It can be traced to me."

"Jerry, why are you hiding? What have you got to hide?"

"I was in that thing out there. Inside of it. Something reached down and jerked me inside of it."

"Inside of it? But you got away."

"It threw me out," he said. "I landed in a tree. That saved me."

"Jerry, I don't understand any of this. Why should you be jerked inside of it?"

"To find out what I was, I think. I'm not sure. Not sure of anything at all. I spent all night, lost, huddled in the woods. I damn near froze to death. I did a lot of thinking."

"You thought and got something figured out. Tell me what it was."

"I figured out I can't be one of those kooks who have been inside a flying saucer."

"This is no saucer, Jerry."

"It's the next thing to it. It's from outer space. It's alive. I know."

"You know . . ."

"Yes, I know. No time to tell you now."

"Why don't you come with me. I don't want you running around in the woods alone."

"Those are newspaper people out there, aren't they?"

"Yes, of course, they are."

"They'd take me apart. They would ask me questions."

"No, they wouldn't. I wouldn't let them."

"And there are state troopers at the bridge."

"Yes. Two of them."

"More than likely they are watching for me. They probably figured out someone had parked his car to go fishing in the pool. These waders—they'd know me from the waders."

"All right," she said. "All right. What do you want to do?"

"I scouted down the stream," he said. "When I saw the troopers, I knew I couldn't get across. There's a shallow stretch of water I can wade across. A quarter mile downstream. Just opposite the far edge of the town. Later on, you can meet me there."

"If that's the way you want it, Jerry. I still think you could walk right out with me."

He shook his head. "I have it figured out. I know what will happen if anyone ever finds out I was inside that thing. I'll see you later. Now get back before someone comes looking for you."

"Kiss me first," said Kathy. "You big lug, you never even kissed me."

10. WASHINGTON, D.C.

When Dave Porter entered the conference room, the others were there. Some of them had just arrived and were getting settled at their places. The President sat at the head of the table. General Henry Whiteside, army chief of staff, sat at his right hand, John Hammond, White House chief of staff, at his left.

John Clark, the President's military aide, was sitting near the end of the table opposite the President. He pulled out one of the few remaining chairs as an invitation to the press secretary to sit down.

"Thanks, Jack," said Porter, sitting in the chair and pulling it up to the table.

"Dave," asked the President, "is there anything new on the wires?"

"Nothing, sir. I imagine everyone knows that our visitor is chewing up trees and turning them into bales of cellulose."

"Yes, I think everyone does. That news came early this morning. There is nothing else?"

"A lot of copy is moving," said Porter. "Nothing significant. The new object in orbit is getting a fair amount of attention."

"All right, then," said the President, "let's try to figure out what we know of the situation. General, would you care to go first."

"Everything still seems to be quiet," said Whiteside. "The public has a lot of interest, but there's been no panic. Not so far. It might not take much to set it off, for everyone is keyed up. Tension, I would suspect, is running fairly high, but so far is under control. A few kooks are doing a few outrageous things. There have been demonstrations at some colleges, but good-natured demonstrations. Kids letting off steam. Exuberance, mostly. Out in Minnesota, the state highway patrol has the situation well in hand. Lone Pine has been cordoned off. The public seems to be taking it well enough. No big demand to be allowed to go in. The governor has put the National Guard on alert, but there's been no need as yet to use it. The patrol is allowing the press into Lone Pine. Some photographers and newsmen waded the river early this morning and circulated all around the visitor. Nothing happened. It kept on attending to business, whatever its business may be. I don't mind telling you that we've been concerned about the killing of the barber yesterday, but so far this thing has shown no further hostility. I understand a team of FBI agents from Minneapolis is now at the scene. Perhaps the director has heard from them."

Timothy Jackson, FBI director, said, "Only a preliminary report, Henry. So far as the agents can ascertain, the visitor seems to carry no armament of any sort. Or, at least, nothing that can be recognized as armament. In fact, it has no exterior features at all, nothing mounted on it, nothing sticking out of it."

"Then how did it kill the barber?" asked the President.

"That's what we'd like to know," said Whiteside. "So far, we haven't a clue."

"Steve, you're sending out some men, aren't you?" asked the President.

"They should be there by now," said Dr. Steven Allen, the science advisor. "I expect any minute to hear from them. I must warn you, however, not to expect any quick findings or any startling disclosures. We seem to be dealing with something far outside our normal experience."

"Are you saying," asked Marcus White, the Secretary of State, "that we are dealing with something from space, an extraterrestrial intelligence, perhaps?"

"The tendency at first is always to overstate," said Allen. "There is, I must admit, a temptation to say this is an intelligence from space, but we have no proof yet that it is. It did, undeniably, fall from space, and, as I say, it appears to lie outside all present experience, but, as a scientist, I'm reluctant to make any judgment until at least some results are in."

"You're straddling the fence," said the Secretary of State.

"No, Marcus, just withholding judgment. It would seem unlikely, on the face of it, that it originated on Earth, but as yet we simply do not know. I am encouraged, whatever it may be, by the fact that it does not, so far, seem intent on doing any harm. So far, it's been friendly."

"Cutting down trees is not exactly friendly," said William Sullivan, Secretary of Interior. "Do you realize, Mr. President, that the land where it is engaged in its depredation is a primitive wilderness area. One of the most significant such tracts we have, the most representative of what the primitive wilderness really was like. Some thousands of acres of trees, mostly white pine, still stand there today as they stood before white men came to America. Truly, it is a tragic business."

"It seems to me," said Hammond, "that cutting down trees and separating out the cellulose should be considered a mark of intelligence."

"A well-programmed machine could perform such a task quite easily," said the science advisor.

"But someone or something would have had to program the machine."

"That is true," said Allen.

"I would think," said the Secretary of State, "that the loss of a few trees is a small thing to bemoan in the face of what is taking place."

"From your point of view," said Interior, "that may be true, although from my point of view, I can't agree with you. It's the arrogance of the visitor that bothers me. It's like someone entering a man's backyard and chopping down an apple tree that the owner has cherished for years, or stealing the produce from his garden. Not a simple act of vandalism, but acting as if he had a legal right to chop down the apple tree or to rob the garden."

"We're wasting time," said State, "harping on such small matters. We should be considering our national stance, arriving at some sort of policy. If this visitor of ours out in Minnesota should turn out to be an alien intelligence, we, necessarily, must have a policy to guide our handling of it. We can't be sure it is the only one there is. There may be others waiting to hear from it before coming in. And if others did show up, a policy would be paramount. We must have some idea of how we should act toward them. How are we to treat and view them? I don't mean we have to immediately get down to specifics, for so far we don't know what may be involved, but certainly we should determine some broad guidelines on how we should act under certain possibilities. We have the time now to lay out a policy. If we fail to do so, we'll find ourselves reacting to various kinds of situations and not always to our best interest."

"You are talking like this Minnesota thing is the equivalent of a new nation," said Whiteside. "Well, it isn't a nation. We don't know what it is. How can we decide on policy until we know what it is? As a military man, my principal concern is our defense capability against it."

"Defense," said White. "We have no indication so far we stand in need of any sort of defense."

"There's another matter we should be talking about," said Leslie Logan, the CIA man, "and that is security."

"How do you mean, security?" asked State.

"If there is an intelligence involved in the Minnesota object," said Logan, "if we find that it came from a place that is not the least like Earth, reflecting factors of evolution and development at great variance from those we know on Earth, then there is a possibility we may learn a great deal from it. We would be dealing with an alien intelligence and an alien technology. If we could acquire some of its intelligence and technology, undoubtedly we could adapt some of it to our own needs and to our national advantage. Any study that we make of it must be done with this firmly in mind. I would suggest it would be most unwise to share any such knowledge with the world. We should immediately take steps to ensure that nothing we get from it is allowed to leak to other interests."

"So far," said the Secretary of State, "only one visitor has landed. There may be other landings. If there are, the chances would be very good that some of the landings would take place in other countries. If such should be the situation, it seems. to me that we would not be able to squirrel away much knowledge. I think the better course would be to share with the world such knowledge as we can get. If we do this, we then can expect, if there are other landings in other countries, to be in a better position to share in the findings that might be made by others."

"In the first place," said Logan, "we cannot know if there will be other landings. That is a supposition that has been carried too far in this discussion. If there were, not many of the other countries, perhaps none of them, would possess the scientific resources and capabilities that we have to extract knowledge."

"That may be true, but the position you urge would result in an extremely bad world impression if we should be too obviously selective in sharing knowledge or in making public what we find, if we find anything."

"You can rely on our finding a few facts," said the science advisor.

"We could reveal some general findings," said the CIA. "A gesture to world opinion if you think that to our advantage, but I would urge we be in no hurry to do so and that we should be highly selective."

"There is a worldwide interest," said State, "and I am beginning to get some discreet inquiries. Sir Basil, at the British embassy, was on the phone to me this morning. Tomorrow I can expect a call from Dmitri. And others after that. It is my view that it would foster a much better international climate if we were to be aboveboard from the very start. Before too long, we can expect an opinion being expressed that this is not a matter of national concern alone, that it should be international. I would be in favor of issuing an invitation to a panel of world scientists to participate in our observations, studies and assessments."

The CIA man shook his head. "I don't agree at all with you," he said.

"Andy, what have you got to say to all of this?" asked the President.

"I can't comment offhand," said Andrew Rollins, the Attorney General. "So far as I can recall, there is nothing in international law that would apply. There might be something tucked away in some treaties. You'd have to give me a few days."

"You're talking like a lawyer," said State.

"I am a lawyer, Marcus."

"Off the top of your head, then. As a man, not a lawyer. What are your thoughts? Should they go contrary to your precious law books, we'll not hold you to them."

"The thing that strikes me," said Rollins, "is that we have talked about our interests and the world's interests and what sort of policy we should have. Never for a moment have we considered the interests of this visitor of ours. It has dropped in to visit us, whether for good or evil, I don't know. But, until we do know, until we have some indication otherwise, I think that as gracious hosts, we should give it some benefit of doubt."

"Andy," said State, "that is exactly what I have been trying to say. As usual, you say it much better than I could have."

"But it is destroying trees!" wailed Interior.

"While I recognize that we may have some obligation to act the gracious host," said Whiteside, "I still would insist that we must stay alert. We must be on our guard. We are facing something with which we are unfamiliar."

"You still think we may be forced to defend ourselves?" asked State.

"I didn't say that, Marcus. I said we should remain alert."

Porter spoke up. "At the press briefing today, there were a number of questions about the new object in orbit. Wanted to know if we were considering sending a shuttle from the space station to investigate. I could only say that it still was under discussion. Is that still the case? I remember that it was mentioned earlier."

"The shuttle can leave within an hour," said John Crowell, of NASA. "It requires only a presidential order. The station has been alerted and the shuttle crew is standing by."

"How difficult an undertaking would it be?" asked the President.

"A fairly simple exercise," said Crowell. "Both the station and the object are in synchronous orbits, displaced from one another by less than a thousand miles. Using the shuttle for a closer look would seem to be to our advantage. Using the telescope on the station, which is not, as you may know, an astronomical glass, but one of rather limited power, we have been able to pick up some information. The object is much larger than had first been believed. It measures nearly twenty miles in diameter and is five miles thick. In the form of a disc. It seems not to be a single, solid object; rather it is made up of discrete parts."

"The thing that is in the back of everyone's mind, of course," said Porter, "is that it may have something to do with our visitor. That it may be a mother ship."

"I think we should send out a shuttle," said the President, "and find out what it really is." He asked Crowell, "Can you see any danger?"

"Nothing specific that I am aware of," said Crowell. "In the case of an unknown, danger can't be entirely ruled out."

"How do the rest of you feel about it?" asked the President. "See any complications?"

"There may be complications," said the Attorney General, "but it's something we must do. We should know what's out there, what we may have to deal with. But I think the pilot should be ordered to be extremely cautious. Careful to stir up nothing. No overt moves. Absolutely no heroics."

"I agree," said State.

"So do I," said Interior.

A murmur of assent went around the table.

11. LONE PINE

Jerry was across the river and waiting when Kathy came down the hill back of the motel. He was sitting at the edge of a clump of plum trees that screened him from sight of the bridge a quarter mile or so upriver.

Kathy came around the clump of plums and saw him there. She tossed the pair of shoes she was carrying at him.

"You can get rid of the waders now," she said. "I hope I got the right size."

"I wear eights," said Jerry.

"These are eights and a half. I couldn't remember. Maybe I never knew. Better too big than too small. Sightseers are walking in, getting past the troopers. Without the waders, no one will take a second look at you."

"Thanks," said Jerry. "I was worried about the waders."

She came over and sat down beside him. He put an arm around her and pulled her close, bent down to kiss her.

"This is a nice place you have," she said. "Let's stay here for a while and talk. I have a lot of questions. Back there this morning, you never gave me a chance to ask any. Now go ahead and tell me."

"Well, I told you I was inside that thing. I wasn't the only one. There was a fish, a rabbit, a coon and a muskrat."

"You said they wanted to look you over. Did they want to look over the rest of them, too?"

"I think so. You're an alien, say, and you land on

another planet. You would want to find out real quick what kind of life there is."

"Why don't you just begin at the beginning and tell me in detail all that happened."

"You'll interrupt me, ask questions."

"No, I won't. I'll just stay quiet and listen."

"And you won't write me up? You won't write a story about me?"

"Depends on how good the story is. And if it can be written. But if you say no, I won't. I may argue with you about it, but if you still say no, I won't."

"That's fair enough. I drove out of my way yesterday to get to this place because I'd been told about the big rainbow in the pool below the bridge. When I got here, I knew I could spend no more than half an hour because there was this concert you wanted to go to and . . ."

"So you did remember the concert?"

"How could I forget it? You'd bullied me and threatened me . . ."

"All right, go on and tell the rest of it."

He went on and told her, with only a few interruptions.

"Why didn't you come back to Lone Pine last night?" she asked when he was finished. "You knew about this place where you could wade the river."

"Not then," he said. "Not until later. Not until this morning. I was lost last night—all night. When the thing threw me out, I lost all sense of direction and it was dark. I couldn't even find that thing you call the visitor. So I found what seemed to be a path. The only way I could follow it was on my hands and knees. When I tried to walk, I kept blundering into trees. Crawling, I could feel the path with my hands. I followed the path because I thought it might lead me somewhere. But it didn't; it finally petered out. When that happened, I knew I had to wait for morning. So I crawled under a small conifer. Its branches hung down to the ground and sheltered me from the wind. But, even so, it was cold. I had no matches to start a fire . . ."

"And you stayed until it was light?"

"That's right. Then I heard trees falling and that growling sound the visitor makes when it chews them up. I didn't know, of course, that it was the visitor doing it. I didn't know what was going on. This is a primitive wilderness area and no one is supposed to be chopping down trees. But I didn't think about that at the time. I only knew there'd be someone who could tell me how to get to Lone Pine."

"Then you saw the troopers at the bridge and got scared off?"

"Exactly. So I scouted down the river and found this place where I could cross. Then I heard people on this side of the river and went back to have a look. That's when I spotted you."

"I still don't entirely understand," she said, "why you don't want anyone to know you were inside the visitor."

"Don't you see? I haven't a shred of proof to back up my story. I'd just be another jerk trying to capitalize on a flying saucer landing. The country must be all stirred up by now."

"It is," said Kathy. "Washington, perhaps, the worst of all. I told you about the FBI who are here. A team of scientific observers got in this afternoon."

"If anyone suspected I had been inside that thing," said Jerry, "they'd snatch me up and question me. I could tell them with a good conscience, of course, but I couldn't prove my story. I'd feel like a fool and they probably wouldn't believe me and sooner or later, I would get into the news and half the people would think I was lying and what is worse, the other half would believe me . . ."

"Yes, I see your point," said Kathy.

"What I have to tell wouldn't help much," he said, "but once they got me, they wouldn't let loose. They'd keep on pestering me and questioning me, trying to trap me in lies. Like as not they'd drag me off to Washington and I have my thesis that I am working on . . ."

"Yes, you're right," said Kathy. "I don't know. I think just possibly you made the right decision."

"You mean, then, that you're not going to argue about making a story out of me."

"I don't think I would dare to," she said. "It would sound like sheer hogwash, pure sensationalism. No evidence at all to document the story. Just your unsupported word for it. I can imagine what Al Lathrop would say."

"Who is Lathrop?"

"Our managing editor. He's a bear for documentation. Such a story would never get past him. Probably it wouldn't even get by Johnny. Johnny would be drooling over it, but he'd know that Lathrop . . ."

"That eases my mind," said Jerry. "I thought maybe I'd have to fight you off."

"It's a damn shame," said Kathy. "It would make a nice story. God, what a story it would make! It would go out over the wires. Every paper would publish it. Millions of people would read it. You'd be an instant hero . . ."

"Or an instant bum."

"That, too," she said.

She settled back into the crook of his arm. It was nice here, she told herself. The sun, halfway down the western sky, was warm; there was not a cloud in sight. In front of them, the shallow water gurgled as it chattered along its rocky bed. Across the river, an aspen grove shouted the goldness of its autumn leaves against the somber greenery of the pines.

"You realize, of course," she said, "that eventually they will catch up with you. As soon as they unscramble that car enough to get at a license plate. Or when they have the engine number."

"Yes, I know," he said. "I need some time before they do. I have to think about it more. Get my feet under me. Know what I have to do. Maybe by that time the question of who the car belongs to won't seem important."

"Even when they know you are the one," said Kathy, "there's no reason to mention that you were ever inside the visitor. They'll never ask. No one would suspect that it possibly could happen. All you have to do is let the incident blow over to some extent. I would imagine that as time goes on, the visitor may give them a lot more to think about. Within the next few days, you should file an insurance claim on the car. By that time, we'll probably know who hauled it off and why."

"That can wait. I have one problem, though. I should be getting back to the university."

"Chet will be driving into Bemidji in another hour or so with some rolls of film to put on a plane to Minneapolis. One of the kids who hang around the gas station walked out this morning and brought in the car for Chet. It had been stranded in the traffic jam when the troopers closed roads into Lone Pine and has been sitting there ever since. You can ride with Chet to Bemidji and take the plane from there."

"Kathy, I haven't the price of a plane ticket on me."

"That's all right. I have. I picked up a wad of expense money before I left the *Tribune*."

"I'll pay you back later on. You may have to wait."

"No need. I can work it into my expense account somehow. If not all this trip, the rest of it on the next."

"I hate to leave," he said. "It's so peaceful up here. Once I get back, I'll sit hunched over waiting for the phone to ring or for someone to tap me on the shoulder."

"It may take a while. They may not move too fast. There'll be other things for them to do."

"When will Chet be leaving?"

"Not for a while. We still have a while."

"When will you be back at the *Tribune*?"

"I have no idea. Not too long, I hope. I've been thinking about one thing you said. The thought of home you said the visitor projected into your mind— if that is what it did. What do you make of it?"

"I've thought and thought of it," he said. "It was a curious thing to happen. Not something one would expect. All I do is think around in circles. I can't seem to get a handle on it."

"It does seem strange."

"It all seems strange. If it hadn't happened to me, I'd say it couldn't happen."

"Any overall impressions? Any idea of the kind of thing this visitor could be?"

"It was all so confusing," he said. "I've tried to figure out if it is some sort of machine controlled by an intelligence or if it is actually a live creature. Sometimes I think one way, sometimes another. It all stays confused. Yet, I'm haunted by it. Maybe if I could tell it all, describe exactly what I saw and felt, to some scientist, an exobiologist perhaps, he might see something that I missed."

"Talking to someone about it is exactly what you are trying to dodge," she reminded him.

"What I'm trying to dodge," he said, "is public exposure, questioning by governmental agencies, being sneered at or treated like an over-imaginative child, beaten to death by people who have no imagination, no concept of what may be involved."

Kathy said, trying to comfort him, "Maybe in another day or two, our visitor will just fly off and leave. We may never see its like again. It may have dropped by only for a visit, a short rest before it goes on to wherever it is going."

"I don't think so," said Jerry. "I don't know why I think this, but I do."

"There's a man at the university," said Kathy. "Dr. Albert Barr. An exobiologist. Not widely known, but he has published a few papers. Maybe you should talk with him. Jay wrote a story a year or so ago about him. He sounded like a good guy."

"Maybe I'll look him up," said Jerry.

12. SPACE

"Do you see anything?" the pilot of the shuttle asked the co-pilot. "Our beam says we're close, but I can't see a thing. We should be seeing something. Some glint, some reflection. The sun is straight behind us."

"I see nothing," said the co-pilot. "I thought I did a minute or so ago. But there's nothing now."

"I'd hate to run into the damn thing," the pilot said. "Why don't you get on the horn, check with the station?"

The co-pilot picked up the mike. "Station," he said. "Station, this is Shuttle. Can you tell us where we are?"

"Shuttle," said a voice, "our readings put you right on top of it. Don't you see anything at all? Can't you spot it?"

"Negative. We cannot see it."

"Sheer off," said Station. "To the left. You're too close. Try an approach from another angle."

"Sheering off," the pilot said. "We'll get out and try a new approach."

The co-pilot grabbed his arm. "My god," he said, "do you see what I see? Will you look at that!"

13. WASHINGTON, D.C.

Once again, as he always did, to his continuing grati-
fication, Dave Porter felt a deep, quiet pride in Alice
Davenport, pride in being seen with her, in knowing
that this splendid, lovely woman would consent to
spend some time with him. She sat across the table
from him in one of the dim, far corners of an intimate
Washington restaurant, with candles on the table and
music coming from some place far away. She lifted
her glass and looked across it at him.

"It can't be too bad yet," she said. "You've not taken
on that terrible haggard look that I see too often. Did
everything go all right today?"

"The news briefing went off fine," he said. "They
didn't beat me up. They were almost buddy-buddy.
There were no awkward moments. I hope it can keep
on that way. I've told the President that on this one,
we have to come out clean. No holding back on anything. The meeting with the President and his men
was something else again. Some of those bastards are
positively paranoid."

"They want to muffle the news?"

"Well, not really. Although I suspect some of them
would be happy if I did. No, it was other things. Sullivan screaming off his head about a few trees being cut
down, as if a few trees are of any great account. State
insisting that we immediately set up a policy for dealing
with the visitor. The CIA counseling that we keep
secret all that we may learn from it. Whiteside worrying about how we can defend ourselves against it."

"Dave, you say the President and his men, as if you
were not one of the President's men. You don't really

like these men, do you. The men the President has around him."

"It isn't a question of whether I like them or not. I have to work with them. But on my own terms. More and more I am seeing that I have to do that. Some of them I like. Jack Clark, the presidential military aide—I like him. We generally see eye to eye."

"Actually," said Alice, "we don't know what our Minnesota visitor is."

"No, of course we don't. Not the slightest idea. It seems quite apparent that it came from space, but that is all we know. Some of these men we were talking about aren't even willing to admit that much, including our science advisor. Not knowing what it is is not to be wondered at. It landed just a little more than twenty-four hours ago. We'll be lucky if we have any real idea of what it is by this time next week. It may take months to know."

"If it stays that long."

"That, too. It may not stay more than a day or two. If that should be the case, it will give us something to talk about and argue about for years. All sorts of conjecture. All sorts of ideas about how its reception could have been handled differently. All sorts of theories about what we should have done. I hope it stays long enough for us to get a few things nailed down."

"What I am afraid of, if it stays long enough," said Alice, "is that we'll get angry at it, for cutting down some of our precious trees or for some other reasons. Dave, we can't afford to hate this thing. We can't allow ourselves to become filled with a blind hatred for it. We may not love it, but we must respect it as another life form."

"There," said Porter, "speaks the true anthropology student."

"You can make fun of me if you want to," she said, "but that's the way it has to be, for our own good. There probably is other life in the universe and if there's life, there should be some intelligence—but it's unlikely there are too many intelligences . . ."

"Alice, we don't even know if this thing is alive, let alone intelligent."

"There must be intelligence. It landed on a road; it picked its landing site. It is cutting down trees and extracting cellulose. That would argue some intelligence."

"A pre-programmed machine . . ."

"I can't accept that," said Alice. "It requires too much. A pre-programmed machine would have to be programmed to respond to millions of situations and environments. I doubt that could be done. When the visitor landed, it could have had no preconceived notions of what kind of planet it was landing on. A general idea, maybe, but that is all. Even if it were only a machine and was capable of all these things that seem so impossible, there would have to be, somewhere, an intelligence that put the program into it."

"I know. You can talk around in circles on it."

"You cannot sidetrack the conclusion," said Alice, "that an intelligence somehow is involved. We shy away from it, of course, because of our biological bias. Such a thing as that big black box, we say, cannot be alive. There's no living thing on Earth like it, so it cannot be alive. It's so illogical, too. That's another reason we recoil from it. It's processing cellulose and why should it want cellulose? We use cellulose to make paper and perhaps other things as well. I'm not up on cellulose. But this thing can't be intending to make paper, so it makes no sense. No one has stopped to consider that cellulose may be a treasure to it, that trees are a bonanza. Just like gold or diamonds would be to us. It may have traveled across many light-years to find a planet where cellulose exists. There wouldn't be, throughout the galaxy, too many planets where trees, or the equivalent of trees, would grow."

"I have the horrible feeling," said Porter, "that you are leading up to something."

"Yes, I am," she said. "A parallel in history that may teach a lesson. Here is a thing that plops down on top of us and begins to take what it wants, without asking us, ignoring us—doing the same thing the white men did when they came to the Americas or to Africa or wherever else they went. As arrogant as we were, as self-satisfied, as assured as we were of our right to do it."

"I'm afraid," he said, "that there are others who will be saying the same thing. You are the first, but there will be others. The Indians, for one."

"The native Americans," said Alice.

"All right. Have it your way. Native Americans."

"There's another thing," she said. "We have to make every effort to communicate with our visitor. It may have so many things to tell us. Some things, perhaps, that we have never even thought about, have never conceptualized. New viewpoints and perspectives. What we could learn from it may change our lives. Turn us around. I have always thought that somewhere along the way, we got off on a wrong track. The visitor, just possibly, could put us back on the right track."

"I agree with you," he said, "but how do we go about talking with it? To do any good, if it's capable of doing us any good, it couldn't be just pidgin talk. It would have to be a meaningful conversation. That might be hard to come by—if we can talk with it at all."

"It would take time," she said. "We'll have to be patient. We must give it, and ourselves, a chance. Above all, we should do nothing to drive it away. We should hang in there, no matter what it takes."

"So far, Alice, there has been no suggestion that we should drive it away. Even if we wanted to, there's no one who has the least idea of how to go about it."

14. LONE PINE

Kathy woke in the middle of the night, huddling in the bed, cringing against the darkness and the cold of the motel room pressing down upon her.

The cold, she thought, the cold and darkness. And knew that she was not thinking so much of the present cold and darkness, here in this small room, as of the cold and darkness through which the visitor had passed to arrive on Earth.

Had she been dreaming of it, she wondered, the dream, now forgotten, translating into this first waking moment? If so, she had no recollection of the dream.

But the thought of the visitor and of the chill emptiness of outer space still continued to persist. From how far out, she wondered, had it come? Perhaps across light-years, with the glint of unknown suns faint specks of hazy light in the all-engulfing darkness. Propelled across the cosmos, driven by a purpose of its own, driven by an emptiness of soul as deep and wide as the emptiness of galactic space, driven by a hunger unlike the hunger that an inhabitant of the planet Earth might feel, seeking, perhaps, the Earth or another planet like the Earth. And why the Earth, or a planet like the Earth? Because it would have trees? Fiercely, she shook her head, for it must be more than that. There must be something more than trees.

Maybe, she told herself, it was doing no more than exploring, mapping the galaxy, or following some dim, cobbled-together chart that some earlier traveler might have put together, following it in the fulfillment of a mission that the human mind might not have the capability to grasp.

The cold and dark, she thought again, wondering why it was that she continued to come back to the cold and dark. But there would be more, she thought, than the cold and dark. There would be, as well, the loneliness, the smallness of one's self in the never-ending gulf where there could exist no flicker of compassion or even of awareness, but only a great uncaring that took no notice of anything that moved or made its way across it. What kind of creature, she wondered, could stand up in the face of this great uncaring? What kind of creature could consign itself to the maw of nothingness? What sort of motive must it have to drive itself into the continuing emptiness? Perhaps it had a purpose—for to do what it had done, there must be a purpose. But if its purpose were the Earth, then it could not have known when it started out that it would achieve its purpose. Certainly, no one in even the most shallow depths of space could know of Earth, or have any inkling of Earth.

Poor, lonely thing, she thought. Poor frightened eater of the trees. Poor creature of so far away, coming into Earth from the great uncaring.

15. WASHINGTON, D.C.

Porter had gotten into his pajamas and was turning down his bed when the phone rang. He glanced at the clock on his bedside table; it was almost two o'clock.

"This is Jack," said the voice on the other end of the line. "Jack Clark. Were you asleep?"

"In another minute, I would have been."

"Dave, I think this is important. Can you come down to the White House? Meet us in your office."

"Who is us?"

"Me, NASA, the science advisor, Whiteside."

"Not the President?"

"He's asleep. We don't want to wake him. There are a few things we should talk out."

"Such as?"

"Your line is not secured. I can't tell you. I repeat, it is important."

"Be there in ten, maybe fifteen, minutes."

"On second thought, maybe I should get the White House chief of staff in on this too. You have any objection?"

"Hammond? Sure. Why not? By all means, get him in."

"All right, then. We'll be expecting you."

Porter put the phone back in the cradle. Now what the hell? he wondered. Clark was excited and concerned; it could be heard in his tone of voice. Perhaps, Porter thought, no one else could have known. But he did. He'd known Jack Clark for a long time.

He took another look at the bed. Why not just sack out, he asked himself, and to hell with Clark and the others? God knows, he needed the rest. In the last twenty-four hours, he had logged little sleep. But he knew that he was only trying the thought on for size. In fifteen minutes, he would be walking down the corridor toward the press office. He started taking off his pajamas, heading for the chest of drawers to get socks and underwear.

In the driveway, before he got into the car, he stood for a moment, looking at the sky. Somewhere to the north, some distance off, he could hear the mutter of a plane coming in to land. He looked for the blinking lights of the craft, but they could not be seen. Out in the street, fallen leaves made a rustling sound as they were driven along the pavement by the wind.

Everyone except Hammond was present and waiting when he entered the door of the press room. Against the wall, the wire machines made soft chortling noises. The kitchen had brought up coffee; a gleaming urn sat on one of the desks, with white coffee mugs ranged in a huddled group.

Whiteside had taken the chair behind Porter's desk, was teetering back and forth in it. Crowell, the NASA man, and Dr. Allen sat side by side on a small sofa. Clark was filling coffee cups preparatory to passing them out. Hammond came striding briskly through the door.

"What is going on?" he asked. "You sounded urgent, Jack."

"I don't know how urgent," said Clark. "It's something we should talk over. The shuttle went out and the station has sent the word."

"What kind of word?"

Clark gestured toward Crowell. All eyes in the room turned to the NASA man.

"The new object in space," said Crowell, "as many of us must have suspected, but didn't want to talk out loud about, very definitely has a connection with the visitor that came down in Minnesota."

"How connected?" asked Hammond.

"It's not an object at all, in the classical sense of the

term. It is a cluster of the visitors, hundreds of them, perhaps thousands. No one so far has taken the time to compute how many there could be."

"You mean a swarm of them clustered in the form of a wheel?"

Crowell nodded. "We should have known without even going out to look. Telescopic observation from the station should have tipped us off. The observers saw no solid object, what they saw was a collection of discrete particles."

"Not exactly discrete particles," said Clark.

"From the distance of a thousand miles, they would have seemed to be."

"But they're still remaining in the cluster," said Hammond. "What I mean, they're not beginning to break up."

"We can't be sure," said Crowell. "The two men on the shuttle said they seemed to be sort of unraveling at the edge. All the visitors—visitors is an awkward word, but I don't know what else to call them—all the visitors at the edge of the disc didn't seem to be as neatly tucked away as they should have been. Whether this means the swarm is beginning to break up, we don't know. If you carry the analogy to that of a swarm of bees, that situation could be quite normal. In a swarm of bees, while the swarm itself may be intact, there are always quite a number of bees in motion around the edges of the swarm, jockeying around to find a more secure place where they can fit themselves. That may be the case with our swarm out there. The men in the shuttle couldn't be sure. They had trouble seeing."

"Couldn't see?" asked Whiteside. "What could prevent their seeing?"

"In space, objects often are hard to detect," said Crowell. "There's not a proper background against which to see them. You see mostly by reflected light."

"But there's the sun," said Whiteside. "The swarm would have been in full sunlight. There should have been plenty of reflection."

"General, there simply wasn't. Which leads me to

believe that we may be dealing with what amounts to black bodies."

"Black bodies? I've heard the term, but . . ."

"Bodies that absorb all energy, in this case, the radiation from the sun. A perfect black body would absorb all energy, reflect none at all."

"Why, certainly," said Allen. "I should have suspected that. Should have known it, in fact. To navigate through space, a fair amount of energy is needed. That's the way these things get their energy. There isn't much, but they get all there is. Not only from the suns in space, however feeble the radiations from those suns may be, but from anything else from which they could extract energy. The impact of micrometeorites would give them some. Kinetic energy, of course, but probably they could transform that into potential energy. Cosmic rays, and cosmic rays have a lot of energy. All other kinds of radiation. They'd gobble it all up. They'd be energy sponges."

"Doctor, you're sure of that?" asked Hammond, drily.

"Well, no, not exactly. Certainly I'm not certain of it. But the hypothesis is sound. It could be the way it works. There'd have to be some such means for a space-going machine to extract sufficient energy to keep going."

He said to Crowell, "Even before you told us what the object is, I had a hunch we'd find what you describe. My men at Lone Pine report the visitor there is sending out signals, modulated signals, which would argue that it is in communication with something. And I asked myself what could it be communicating with. The answer seemed to be others of its kind. No one else could decode the garbage that it's sending."

"Which means," said Whiteside, "that it is telling all of its relatives out there what fine forests it has found. Inviting them in to eat their fill. In a little while, there may be others tumbling down, landing in our forests and tucking their napkins underneath their chins."

"Henry," said Hammond, "you're jumping to conclusions again. We can't be sure of that."

"The possibility exists," said the general, stubbornly. "We can't close our eyes to it. My god, what a horrible situation!"

"What else did your men find?" Porter asked Allen.

"Not much. The visitor is not metal. We are sure of that. We don't know what it is. We tried to get samples . . ."

"You mean your men just walked up to it and pried away at it and scraped away at it?"

"Hell, man, they climbed all over it. They examined every inch of it. It paid them no attention. It never even twitched its hide. It just went on with its lumbering."

"For the love of God," asked Clark, "what are we dealing with?"

No one answered him.

Crowell said, "One other thing puzzles me. How the swarm up there got into orbit. It takes a while to eject an object into orbit. Several times around the Earth until it's where you want it and moving at the speed you want it. If this new object, if this swarm did any jockeying preliminary to getting into orbit our spotters would have caught it well ahead of time. But they didn't. When they found it, it already was in a settled orbit. And, another thing: It would have had to know quite a lot about the planet around which it intended to set up an orbit—the planet's speed, its rotation rate, its gravitational attraction. This would apply to any kind of orbit, but to set up a synchronous orbit, it would have had to have all the factors figured to a fraction. Apparently, it just plopped in and settled to the correct altitude at the correct speed and how the hell that could be done, I don't know. I'd say, offhand, it would be impossible."

"So now that we have all the bad news," said Hammond, "what are we going to do about it? That's what this meeting is for, isn't it? So we can map a course of action. In the morning, I'd like to be able to tell the man upstairs that we have some answers for him."

"One thing we should do is to notify all the governors to put the National Guard on alert," said Whiteside.

"That would be guaranteed," said Hammond, "to scare the country senseless."

"And make some of our international neighbors nervous," said Clark.

The general asked, "How about passing the word along quietly? Telling the governors to be prepared to call out the guard at a moment's notice."

"It would leak," said Porter. "There's no such thing as secrecy among forty-eight governors—fifty if you were to include Hawaii and Alaska and I suppose Hawaii and Alaska would have their noses out of joint if we passed them by. Governors are political creatures and some of them are blabbermouths. Besides, they all have staffs and . . ."

"Dave is right," Hammond told Whiteside. "You'd simply be asking for it."

"If it comes to that," said Porter, "the country should be told, not only about what we are doing but why we're doing it. They'll find out in a few days in any case and it would go down better if we told the people at once. Let the news come from us rather than from someone else."

"Otherwise than the National Guard, what can we do?" asked Whiteside.

"You persist," said Allen, "in regarding these things as enemies."

"At least, they're potential enemies," said the general. "Until we know more about them, we must be prepared to recognize them as possible threats. If they should invade us, then, automatically, they are enemies."

"Maybe it's time for us to lay out the situation to some of our international friends," said Hammond. "We've held out from doing this, but if that swarm up there starts coming down, we're not going to be the only ones involved. Maybe we owe it to the others to let them know what is going on."

Whiteside said, "The President should be sitting in with us on this."

"No," said Hammond. "Let him sleep. He needs the rest. A long, hard day is coming up."

"Why do we assume that we are the only ones who sent out a shuttle to have a look at the swarm?" asked Porter. "The Soviets also have a space station. They could have sent out a shuttle. We announced the new object in space more than twenty-four hours ago. They'd have had the time."

"I can't be sure," said Hammond. "I think it is unlikely. Their station is a considerable distance from ours, the shuttle trip would be longer. Not that distance makes that great a difference, but somehow I don't think so. For one thing, they'd have less reason to react. The visitor is in our country, not theirs."

"What difference does it make, anyhow?" asked Clark.

"We wouldn't want to go to them," said Porter, "and say, 'Look, pal, we got these things up there' if we had any reason to believe they knew as much as we do, maybe more than we do."

"I think your objection is academic," said Hammond.

"Perhaps so," said Porter. "We just don't want to look any sillier than we have to."

"Let's get back," said Whiteside, "to the matter of defense. You vetoed the National Guard. If we can't do that, the regular military establishments should be alerted."

"If it can be done without publicity," said Hammond. "If you can guarantee no leaks."

"That can be managed," said Whiteside.

"What I'm worried about is public panic," said Hammond. "It's been all right so far, but touch the wrong button and the country can go sky-high. There's been so much talk, so much controversy, all these years, about the UFOs, that the country's ripe."

"It seems to me all the UFO talk works to our benefit," Porter told him. "The idea of aliens coming to Earth is a bit old hat. Many people are reconciled to the thought that some day they will come. Thus, they are more prepared for it. It will be less of a shock.

Some people believe it would be good for us if they did come. We no longer have the H. G. Wells' War of the Worlds psychology. Not in full force at least. We have some philosophical preparation."

"That may be so," said Clark, "but one damn fool saying one wrong thing could trigger a panic."

"I agree," said Hammond. "Maybe your approach is correct, Dave. Tell the people what we know. Give them a little time to think it over, so if more visitors come the people will be half accustomed to the idea. A soothing word here and there, being careful not to overplay the soothing syrup. Buy some time for sober reflection. Time to think it out and talk it over."

"So what we have is this," said Clark. "Military installations will be informed of the situation. Nothing will be done at the moment with the guard, but we'll be ready to put it on alert, throughout the country, on a moment's notice. We'll give earnest consideration to informing and consulting with other governments. We'll tell the people as many facts as we can. How about the U.N.?"

"Let's leave the U.N. out of it for a time," said Hammond. "They'll come charging in fast enough. And it is understood the man upstairs has to put his stamp of approval on all of this. He'll be waking in a couple of hours. We won't have to wait long. When we do move, we should move fast."

"John, I'd like to get the word to my boys right away," said Whiteside. "I can't imagine you would object to that. It's all in the family, so to speak."

"No objection," Hammond said. "That's your turf."

Allen said to Crowell, "The station is keeping watch, I'd assume. They'll let us know if anything is beginning to happen? Or looks as if it is beginning to happen."

"That's right. The minute there's anything going on, we'll know."

"What if one of our international friends gets trigger happy and proposes boosting off a nuke to blow the swarm all to hell?" asked Whiteside. "Or worse, acts unilaterally."

"Henry, you think of the damnedest things," said Hammond.

"It could happen," said the general. "Let someone get scared enough."

"That's something we'll just have to hope doesn't happen," said Porter.

"I think it's most unlikely," said Hammond. "Maybe I should get State out of bed. He'll have to be briefed. Perhaps he could have breakfast with the President. He and a few others. The Attorney General, for one. I'll make the calls."

"And that's it?" asked Crowell.

"It would seem so."

"It's barely worth going back to bed," said Clark. "In an hour or two, it will be morning."

"I'm not going back," said Porter. "There's a comfortable couch in the press lounge. I'm going to stretch out there. In fact, come to think of it, there are two. Anyone care to join me?"

"I think I will," said Clark.

16. LONE PINE

Stiffy Grant shuffled into the Pine Cafe, hoisted himself onto one of the stools at the counter. At the sound of the slamming front door, Sally came out of the back.

"You working in the morning?" asked Stiffy. "I thought Judy worked in the mornings."

"Judy has a cold," said Sally, "so I'm filling in for her."

The place was empty except for the two of them. "Where's everyone?" asked Stiffy. "With all the people who are in town . . ."

"They sleep late," said Sally. "Those who are here. A lot of them are staying in Bemidji, driving here and back. There's no room for them here."

"Those two folks from the *Tribune* are here," said Stiffy. "The camera fellow and that girl writer."

"They got here early when there was still room at the motel."

"They're all right," said Stiffy. "Real white folks. That girl gave me five dollars for just answering a phone and then hanging on so no one else could get the line. Yesterday, the camera fellow slipped me a bottle for keeping watch of what was going on across the river so he could grab some sleep. Was supposed to run and wake him if anything happened. But nothing did. Good liquor, too. None of your cheap stuff."

"Most of the folks are nice," said Sally. "They tip good. Most folks around here don't tip at all."

"They ain't learning much, though," said Stiffy. "There don't seem much to learn from that thing out there. The men from Washington are working real hard at it and not coming up with much. I talked with one of them the other day. He'd been pawing through some of the rubbish the thing is throwing out, what's left after it makes those bales of white stuff. He was all excited about what he was finding but it didn't sound like much to me. He said he wasn't finding any pine seeds, or almost none. The cones had been broken up and the seeds were gone. He said that was unnatural. He seemed to think the thing was collecting the seeds and saving them. I told him maybe the thing was eating them; squirrels and such eat them. But he shook his head. He didn't seem to think so."

"What can I get you, Stiffy?"

"I guess some cakes."

"Sausage or bacon?"

"Naw, you charge too much for them. I can't afford it. Just the cakes. And plenty of syrup. I like lots of syrup."

"The syrup is there in the pitcher. You can use as much as you want."

"All right. Plenty of butter, then. A little extra butter. But don't charge me for it."

Sally went back into the kitchen to give the cook the order, then came back.

"How far has the visitor cut into the woods?" she asked. "I haven't seen it for a while."

"More than a mile, I'd say. It moves right along, day and night. Spitting out those bales of white stuff every few minutes. Leaving a long trail of them behind it. I wonder why it's doing that. It don't make no sense to me. Nothing about it makes any sense to me."

"There must be a reason for it."

"Maybe there is, but I don't see it. I wonder, too, why it picked us out."

"It had to be some place. It just happened to be us. If it was trees it was looking for, it picked a good place."

"I imagine," said Stiffy, "them forestry people ain't

too entranced with it. They set a lot of store by them trees. I don't see why. They're just trees, like any other trees."

"It's a primitive wilderness area," said Sally.

"Yeah, I know," said Stiffy. "A lot of foolishness."

17. LONE PINE

The visitor had gotten lumpy. It had bumps all over it, but it kept on chopping down the trees and masticating them, or at least ingesting them, and at regular intervals the rear section of it slid up, ejecting bales of cellulose and great gobbets of waste from the chewed-up trees.

"We don't know what is going on," one of the two troopers told Kathy. "Maybe some of the people from Washington do, although I'm inclined to doubt it. In any case, they're not talking, so we don't know if they do or not. The lumps on the visitor were there this morning when it got light enough to see. They must have started in the night and they've been growing ever since. They are a lot bigger than they were when I first saw them."

"Any reason why I can't get closer?" asked Kathy. "Some of the other newsmen are."

"Just watch yourself," said the trooper. "Don't get too close. We don't want people getting hurt."

"The visitor has made no move to harm anyone," she said. "We've been practically living with it ever since it landed and it doesn't even notice us."

"You can never tell," the trooper said. "If I were you, I wouldn't push my luck. It killed a man, remember?"

"But he shot at it."

"Even so, I don't trust it. Not entirely, that is. This ain't one of us."

Kathy and the troopers stood midway between the visitor and the river, now spanned by the temporary structure laid down by the army engineers. Behind them and in front of them the wide swath cut through the forest by the visitor was littered with white bales and clumps of tree debris. Both the bales and the debris were regularly spaced, laid out very neatly.

"The other troopers," said the trooper, "are holding the sightseers the other side of the river. We're only letting in the official people and the press. You people know you're here on your own responsibility. That's been explained to you."

"Yes, of course, it has."

"I don't see," said the trooper, "how all these sightseers got here. There seems to be a couple hundred of them. We have all the roads blocked. But they just seep through, sort of."

"They park their cars short of the road blocks," Kathy said, "and walk in through the woods. It would take a picket line to keep them out."

"I suppose so," said the trooper. "They can be a nuisance."

"Here come Frank Norton and Chet, my photographer," said Kathy. "As soon as they reach here, we'll be going in."

The trooper shrugged. "Take it easy, now," he said. "Something's about to happen and I don't like it. I can feel it in the air."

Kathy waited for Norton and Chet to come up and the three of them walked up the swath.

Kathy asked Chet, "Did Jerry get on the plane all right?"

Chet nodded. "We just made it. Only minutes to spare. I gave him the film. He said he'd deliver it. Meant to ask you—how come he showed up here? I seem to remember he turned up missing and you were hunting him."

"His car broke down and he walked into Lone Pine, looking for a phone. We ran into one another. It was a surprise to the both of us. Neither of us knew the other one was here."

"Seems to be a nice guy."

"Yes, he is."

"Not very talkative, though. Didn't have much to say."

"He never does," said Kathy.

They walked up on a group of newsmen clustered to one side of the visitor.

"Did you talk to Johnny this morning?" Kathy asked.

"Yeah, I did. Checking on the film. He said someone delivered it, in plenty of time for the first edition, to the photo lab."

"He didn't say anything about sending someone up to replace me?"

"Not a word. Did you expect he would?"

"Well, I don't know," said Kathy. "There are others he might think would do a better job. Jay, for instance. He only pointed the finger at me because there was almost no one else in the newsroom at the time."

"I don't think you need to worry any. Johnny is a fair man. As long as you do the job, he will leave you here."

"If he tried to send someone else," said Kathy, "I'd yell like hell. This is my story, Chet, and I mean to keep it that way."

"You'd fight for it?"

"You're damn right I would."

"Look," said Norton, "someone has painted a number on the visitor. See it. It reads 101. On the side, up near the front of it."

Kathy looked and saw the number, in green paint, the numerals a foot high or so.

"I wonder who did that," she said.

Chet snorted. "One of them jerks from Washington, most likely. One of them observers. Science types. They got to have everything numbered for the record."

"It seems a funny thing to do."

"We can't presume to judge how the observers go about their work," said Norton. "There probably is a valid reason for the number."

"I suppose so," said Kathy.

"You have any idea what those lumps may be?" asked Norton.

Kathy shook her head. "I can't imagine. It's a shame. It was such a nice, neat thing before, so symmetrical, and now it's got all lumpy."

"You sound like you thought it was pretty."

"Maybe not pretty. But appropriate. The kind of thing you'd expect to come from space. Nice, neat, not spectacular."

"Good Lord," said Norton, "will you have a look at that!"

One of the larger lumps that had grown on the visitor was beginning to burst open and from it was emerging a small replica of the visitor. The thing that was emerging from the lump was three or four feet long, but, except for its size and for the absence of bumps on it, it was an exact copy of the big black box. The lump lengthened and widened even as they watched and the thing that was emerging from it fought free and came tumbling to the ground. It landed and rolled and came upright. It was a shiny black, not the deep black of the visitor, but shiny as if it might be wet. For a moment it crouched on the ground, unstirring, then swiftly it wheeled about and set itself in motion, racing toward the back of the visitor, flowing smoothly and silently.

The group of people surged back to clear the way for it. A TV cameraman was shouting savagely, "Down in front. Down in front, goddammit. Get out from in front of the camera. Give me a chance, will you?"

Kathy, backing away with the others, was thinking furiously: That settles it! It is biological. Not a machine, but a biological being. A live creature, for it is giving birth. It is having babies!

Another of the lumps was splitting open and another small replica of the visitor was fighting free of it. The visitor, itself, was paying to attention to what was taking place. It went on chomping trees.

The first baby to emerge whipped around the rear of the visitor, heading for one of the bales of cellulose. It reared up and attacked the bale, tearing it apart, gulping down the cellulose in much the same manner as its "mother" was gulping down the trees.

Chet was racing toward it, his camera lifted and ready. Sliding to a stop, he braced himself, plastered the camera to his face and began shooting pictures, sliding along after a few exposures to get shots from different angles. Other cameramen also were running frantically, joggling one another for position, forming a ragged circle around the little creature.

"I should have guessed," said a man standing beside Kathy. "When I saw those lumps I should have known. The thing is budding. And that answers the question all of us have been asking ourselves . . ."

"That's right," said Kathy. "It's biological."

He looked at her, apparently for the first time. He raised a hand and touched it to his forehead in salute.

"Quinn," he said. "New York *Times*."

"Foster," said Kathy. "Minneapolis *Tribune*."

"You got here early then," he said. "From the first, I would suppose."

"Late on the day it landed."

"Do you realize," he asked, "that we may be covering the story of the century. If not of all time."

"I hadn't thought of it," said Kathy.

Then, ashamed, she said, "I am sorry, Mr. Quinn. I was being flippant. Yes, I had thought of it."

There were more of the babies now, running wildly to find the bales so that they might feed. The newsmen and photographers were scattering, no longer huddled in a group.

One of the babies had fallen and was not running. It lay jiggling and quivering, like an animal that had fallen and was struggling to get up. It lay close against the visitor, but the visitor was paying no attention to its plight.

It's fallen on its side, thought Kathy. The poor thing has fallen on its side and can't get to its feet. Although how she might know this, she did not know, for, truth to tell, there was no way one could know. No one could tell which part was top or bottom.

Quickly she stepped forward and, stooping, laid hold of it and tipped it. Swiftly, it flipped over and quickly scurried off, heading for the bales.

Straightening, Kathy reached up a hand and patted the barn-like side of the visitor.

"Mother," she said, softly to herself, not really speaking to the visitor, for how was the visitor to hear? "Mother, I helped your baby to its feet."

Underneath her hand, the hide of the visitor twitched and then folded over to grasp her hand, still against its side, folding over gently, covering her outspread hand, to hold it for a moment. Then the hide unfolded and became hard and smooth again.

Kathy stood stricken, shaken, not believing it had happened.

It noticed me, she thought in a wild panic of churning emotion. It knew I was here. It knew what I had done. It tried to shake my hand. It was thanking me.

18. WASHINGTON, D.C.

"What do you have on this pupping business?" the President asked Porter.

"Pupping, sir?"

"Yes, the visitor out in Minnesota, having pups."

"All that I have is on the wires," said Porter. "Fourteen of them so far, and a few more to go."

"A fair litter," said the President.

"You probably know more than I do about it," the press secretary said. "Dr. Allen has his men out there. He probably has reported to you."

"Yes, of course he has. But Allen is an old woman and those observers of his are thin-lipped science people. They won't tell you anything until it's all nailed down. They won't tell you what they're thinking because if they were wrong, their beloved fellow scientists would laugh them out of court. What they do tell you is so filled with scientific lingo and so many ifs and maybes and so much double-talk, you can't tell what they mean."

"You can't mean that Dr. Allen is incompetent," said Hammond. "He is a top-notch man. He has the respect . . ."

The President waved his hand. "Oh, he's competent, of course, and his fellow scientists are filled to overflowing with their respect of him, but he's not the kind of man I cotton to. I like straight talking men who tell you what they mean. With Allen, there's a lot of times when I wonder what he is talking about. The two of us don't talk the same kind of language."

"Barring all this," said Hammond, "cutting through

all the lingo and the double-talk, what does he think of it?"

"He's puzzled," said the President. "A very puzzled scientist. I think he was convinced, when this first started, that the visitor was a machine and now he has to admit, at least to the probability, that it probably isn't. This pupping business has done violence to his little scientific mind. Really, I'm not too concerned with what he is thinking of it because he's going to change his mind a couple of more times before the week is at an end. What I'm more interested in is how the country's taking it."

"It's too soon to know," said Porter. "There are as yet no solid indications, no way to gauge reactions. There've been no outbreaks of any kind. Whatever may be happening is happening underneath the people's skins. They are still busy sorting it all out, holding in their feelings until they get it sorted out. But I have a hunch . . ."

He broke off his words and looked at Hammond and the Secretary of State.

"Well, go ahead," said the President. "What is this hunch of yours?"

"It's probably silly. Or will sound silly."

"Well, go ahead and be silly. I hear a hell of a lot of silly things. I've listened to and profited from many of them. Anyhow, it's among us boys. John and Marcus won't mind. They've said their share of silly things."

"The hunch is this," said Porter, "and I'll not guarantee it, but I have the feeling that this pupping business, as you call it, may serve to somewhat endear the visitor to the people. This country goes all soft on motherhood."

"I don't know about that," said Marcus White, the Secretary of State. "It scares me spitless. Not only do we have hundreds, perhaps thousands, of those creatures out in space, but the one that's here is spawning. What happens if they all come down and spawn?"

"The public won't think of that," said Porter. "Not now. Not right away. The spawning may give us a little time."

"Marcus," said the President, "I know you talked with the Russian. What did he have to say?"

"Not a great deal. Sounded as if he still was waiting for instructions from Moscow. Maybe Moscow doesn't know as yet quite what line it should take. Rumbled around a lot without getting anywhere. Gave some indication that his government might demand some hand in the study of this visitor of ours. I gave him no indication of what our policy might be. For starters, I told him we still considered it an internal matter. Personally, I still think we should give some thought to inviting foreign scientists to participate. It would make for better international relations and we probably wouldn't be hurt too much, if at all."

"That's what you said the other day," the President told him. "Since that time, I've given considerable thought to your suggestion. I'm inclined to be against it."

"What Ivan is afraid of is that we'll find out something from the visitor that will give us a defensive edge," said Hammond. "That's why the ambassador did his rumbling about being counted in. My feeling is that we should hold up until we at least have some inkling of what we might have."

"I talked with Mike at the U.N. just before you all came in," said the President. "He tells me we'll have a fight to keep the U.N. from declaring this an international situation. All our little brothers in Africa and Asia and some of our good friends in South America think, or at least are saying, that this is something that extends beyond national interest. The arrival of a visitor from space, they argue, is of international concern."

"Well," said Hammond, "we can fight them off for a while. There isn't much that they can do beyond attempting to amass worldwide opinion. They can pass resolutions in principle until they are purple in the face, but there's not much they can do to implement the resolutions."

"We'll hold the line for a time," said the President.

"If some others of the visitors drop in on us, that may be a different matter."

"You are saying, Mr. President," asked State, "that you'll not even consider my suggestion of a cooperative international study?"

"For the time," said the President. "Only for the time. We'll have to think about it and await further developments. The subject is not closed."

"What's vital for us to learn," said Hammond, "is the intention of these things. What is their purpose? Why are they here? What do they expect? Are they a band of roving nomads looking to pick up whatever's loose or are they a legitimate expedition out on an exploration flight? Do they represent a contact with some other civilization out in space or are they a pack of freebooters? How we react, what we do, must depend to a large extent on who and what they are."

"That might take a lot of finding out," said Porter.

"We'll have to try," said Hammond. "I don't know how it can be done, but we'll have to try. Allen's boys in the next few days may start turning up a few facts that could be significant. All we need is a little time."

The intercom on the desk purred and the President picked up the phone. He listened for a moment and then said, "Put him on." Again he listened, a frown growing on his face. "Thank you," he finally said. "Please keep in close touch with me."

He put down the phone and looked from one to the other of them.

"We may just have run out of time," he said. "That was Crowell at NASA. He's had word from the station. There seems to be some indication that the swarm in orbit is beginning to break up."

19. LONE PINE

"They're cute," said Kathy.

"I can't see anything cute in them," said Chet. "They're just little black oblong boxes scampering around."

Scampering they were, hastening from bale to bale, ingesting each bale in turn, doing it neatly and precisely, down to the last shred of cellulose. There was no scuffling or fighting among themselves for possession of a bale; they were well mannered. If one of them was working on a bale, another did not try to horn in, but found another bale. They had eaten a number of bales, but there were still plenty of bales left. The voracious youngsters had barely made a dent in them. A mile or more of bales was spread along the lane cut through the forest and the adult visitor, at the far end of the swath, still was burrowing its way into the forest, regularly ejecting bales.

"It seems to me," said Kathy, "that they are growing. Would that be possible? They seem bigger than they were just an hour or so ago."

"I can't think so," said Chet. "They've been feeding for only a few hours."

"It seems to me, too, that they are growing," said Quinn, the New York *Times* man. "I suppose it could be possible. They may have an extremely efficient metabolic system. Much more efficient than any kind of life on Earth."

"If they are growing now," said Kathy, "it won't be more than a few more days before they can be cutting their own trees and extracting cellulose."

Norton said, "If that is the case, there goes the wilderness area."

"I suppose that somewhere along the line," said Quinn, "the forestry people will have to make up their minds what they want to do about it. This thing is our guest at the moment, I would think, but how long can we put up with a guest that eats everything in sight?"

"Or a guest that litters a brood of young on your living room floor," said Norton.

"The problem is," said Chet, "what can be done about it. You can't just shoo this thing out of the woods like you'd shoo a pig out of a potato patch."

"No matter what you say," said Kathy, "I think those little things are nice. They are in such a hurry and they are so hungry."

She tried again, as she had tried unsuccessfully before, to pick out the one she'd helped to regain its feet. But there seemed to be no way to distinguish one from the other. They were all alike.

And she remembered, too, that moment after she had helped the youngster to its feet and then reached out to pat the mother. She could still feel, in the imagination of memory, the gentle twitching of the hide and then the hide folding over her hand in a soft embrace. I can't believe, she told herself fiercely, that there can be too much wrong with a creature of any sort at all that would respond like that—a gesture of recognition? a sign of gratitude for a service rendered? the friendliness of one life to another? or an apology for subjecting another intelligence to the trouble it had brought?

If only, she thought, she could put this in the story that in another couple of hours she'd phone into the *Tribune*. But there was no way that she could. If Johnny didn't throw it out to start with, the ogres on the copy desk would not let it pass. It would be an intrusion of the reporter into the story. It was something for which there would be no kind of proof, no documentation. How, Kathy asked herself, does one document a handshake with an alien?

Norton was asking Quinn, "Have you folks gotten anything out of the governmental observers?"

"Nothing much," said Quinn. "They've taken the visitor's temperature, or at least the temperature of its skin. They may have looked for a heartbeat, and I suspect they did, although they won't own up to it. They know it isn't metal, but they don't know what it is. It hasn't any treads or wheels to move on. It just floats along a few inches above the ground. As if it were disregarding the force of gravitation. One observer was speculating that it may know how to control and use gravity and his fellow observers probably will pin his ears back for his ill-considered muttering. And they know it is sending out signals. And that's about all they know."

"I'm not sure," said Chet, "they'll ever know much more. I wouldn't know where to start to find out any more."

"They have ways," said Quinn. "They'll learn other things but probably not all we need to know. We may be dealing here with something outside our knowledge. We may have to change some of our thinking before we understand it."

A silence fell—a relative silence. The growling and the crunching of the visitor in its chewing up of trees had stopped. Now the sounds that had been drowned out by the chomping of the trees came through—the chirps and calls of distant birds, the sough of the wind blowing through the pines, the chatter and gurgle of the river.

The newsmen and photographers who were in the cleared swath swung around to look. For a moment nothing happened. Maybe, Kathy told herself, it is only resting for a moment. But why, she wondered, should it be resting now? Since the time it had started on its strange harvest of the trees, it had not stopped to rest, but had continued to bore into the forest, lengthening the swath that it left behind it.

The visitor began to lift, so slowly that at first its movement was barely perceptible, then gathering speed. It rose above the pines and hung there for a moment—and there had not been any sound. There had been no roar of motors, no noise omitted by propulsive mechanisms. There was no flame, no smoke, no sign that any propulsive device had been used. It had simply floated up until it hung above the trees, hanging there as silently as it had risen. In the light of the westering sun, the green 101 that had been painted on its side stood out in sharp relief against its blackness.

So slowly that it seemed to be doing no more than drifting in the wind, it began to move eastward and upward. It built up speed and swung from the east to the south, its apparent size diminishing as it moved.

So it is going, Kathy thought; it is leaving us. It came and stayed a while. It processed food for its babies and now is on its way, its purpose filled, its function done.

She stood and watched until it was a small dot in the sky and finally the dot was gone. She brought herself back to the cleared swath in which she stood. And the place, she thought, somehow seemed lonelier, as if a valued friend had left.

The youngsters that it had left behind it still continued their scurrying about, feeding greedily on the bales of cellulose. One of the observers was busily painting numbers on them, but on them the paint was red, not green.

20. MINNEAPOLIS

It was after midnight before Johnny Garrison got away from his desk. Now, driving west on Highway 12, he tried to relax. Relaxation, he found, came hard. There was nothing to worry about now, he told himself. The final edition was all wrapped up and Gold would stay on until the presses had started and he could have a look at one of the first copies from the pressroom. Gold was a good man; he could be depended upon to know what to do if something should come up. The chances were that nothing would occur. At the last moment before closing, it had been possible to squeeze out a few inches of space on page one to put in a bulletin carrying the NASA announcement that the new object in orbit appeared to be breaking up. As a matter of fact, the bulletin of the announcement was all that had appeared. There had been no official elaboration. When Garrison phoned the *Tribune*'s news bureau in Washington, to catch Matthews standing the dog watch (a procedure that was followed only when big news possibly might be breaking), Matthews had been upset and slightly bitter.

"The bastards knew about it hours ago," he fumed. "I am sure they did, but they held the announcement up. Waiting for that sewing circle at the White House to figure out how it should be handled. They finally wound up letting NASA make the announcement, probably figuring it would have less impact than it would have coming from the White House. If you ask me, the White House doesn't know what to do. They're scared down to their toenails. I tried to reach Dave Porter, but he couldn't be found; neither could any of his staff. I imagine Dave is crisped to a cinder. He has spent the last two days assuring us that the White House would come clean on this one."

"What's the matter with them down there?" Garrison asked.

"It's too big for them to handle, Johnny. Too big and too different. They are afraid of making mistakes. I have a feeling that there is a hell of a squabble going on among the President's men, arguing what should be done, and not being able to get together on it. It's something entirely new, a situation that has never come up before, and there is no precedent. It's not simple; not like the energy situation."

"The energy situation's not simple, either."

"Well, hell, Johnny, you know what I mean."

"Yes," said Garrison. "Yes, I guess I do."

The highway was relatively deserted; only occasional cars moving on it. A few of the eating places that dotted the road were still lighted, but the other places of business were dark, the gas stations faint glows with the single light in the office burning. Off to the north, the twinkling glimmer of street lights swaying in the wind marked a suburban housing development off the highway.

We did it right, Garrison told himself, running the events of the past two days across his mind. Getting Kathy and Chet up to Lone Pine shortly after the landing had been a move that paid off. Kathy had done well. There had been a time, he recalled, when he had considered sending Jay to replace her; now he was glad he hadn't. Jay might, in certain regards, have done a slightly better job, he thought, but not enough to justify the shattering of Kathy's confidence. An editor, he reminded himself, did not have the sole job of getting stories in the paper; it also was his job to build a staff.

And aside from that, he thought, we kept the news objective. We wrote it as we saw it, we played it responsibly. We shunned any hint of sensationalism—straight, responsible reporting all the way. And there had been times when it had been difficult to determine that fine line between sensationalism and responsibility.

The sky was clear. A large, bright moon sailed halfway down the western sky. Here, beyond the glow of the inner city, the sky was speckled with a million stars. Cool, sharp air blew through the window at his left. He debated whether he would take the time for a good, stiff drink before he went to bed. Jane would be awake, perhaps in bed, but still awake, waiting for the sound of the car coming up the driveway. She would be up and waiting for him when he came in the door. He went a little soft inside, thinking of all the years Jane had been up and waiting for him, no matter what the hour. The kids would be in bed and fast asleep and the house would have that strangely empty feeling with the clatter of their running stilled and it would be good to sit in the living room a while and have a drink with Jane.

Ahead of him the moon was blotted out. A cloud, he thought, staring through the windshield in amazement. A tingle went along his spine, for a cloud was wrong. A cloud would not have dropped from overhead and it would not have moved so quickly and even if it had, it would be fuzzy at the edges, not so black, so sharp, so regular. He took his foot off the accelerator, began gently braking. The darkness that had swallowed the moon was blacking out the stars that gleamed above the horizon straight ahead of him. The car rolled to a stop in the right hand lane. Ahead of him, no more than half a mile ahead of him, the darkness that could not be a cloud came down to sit upon the road.

He opened the door and stepped out to the pavement. Another car came up beside him and stopped. A woman thrust her head out of the right hand window and asked, in a shrill, excited voice, "What is going on? What's that up ahead?"

"I think it's another visitor," said Garrison. "Like the one up north."

"Oh, my god!" the woman shrilled. "Let's get out of here."

The man behind the wheel said, "Take it easy, Gladys. It may not be a visitor."

He got out of the car and joined Garrison, who had walked out ahead of the cars, standing in the glare of the headlights. He ranged himself alongside Garrison and stood staring at the thing that loomed on the road ahead.

"How sure are you?" he asked.

"Not entirely," Garrison told him. "It looks like one. It popped into my mind it could be one of them."

"It's big," said the other man. "I read about the one up north and saw pictures of it. But I had no idea it could be that big."

It was big. It blocked both the traffic lanes and the grassy median that ran between them. It was black and rectangular and loomed high against the sky. Once having settled, it did not move. It sat there, a lump of blackness.

The woman had gotten out of the car and came up to them. "Let's turn around and get out of here," she said. "I don't like it."

"Goddammit, Gladys," said the man, "quit your caterwauling. There's nothing to be afraid of. That one up north never hurt no one."

"It killed a man. That's what it did."

"After he shot at it. We ain't shooting at it. We're not going to bother it."

It must be a visitor, Garrison told himself. It had the square blockiness that the photos had shown. It was exactly as Kathy had described the one at Lone Pine. Except for its size; he was not intellectually prepared for the sheer, overwhelming size of it.

Two other cars had come up behind them and stopped, the people in them getting out to walk up the road to where the three of them stood. Another car came along, but did not stop. It ran off the road, crossed the median, gained the eastward traffic lanes and went roaring off.

The NASA announcement had said that the object in orbit appeared to be breaking up. It was doing a hell of a lot more, Garrison told himself, than simply breaking up; the visitors that had clustered in the orbiting object were coming down to Earth. There was one here, spraddled across the road, and the likelihood was that it was not the only one that had come to Earth. There would be others, scattered all over the world. That first landing at Lone Pine probably had been no more than a test attempt at landing, a preliminary probing to have a look at the situation. The Lone Pine visitor, before it had spawned and then had taken off, had been sending signals to its fellows orbiting in space and now the invasion was on. If it could be called an invasion. Garrison reminded himself that probably it was not an invasion in the classical sense of the term. A reconnaissance in force—could that be what it was? Or simply a visit, intelligences of another world dropping in to say hello?

He started walking up the road toward the visitor. Looking back over his shoulder, he saw that only one of the others who had been standing with him was following. With only a quick glance at the follower, he could not be sure which one of them it was. Perhaps, he thought, he should slow down and let the other man catch up with him, but decided against it. He did not feel like engaging in the meaningless chit chat that would come from the other, filled with questioning and wonder. Why do you think it landed here? What does it want? What kind of thing is it? Where do you think it's from?

He increased his stride, almost running down the pavement. When he came to within a few yards of the huge blackness, he swung to his right, to the far shoulder of the highway, and began making his way around it. There now was no question in his mind that it was a visitor—a huge black oblong box with no gadgets attached to it, with no external features at all. It sat there. It did not move. It did not click or purr. Going up to it, he laid his hand, spread wide, against its hide. The hide was hard, but not with the hardness of metal. It was warm, with a warmth that somehow had the feel of life. Like touching a man, he thought. Like stroking a dog or cat. A soft warmness, despite the hardness of the skin, that spoke of life.

Standing there, with his spread out hand against the warmness of the hide, a sudden chill ran through him, a chill that set his teeth on edge and made his face feel, for a moment, stiff and hard, as if it might be changing into stone. And, even as he felt the chill, his suddenly racing brain launched into a frantic scurry to analyze the chill. Not fear, said the analysis, not terror, not panic, no inclination to burst out screaming, no urge to run, no buckling of the knees—only that terrible coldness which was not the coldness of the body only, but a coldness of the mind, and a coldness of the mind that the mind could not understand.

Slowly he pulled his hand away from the hide and there was no need to pull it, for nothing held it there.

He let his arm drop to his side, but, otherwise, he made no movement and he felt the chill ebb out of him, not going quickly, but draining slowly from him until it was gone, although the memory of how it had been stayed with him.

A touch of strange, he thought, but more than a touch of strange. Rather a brush against something that he could not understand, that no human might be able to understand. A touch that was composed of the coldness and the vastness of deep space, of the glare of distant suns, of dark planets that were unlike the Earth, and the incomprehensibility of a life that had been spawned in the darkness of those planets. As if he had been hurled into a place that he did not know and perhaps could never know, that he could not even begin to know no matter how long a time he spent there. Incomprehensibility, that was it, he thought.

And, yet, the damn thing looked so ordinary, was so unspectacular, an almost old shoe structure.

He backed away from it, staring up at the great black wall of it that rose so high above him. And the hell of it was, he found, that he wanted once again to step close to it and lay his hand against it so that he again could feel the warmness of it, and perhaps the chill as well.

But he did not step closer to it, did not lay his hand against it. He backed a few steps away from it, then turned around and hurried back the way that he had come. Not running, for he sensed there was no reason he should run, but taking long, deliberate steps to get away from it as quickly as he could.

Out on the highway and clear of the visitor, he saw that several other cars had stopped and the cluster of people standing in the road had grown. He did not see the man who had followed him. Even had he seen him, he would not have recognized him, for he had caught only that one, quick, over-the-shoulder glimpse of him.

One man stepped out of the cluster to intercept him as he came down the road. "What did you see?" the man asked. "Is there anything going on?"

"Why don't you go and look?" Garrison asked him brusquely, brushing swiftly past him.

It was strange, Garrison thought, that there was so little panic. If there was fear, it was being hidden. What was it about the visitors that seemed to inspire no fear? Maybe it was because the big black box had so few alien connotations. Perhaps because it was so totally unlike the common concept of something out of space. To a people brought up on the idiocies of TV and movie imaginations, the reality must seem quite commonplace.

His car was standing with the headlights burning and the engine running. He got into it, pulled up the road a car length or so, then cut to its left, drove across the median to reach the eastbound lanes. A mile down the road he pulled into a flanking service lane to reach a roadside phone booth.

Gold answered, his voice slightly flustered, on the second ring.

"I am glad you called," he said. "I was tempted to call you, but hesitated, because I thought you'd be asleep."

"Why should you be calling me?"

"Well, another visitor has landed. Right in our lap

this time. It's sitting on one of the runways at the airport."

"That's only half of it," said Garrison. "There's a second one. Came down on Highway 12, about a mile east of Ridgedale shopping center. It's blocking off the road."

"You there now?"

"That's right. It landed half a mile or so ahead of me. I better come on in. These may not be the only landings in the area. You have someone you can send out to keep an eye on this one?"

"I don't know. I'll look around. Jay was still here, so I sent him to the airport. Have a photographer out there as well."

"What's happening at the airport?"

"Not much, so far. The visitor is roosting out there, not bothering anyone, but the men in the tower are up tight. Not much air traffic out there now, but it'll pick up in a few hours. The visitor being there means there's one less runway to handle the planes."

"Anything on the wires? Any other landings in other places?"

"Fragmentary reports. Nothing solid. Nothing confirmed. Someone in Texas phoned the police to report one down. Another report from New Jersey. Simple reports of sightings, nothing official yet."

"I'm afraid the swarm that was in orbit out there is beginning to come in."

"Look, Johnny, why the hell don't you go on home, get some rest. There must be ways to bypass the visitor blocking the road. It'll be twenty hours before we can go to press again."

"No. If need be, I can go down to medical service and stretch out on a cot, get a few hours sleep later on. Any word from Kathy?"

"None. Why would you expect her to be calling? She's probably been asleep for hours."

"I think when she does phone, we should call her in. The Lone Pine thing is finished. The action will be down here so far as we are concerned. Anything happen at Lone Pine, Norton can fill us in. We need Kathy. She's the one who knows about these things."

"O.K. I'll tell her if she calls."

"I'll see you in a while," said Garrison.

He hung up, fished in his pocket for another dime, inserted it in the slot and dialed.

Jane answered. "Johnny, I'm sitting up, waiting for you. When will you be home?"

"I started out," he said, "then something happened."

"And you aren't coming?"

"Not for a while. One of the visitors landed on the road just ahead of me. I have to get back to the office. Jim tells me another one landed at the airport."

"You mean one landed on Highway 12?"

"That's right. Just east of Ridgedale."

"Johnny, that's only four or five miles from here."

"Yes, I know. But there's nothing . . ."

"Johnny," she said, "that's too close. I'm getting scared."

21. THE UNITED STATES

They came down through the night, like homing birds, although they were not homing birds, but were settling on a terrain that was alien to them. They came seeking through the dark, although it was not dark to them, and picked out their landing places with a certain care. There was little interference, for there was nothing, at this time of night, to interfere with them. They kept in touch with one another, talking back and forth, and there was nothing that one sensed the others did not know.

They landed in the watery delta lands where the Mississippi flowed into the Gulf, on the broad plains of Texas, the deserts of the American Southwest, the sandy beaches of Florida, the wheatlands of the West, the rustling cornfields of the Central States, the commons of New England villages, in Southern cotton fields and sweet potato patches, on the concrete of large airports, astride the great highways that spanned the continent, along the Western seaboard, in the forests of Oregon, Washington and Maine, in the woodlots of Ohio and Indiana.

They came down and landed silently with no more noise than the whisper of the air disturbed by their passage. They landed softly, then rose an inch or two from where they had landed and floated just above the surface. They disturbed few of the sleeping millions they passed over and landed among. Only on occasion were they sighted and, except when they landed on airports or highways, that by accident.

They made a flurry of soft, fluttering, moth-like tracks across the screen in the war room of the Strategic Air Command, but there the watchers of the screens, maintaining an intent, militarily professional surveillance, had been warned and were prepared for them, their only real concern being that the coming of the visitors cluttered up the board and might mask other kinds of incoming objects.

In those instances where they landed in forested areas, they almost immediately set to work harvesting cellulose. In a suburban Virginia housing tract, not far from Washington, one of them, in lieu of trees, began the harvesting of houses. Another, in Oregon, landed adjacent to a huge lumberyard and began the chomping of stacked lumber. But the most of them, coming to rest in less productive areas, simply squatted down and waited.

22. MINNEAPOLIS

Gold was on the phone when Garrison came into the newsroom. The only other people in the room were three copyreaders and two sleepy dog-trick copy aides.

Gold hung up the phone and said to Garrison, "That was some screwball, calling to tell me that a group that calls themselves the Lovers are going to go out to the airport, sit down in front of the visitor there and love it all to hell. Isn't that the silly bunch that Kathy wrote about?"

"That's right. Did Kathy's story ever make the paper?"

"I never saw it. Just knew you sent her out on it."

"It's probably still in her typewriter. She was working on it when I interrupted her to ship her off to Lone Pine. Now that I am here, why don't you take off?"

"Not on your life," said Gold. "I wouldn't miss this for a million dollars."

"All right, then, if that's the way you feel, why don't we settle down and figure what we should be doing. Probably, in the next few hours, we should start calling in some of our people early. You have any ideas?"

"Jay's out at the airport now," said Gold. "I caught Sloane before he left and sent him out to Highway 12. Jones just got back from South Dakota and he'll have to write his Black Hills-Indian story for the Sunday paper."

"Let's forget the Black Hills piece," said Garrison. "We'll have plenty else and it can wait. Jones is a good man and we'll need him. He's had a good night's sleep. Call him in another hour or two."

"Freeman is another man we could use early," said Gold. "He knows his way around the statehouse. The governor, most likely, will be calling out the guard. We need someone who can sit here at a desk and keep tabs on what the state is doing. I phoned the highway patrol and it is on the job. They'll probably have troopers three deep around the visitor on Highway 12. Some at the airport, too, but the airport has its own security force and may not need much help."

"They'll have real problems out there when the traffic picks up later in the morning."

"They have problems now. It puts a crimp in handling air traffic when you have a runway out."

"Why the hell do you think that thing landed at the airport?"

Gold shook his head. "For that matter, why should one land on a highway? Why do they land in any one particular place?" He reached out his hand and picked up a sheaf of paper ripped off the teletypes. "All over the country," he said. "Mostly reports of sightings, but some of them now are being verified. One reported here, another there. Reports from truck drivers, late people driving home from work, night watchmen, from all kinds of night owls."

"Like us," said Garrison.

"That's right. Like us."

"We'll need coverage of state and federal agencies," said Garrison. "Anyone or any agency that can be possibly involved. Williams is our man to contact the local FBI. No one is going to get much out of the FBI, but Williams will come closer than any other man. He seems to get along with them."

"Campbell, maybe, could tackle some of the people at the university," said Gold. "Physicists, psychologists, engineers, aeronautic people. They might be able to give some insight on what is going on. Maybe some of the sociologists and psychologists may be able to make some sort of an assessment on what the public impact will be. And we can't forget the churches. Will this business have any impact on religious thinking?"

"We'll have to pick our sources carefully," said

Garrison. "Some of these churchmen are inclined to shoot off their mouths in all directions and endlessly and without thought on any given subject."

"Roberts might be the man for that," said Gold.

The phone rang and Garrison picked it up.

Kathy's voice asked, "Is that you, Johnny? What are you doing there this time of night?"

"We have some of your visitors down here. How about yourself? We talked about phoning you, but figured you were asleep."

"I was, but Stiffy came pounding at the door and woke me up."

"Stiffy?"

"That old man who took the call and held the phone for me."

"Now I remember. Why should he be pounding at your door?"

"He was sleeping off a drunk and woke up and saw them."

"Them?"

"More of the visitors. A dozen or so of them, all coming in a bunch. They landed across the river, in the wilderness area. They're lined up abreast, mowing down the trees and turning out cellulose."

"But Stiffy . . ."

"I gave him five dollars for holding the phone. Chet gave him a quart of booze. We've bought the man for life."

"We need you and Chet down here, Kathy. I think there's an early morning plane out of Bemidji. Can you manage it?"

"It doesn't leave until six or so. Plenty of time. Even time to go out and have a closer look at these new visitors. Stiffy's pounding Chet awake right now."

"Okay. Whatever you can manage. But don't miss that plane. All hell is set to let loose down here."

"I should give Stiffy another five."

"Give him ten," said Garrison. "Norton can keep an eye on things up there for us and Stiffy maybe can do some legwork for him."

People woke and turned on their radios to learn what kind of weather they might expect that day. There was no weather news; instead a running commentary, half news, half wonder and speculation, spewed out of the sets.

The people listened, prickled by the first faint touch of fear. The Minnesota visitor had been a novelty, an event that brought twinges of excitement and well-hidden apprehension, but there had been only one of them. It had stayed for a time and then had flown off and, except for the young that it had spawned, that had been the end of it. But now, suddenly, a horde of the things had descended on the Earth. Well-behaved, of course, not really causing trouble, but posing an uneasy wonder as to what kind of things they were, what they might expect of Earth.

The people went about their work, but all day long they met other people who were prone to stop and talk about the wonder of the visitors. Throughout the day, the uneasiness kept growing as rumor piled on rumor, as speculation grew, with each speculation adding to the sense of uneasiness and, at times, the sense of fear. Little work was done.

An Iowa farmer, not bothering to turn on his radio, went out in the early dawn to do the morning chores and was stopped in his tracks by the sight of the huge black box that was sitting in his cornfield. He hurried back into the house and came out again armed with a twelve-gauge shotgun, his jacket pocket sagging with a handful of shells. Riding a small farm tractor, he went to the cornfield and parked outside the fence that enclosed the field. Climbing from the tractor, he crawled through the fence and walked toward the visitor. It made no sign that it noticed his approach. Cautiously, he made his way around it. Apparently, it was doing nothing; it was only sitting there. Twice he raised the gun, his finger on the trigger; each time he decided not to shoot. There was no way of telling, he reminded himself, what it might do if he shot at it. Finally, having circled it, he climbed through the fence, clambered on the tractor and went back to the morning chores.

Looking to his left, the airliner pilot spotted the visitor several miles away. He reached out a hand and nudged the man sitting next to him. "Look over there," he said. The other looked. "It's paralleling us," he said. "I thought all of them were down," the pilot said. "Sitting on the ground." They continued to watch it. It continued on course with them, matching their speed, moving no nearer or no farther off.

A man stood on a street corner in a ghetto area and raised his arms above his head. He bellowed to the others in the street. "Our brothers out of space," he howled, "have come to rescue us. They're dropping down to confront those who hold us in our bondage. Let us rejoice, brothers, for help has finally come." The people gathered to listen to his mad ranting, grinning or scowling as the words might strike them, but not believing him, for these people of the street believed no one at all, but sensing in him a primitive excitement that stirred in them a savage anger at their hopelessness. An hour later, there was looting and burning in the area.

In one New England village, someone (never identified) went into a church and began ringing the bell. Curious people came to learn why the bell was ringing. And to many of them, it seemed good to be there, proper to be there when visitors had come upon the Earth. So they went into the church and the minister, hurrying from the parsonage, found them there. To him, as well, it seemed proper that they should be there, so he led them in prayer. In other villages, other church bells rang and other people came to be led in prayer. Across the land suddenly godstricken people flocked to church.

National guardsmen cordoned off the visitors that were sitting on the ground. Highway patrolmen worked to keep traffic moving as thousands of sightseers converged upon the sites where the visitors were sitting. And in some scattered places visitors, floating easily along, only a few hundred feet above the ground, patrolled the highways. Motorists stopped their cars to get out and gape and tangled traffic jams resulted. There were many accidents.

24. WASHINGTON, D.C.

Winston Mallory, Secretary of Defense, said to the President, "Whiteside thinks we should run a test of how these things react to firepower. Under the circumstances, I recommend that we should turn him loose. It didn't make much sense when there was only one of them, but now that they've invaded . . ."

"I object to your use of the term 'invasion' for what is happening," said the Secretary of State. "A fair number of them have landed, but there has been no violence. They're not killing our citizens, they're not burning our cities."

William Sullivan, Secretary of Interior, said, "They chewed up a housing development across the Potomac. One of them gobbled up a lumberyard out on the west coast. They're eating our forests in Michigan, in Maine, in Minnesota, in Washington and Oregon."

"But they haven't killed anyone," said State. "The only thing they've done is steal a little cellulose. They haven't . . ."

"Just a minute, Marcus," said the President. "I want to hear more about this weapons test. What does Whiteside propose to do? Open up on them with tanks?"

"Nothing like that," said Mallory. "Just a simple test, that is all. We've got to know how these things respond. You remember, out in Minnesota, a man fired at the one that landed there and it fired back, killing him. He used a deer rifle, probably a .30 caliber. The thing about it is that we don't know what happened, how the visitor did it. It carried no apparent weaponry. It was bare of any external features. Yet when that man fired at it . . ."

"What you want to do is fire another .30 caliber, probably by remote control, then try to determine how the visitor fires back?"

"Precisely. We'll use cameras. High speed cameras. Some of them can take up to thousands of frames a second. That way we can track the bullet, record the moment of impact, see what happens on impact. A study of the film . . ."

"Yes, I see," said the President. "If you can be sure the general will stop with a .30 caliber."

"He will stop at the .30 caliber. All we want, all he wants, is some idea of how the visitor shoots back. Once we know that, we can go on from there."

"If it seems necessary."

"That's right. If it seems necessary."

"And, for Christ's sake, tell Henry to go easy. Take all possible precautions. Exercise all restraint. Only the one shot to get the data."

"He'll go easy. I have talked with him about it."

"I'm impressed by what Marcus was saying," said the President. "Except for this cellulose business, nothing actually has happened. The closest to anything disastrous was the Virginia housing development . . ."

"People could have been killed," said Sullivan. "It was just plain dumb luck that everyone got out of the houses in time. There were people sleeping in those houses. A lot of them could have lost their lives. And they're sitting down at airports, closing runways. Let one plane crash because of that and we'd have casualties. Also, I understand they are flying along with planes, as if they might be studying them. So far nothing's happened, but it could."

"What would you have us do?" asked State. "Wheel out our artillery?"

"No, of course not. But we should be doing something. We shouldn't just be sitting here."

"We've called out the National Guard," said the President. "Troops are keeping each of our visitors isolated, keeping the public away from them. That way we probably will avoid incidents."

"What if our visitors start in on other housing developments?" asked Sullivan. "What if they move into the residential areas of our cities, leveling houses to get cellulose? What will we do then? How will we take care of the people who will be homeless?"

"They haven't done that yet," said Marcus White. "Virginia apparently was an isolated example. And the visitor stopped after chewing up a few houses, as if it realized it had made a mistake."

"We have to take care of emergencies as they arise," said the President. "Meanwhile, we'll have to do everything we possibly can to find out more about our visitors."

"The thing that puzzles me," said White, "is that so far they've landed only in the United States, with some small slop-over into Canada. None in Europe. None in Africa. None anywhere else. Why us? Why just us?"

"I think I may have a suggestion," said Dr. Steven Allen, the science advisor. "Let's put ourselves in the place of the visitors. Let's say we have sent out an expedition to some other planet. A half a dozen ships, a hundred—the number's not important. We are looking for one specific thing, like these things apparently are looking for cellulose. We don't know too much about this planet we have reached. A few things by instrument study from some distance off, but that is all. So we send one ship down to study the situation. There are several land masses and we pick one as a starter. The ship goes down and finds what we are looking for. It finds, as well, that the indigenous life in that area seems friendly. At first glance, there's nothing on that particular land mass that is about to cause too much trouble and we, of course, want as little trouble as possible. We know this one land mass is safe; we don't know about the others . . ."

"You make a good point there," said the President. "Don't you agree, Marcus?"

"Yes, I do agree. I hadn't thought of it in quite

that way. I had assumed the visitors might want a rather broad look at the entire planet."

"Have you anything else for us?" the President asked the science advisor.

"A big puzzle," said Allen. "Much as we hate to even think it, there seems to be a fair possibility that the visitors operate by means of some sort of gravitational control. They float an inch or two above ground level. The one that left Minnesota yesterday rose into the air with no sign of using any propulsive units. They come down to land slowly, almost as if they were gliding to a landing, but to glide you have to make use of wing surfaces and they haven't any wings."

"You sound just slightly outraged over it," said Defense.

"I am outraged," Allen told him. "Any scientist would be outraged. We talk about gravity waves, the implication being that they would somehow be akin to electromagnetic waves. And we've looked for them. For a long time, no one could even figure out how to look for them. We're not even sure, right now, that we are using correct methods in our attempt to detect them. So far, none has been detected. At one time many scientists said, and some still say, that there aren't such things as gravity waves. As things stand now, even were we able to detect them, it would be only on a theoretical basis. No one has even the slightest idea of how they might be put to work."

"Your men are still hard at work on the visitors, I suppose," said Defense. "There still is hope that you will be coming up with something. After all, it's been only a couple of days."

"Not only our own men," said Allen, "but every qualified worker I can lure into the study. I've contacted a number of universities and institutes. In a few days, we'll have a large force in the field. The trouble is that we haven't much to work with. All we can do is observe. Stand off to one side and look at them. If we could trap one of them somehow so we could really work on it, we might find something of significance. But, at the moment, that is unthinkable. It probably would be highly dangerous. There has been a suggestion that we try to work on some of the young the Minnesota visitor spawned. But I shy away from that. If the baby started squalling that it was being hurt, adult visitors probably would come in force to its rescue. I can't be sure of this, but I hate to take a chance."

"You say universities and institutes," said White. "In this country only, I assume. Might there not be some scientists from other countries . . ."

"Marcus," said the President, speaking sharply, "let's not get into that again. For the moment, this is our show. The visitors have helped to keep it our show by landing here exclusively."

"There are a few in Canada," said White.

"We can work with Canada. We've always been able to. I know the Russians want in, but I'm opposed . . ."

"A small, token Russian representation might not be a bad thing," said Defense. "If we push them too far, if we shut them out . . ."

"I hope, Winston," said the President, "that you're not thinking what I'm afraid you are."

"The thought had flitted across my mind," said Mallory. "If it seems we are finding something that could tip the balance . . ."

"And if we did find something to tip the balance, as you say, and shared it with them, that would only mean further escalation. How many others feel the same way?"

"I didn't say share," said Mallory. "I said a token inclusion. That is all. Something to save their national pride."

"I think with Winston," said White, "that we can afford to do something to make these friends of ours look a little better."

Hammond, who until now had been sitting silently, spoke up. "What you're talking about is patronizing them. They'd sense that and resent it. It would be worse than nothing. They can understand nothing because that's what they'd give us if the situation were reversed. We either go whole hog with them or keep it for ourselves. One thing we must realize is that there may be nothing to share. With all due respect to Dr. Allen, we may not find out one damn thing that will be useful to us."

"In which case," said White, "there would be no harm in letting them in. It would improve relationships greatly and if we found nothing, it would cost us nothing."

"Marcus," said the President, "you are talking about playing the odds and that could be dangerous."

"Let's forget it," said Mallory. "I'm sorry I mentioned it. It just came off the top of my head."

"The embarrassing thing about all this," said White, "is that we are receiving offers of assistance from good allies and friends to help us in any way they can. They seem to be sincere . . ."

"I just bet they are," said Hammond.

"The only thing I can tell them," said White, ignoring Hammond, "is that later on we may call on them, but that, at the moment, we don't know what we face."

"I think, for the moment," said the President, "we had best leave it at that. Let's forget other countries for the moment and look to our own. There have been a few minor flareups. Small riots, some looting and burning in such places as Chicago, New York, St. Louis. Is there anything new on all of this, Dave?"

"Nothing big," said Porter. "And in this we have been lucky. We should have prepared the country. We should have called in the press when we first found the swarm was beginning to break up. We could have forewarned the country."

"You're still smarting over that?"

"You're damned right I am, Mr. President. We botched it. To let NASA issue that skimpy little announcement was a sneaky thing to do."

"Dave, we talked it over."

"Yes, I know. And you were wrong."

"You went along with it."

"I didn't go along. I protested and there were a few who sided with me."

"But only a few."

"Sir, you can't run a news operation on a majority vote. The rest of you know your business, but I know mine. Right now we've been lucky. I hope we can say the same thing at this time tomorrow. The thing I'm afraid of is the cult outbreak. Every crackpot in the country is up on the stump and shouting. All the evangelists are calling big prayer meetings. Every little backwoods church is filled with clapping, stomping, singing people. Out in Minneapolis, a group of second generation flower people tried to rush police lines. They wanted to squat down on an airport runway and give the visitor that landed there a demonstration of their love."

"I don't think we need to worry too much about things like that," said Hammond.

"There's a lot of emotion boiling around," Porter told him, "a lot of it still beneath the surface. I hope it can be kept from boiling over. Mixed emotions of all sorts. Latent fears that can easily boil up to the surface. Hallelujah emotions that can get out of hand. We're on the edge of something that could produce violent street encounters. Let a bunch of beer drinking hardhats get fed up with the antics of the millennium-has-come dancers in the streets . . ."

"You're exaggerating," said Hammond.

"I hope I am," said Porter.

"I don't like this watchful waiting," said Sullivan. "I think we should act in some positive manner. Something to let the people know we are involved, that we, at least, are taking some action."

"We've called out the National Guard," said the President. "We have investigators in the field."

"That's passive action," said Sullivan.

"The trouble is," said the President, "that anything we did probably would be wrong."

25. THE UNIVERSITY OF MINNESOTA

Dr. Albert Barr said to Jerry Conklin, "Miss Foster phoned to say that you wanted to talk with me, but she wasn't too specific. She indicated it had something to do with the visitors." He said to Kathy, "You assured me this is not an interview for an article in your paper."

"It's not an interview," said Kathy, "and I was not specific because I think that Jerry should tell you what happened."

"I've been worried about it," said Jerry, "ever since it happened . . ."

"Please tell me what happened," said Barr. "Start at the beginning."

He lounged behind his desk, regarding his two callers with a quizzical expression. He was a sandy-haired man, much younger than Kathy had expected him to be, with the build of a football player. Through the open window of his office came the sounds of a late afternoon on campus, the shrill laughter of a girl, students shouting back and forth, the deep humming of a started car and the scream of tires on pavement as it was gunned to a sudden take-off. Golden spangles of light flecked the windows as the westering sun shone through a birch tree decked in bright autumnal color.

"You may have read about the car that was smashed when the first visitor landed at Lone Pine," said Jerry.

"Could it have been your car?" asked Barr.

"It could have been. It was. I had parked at the end of the bridge to get in some fishing. I had been told there were some big rainbow in the pool below the bridge."

Barr did not interrupt as Jerry told his story. A couple of times he seemed to be on the verge of asking questions, but he did not ask them.

When Jerry had finished, the exobiologist said, "There are a number of points I would like to raise and discuss with you, but tell me first, why have you come to me? What do you want of me?"

"There are two things," said Jerry. "This business of home. The visitor thought of home, or made me think of home. I've mulled it over and over and there seems to be no sense to it. I am convinced that it induced the thought I had of home. In a situation such as that, I would not have thought of home. And the thought was real enough—not just a brief impression, but something that continued. As if the visitor or whatever was inside the visitor wanted me to think of home, kept on pressuring me to think of home."

"Are you trying to say that telepathy was involved?"

"I don't know what was involved. If by telepathy you mean that it was talking with me, or trying to talk with me, no, that was not the case. I tried to talk with it, which might have been a foolish thing to do, but something, that under the circumstances, I imagine might have come quite naturally. There I was, trapped in a place that I did not understand and I was reaching out for information, for any kind of information that would help to explain what was going on. So I tried to talk with it, to establish any kind of contact, to seek some answers. Probably I was fairly well aware that it would be impossible to establish contact, but . . ."

"Do you consider yourself in any way telepathic?"

"No, I do not. I have no telepathic ability that I am aware of. The simple fact is that it is something I had never thought about. I would say I'm not a telepath."

"And yet it talked to you. Or you think it talked to you."

"Dr. Barr, that's not what I said," said Jerry. "At no

time did I think the visitor was talking to me. No conscious communication, no words forming in my mind, no pictures, nothing like that at all. There was just this feeling of home, this overpowering sense of home."

"You are convinced the feeling came from the creature?"

"Where else could it have come from? I am convinced the thought of home would not have occurred independently to me. There was no reason for it to. There were a lot of other things that were more important for me to think about."

"You said two things. What was the other thing?"

"It seemed to me," said Jerry, "that the visitor was a tree or very like a tree."

"You mean after you learned about the cellulose?"

"No. I'm convinced the cellulose had nothing to do with it. I don't think that was the case. I imagine there must have been some underlying question of what it was and there seemed to be some familiarity and . . ."

"You're in graduate work in forestry. You must know a lot about trees."

"He's in love with trees," said Kathy. "Sometimes I get the impression that he talks with them."

"She's exaggerating," Jerry told Barr. "But, yes, I do know a fair amount about them and I guess I could say I have a fair degree of empathy with them. There are people who are gone on animals, those who are flower enthusiasts, devoted bird watchers. Maybe you could say I'm a tree watcher."

"You used the word 'familiarity' back there a ways. What made you use that word?"

"Perhaps because I think I could have felt some familiarity with it, not being aware of it at the time. To start with, when I found myself inside it, I was frightened—deep-down, deadly, screaming frightened, although I didn't scream. But in a little time, a far shorter time than one would think, I wasn't frightened, at least not frightened in that way. I got all tense and cold, but I wasn't garden-variety scared any longer. I was even getting interested before it threw me out."

Barr said, "You must realize that an exobiologist is a strange sort of animal. Really, there is no such thing. Rather, they are men in other disciplines, mostly the biological field, although physics and chemistry also could enter into the picture, who because of personal interest have branched out into a study of what might be expected under extraterrestrial conditions. So you understand, of course, that there is no real, precise science of exobiology."

"Yes, of course," said Jerry. "But at least the exobiologist would be thinking about what might be found in space and on other planets."

"So, with such a disclaimer duly noted," said Barr, "I must agree that your idea of an intelligent tree-like organism need not be too far off the mark. In the last twenty years or so, there have been botanists who have contended that on occasion plant life may show some capacity for sentience, possessing powers of sense or sense perception, experiencing sensation and feeling. For years, we have known that certain people seem to have green thumbs, under their care plants will flourish while under the care of others who do not have this capability, they fade and die. There are those who advocate that plant owners talk sympathetically to their plants. If plants, in fact, do have such sensitivity, then it is only a couple of long steps until we arrive at a true intelligence and full sentience. Could you explain a little more fully how you arrived at the realization the visitors could be plant-like, akin to trees?"

"I'm not sure I can," said Jerry. "I get a certain feeling when I look at a tree, or when I work with trees. A sort of kinship to them, which may sound strange . . ."

"And you think you may have felt the same kinship to the visitor?"

"No, not kinship. The visitor was too alien to feel anything like kinship. Perhaps a realization that some of the same qualities I feel in trees were also in the visitor. But skewed around. Not like a tree of Earth, but a tree of somewhere else."

"I think I understand," said Barr. "Have you told anyone else of this?"

"No. Someone else would have laughed at me. You didn't and I thank you for that."

"The government would like to know. The federal observers and other scientists who are investigating the visitors would be grateful for any kind of data."

"I have no data," said Jerry. "Lacking data, they would try to dig it out of me, feeling that I must have some hidden information that I might not be aware of. Either that or they would think I was another UFO crackpot trying to cash in on the visitors."

"I see your point," said Barr. "If I were in your place, I would have the same reservation."

"You sound as if you believe me."

"Why not? Why should I have reason to disbelieve you? There is no reason in the world you should have made up such a story. You felt a need to tell someone who might just possibly understand and take what you have to say at face value. I'm glad you came to me. I haven't been much help, but I'm glad you came. And on this business of thinking about home . . . I've been thinking. Could it be possible you misinterpreted what was going on?"

"I know there was a powerful compulsion to think of home."

"I don't mean that. Maybe the visitor was not talking to you at all, not trying to convey anything at all. You might have cued in on its thoughts. You may be just a little telepathic, whether you know it or not, or the signal, the emotions of the visitor, might have been so strong that no human could have avoided reacting to it. The thought comes to me that it may not have been broadcasting any thought of your home, but of its home."

Kathy gulped. "You mean here, the Earth? That it was thinking of Earth as home?"

"Consider this," said Barr. "It had come from God knows where, over no one can imagine how great a distance, looking for a planet where it could settle down, looking for a new home to replace the one that somehow had been lost. Maybe the Earth is that kind of planet—where it could bud and reproduce its young, find food for them, live the sort of life it perhaps had despaired of ever living again. Saying to itself, 'Home! Home! I've finally found a home!' "

26. THE UNITED STATES

The visitors observed. Some of them, having set down, stayed where they were. Others, after a time, floated into the air and set about their observations. They cruised back and forth over industrial plants, they circled and re-circled cities, they made sweeps of vast stretches of farmland. They escorted planes, maintaining their distance and position, never interfering; they flew up and down long stretches of highways, selecting those areas where the traffic flowed the heaviest; they followed the winding courses of rivers, keeping watch of the boats and other craft that plied the watercourses.

Others of them sought out forests and settled down to eat. They gobbled up a number of lumberyards. In the St. Louis area, three of them landed in a used car parking lot, ingested a dozen or so cars and then took off. But aside from ingesting trees and the cars and gulping down forty or fifty lumberyards, they did little harm. Most people with whom they came in contact were only marginally inconvenienced; no one was killed. Pilots flying planes became jumpy at being shadowed by the visitors. The highway accidents, few of them more than fender benders, fell off as motorists became accustomed to the sight of the great black boxes floating up and down the highways, coming at last to pay but slight attention to them.

The visitors qualified as first class nuisances. They tied up the National Guard, various highway patrols, and other law and order personnel, in the process costing considerable money.

A few riots flared in some of the larger cities where social and economic situations were such that anything at all became an excuse for rioting. In the process of the rioting, there was some looting and burning. A number of persons were injured, a few died. On some college campuses, students mounted good-natured demonstrations, various groups joining in to advance the causes of their special hang-ups, but none of the demonstrations really amounted to too much. Religious fanatics and other fanatics who were not religious held forth at street corners, parks, churches and halls. In certain areas, cult enthusiasms ran high. Newspaper columnists and TV commentators threw out a hundred different points of view, few of which, under any sort of objective scrutiny, made any sort of sense.

Stories grew—always of something that happened somewhere else, the preposterous index increasing with the distance—and embryonic legends began taking form.

The phenomenon of "being taken up" was heard increasingly, the reports coming from all parts of the nation, and snatched up swiftly to be exploited by the cults that had formed, likewise, in every corner of the nation. Various people claimed they had been "taken up," that somehow, never with an adequate explanation of how it happened, they had been introduced into the bodies of the visitors and, having been taken up, were either allowed to envision many wondrous things or were given messages (again, of many different sorts) that they were charged to transmit to their fellow Earthmen. The cult members, and many others, gave varying degrees of credence to these reports of being taken up, while a greater number scoffed. It was recalled that in the early days of UFO appearances, or supposed appearances, there had been many who had claimed direct contact with the crews of the flying saucers.

But however these reports, or other legendary stories, may have been inaugurated or spread, the populace became aware of one fact that could not be denied. The Earth had been invaded by creatures out of space and none of the things had happened that science fiction writers, through long years of scribbling, had foreseen as happening.

It all had turned out, as viewed by one editorial writer on the staff of an obscure little daily published in the depths of Tennessee, to be a sort of cosmic picnic.

In the northeastern corner of Iowa, a farmer had just finished his plowing on a 160-acre field when one of the visitors turned up at the field. It flew up and down the field, making neat turns at the end of each flight up the field, to go back down it once again, flying so low that it barely skimmed the new-plowed surface. The farmer stood beside his machine shed and watched it.

"I swear," he told a newsman who came out from a nearby town to interview him, "it was as if that thing was planting something, or sowing something, in the ground I had just plowed. Maybe it waited until I had the plowing done before it showed up. When it had finished and had set down in a pasture, I went out to have a look—you know, to find out if it had sowed anything or not. But I never got there. That damn thing floated up and came at me—not threatening, you understand, not even moving very fast, but letting me know, plain as day, I was not to go near that field. I tried it several times, but each time it chased me off. I tell you, mister, I am not about to argue with it. It's a lot bigger than I am. In the spring, when it comes time for me to plant, I'll try it again. Maybe, by that time, it may have gone away or may have lost its interest. I'll just have to wait and see."

The reporter eyed the huge blackness of the visitor, squatted in the pasture.

"Seems to me," he said, "it's got something painted on it. Did you get close enough to make out what it was?"

"Yeah, plain as day," the farmer said. "The number 101, painted on it in green paint. Now I wonder what sort of damn fool would have done a thing like that."

In a medium-sized city in Alabama, the building of

a stadium had been a local issue of some intensity for years, the issue fought out bitterly on the basis of funding, location and type of facility. But, finally, the issue had been settled and the stadium built. Despite all the disappointments encountered in the final decision, it was still a thing of civic pride. It had been furbished and polished for the game that would be the highlight of its dedication. The turf (live, not artificial) was a carpet of green, the parking lot a great extent of virgin asphalt, the stadium itself gay with pennons of many colors flapping in the breeze.

On the day before the dedication, a great black box came sailing through the blue and sat down, slowly and gracefully, inside the stadium, floating just above the green expanse of the playing field, as if the smooth carpet, so carefully mowed and tended, had been designed as a special landing space for big black boxes that came sailing from the blue.

Once the shock of rage had subsided slightly, there were great huddlings by official committees and interested civic groups. Some hope was expressed, early on, that the visitor might remain only for a matter of hours and then move on. But this did not happen. It remained within the stadium. The dedication was cancelled and the dedicatory game was postponed, occasioning major violence to the sacred schedule of the league.

The huddlings of the various groups continued and from time to time, suggestions were advanced and, amid great agonizing, all the suggestions were turned down as impractical. Quiet civic desperation reigned.

Sheriff's deputies who were guarding the stadium intercepted and arrested a small group of sport enthusiasts who were trying to sneak into the area with a box of dynamite.

In Pennsylvania, another visitor settled down in a potato patch. The owner of the patch stacked a huge pile of wood against the side of the visitor, doused it with gasoline and set the pile ablaze. The visitor did not mind at all.

27. LONE PINE

Sally, the waitress at the Pine Cafe, brought Frank Norton his plate of ham and eggs and sat down at the table to talk with him. The door came open and Stiffy Grant came fumbling in.

"Come on over, Stiffy," Norton called to him, "and sit down with us. I'll buy you your breakfast."

"That's handsome of you," said Stiffy, "and if you don't mind, I'll take you up on it. I been out watching them visitors of ours mowing down the trees. It was quite a walk, but I got up before light so I could get there early before any tourists showed up. Them tourists kind of take an edge off watching them. I wanted to see if maybe they were starting to bud, like the one that was here before."

"And are they?" asked Sally.

"Well, not yet. It seems to me it's taking them a little longer than the other one. But any day now they'll be doing it. They got long rows of those bales of white stuff strung out behind them. I been trying to think what that stuff is called."

"Cellulose," said Norton.

"That's right," said Stiffy. "That is what it's called."

"Since when did you get so interested in the visitors?" asked Sally.

"I don't rightly know," Stiffy told her. "I guess it was from the very start, when this batch first sat down. You might say I was sort of involved with them. There was this girl writer from down in Minneapolis and that first night, I held the phone for her so she could talk to her editor when she got back and then I was the one who brought word to her when the second batch landed. I was sleeping off a drunk this side of the river and saw them coming down and right away I told myself she would want to know. It didn't seem right to me that I should go pounding at her door in the middle of the night, an old reprobate like me. I thought she might be mad at me. But I went and done it anyhow and she wasn't mad at me. She gave me ten dollars later on. She and that camera fellow she had along with her, they were real nice people."

"Yes, they were," said Sally. "So were all the newspaper and TV people. It seems a little strange that they now are gone. Of course, there are still a lot of people coming to see the baby visitors. Sometimes they go down to see the others, too. But these people aren't like the news people. They're just sightseers. Drop in for a cup of coffee and a doughnut, once in a while a sandwich, but they don't come for meals and they never tip. I suppose that in a little place like this, and not buying much, they don't feel there is any need of it."

"At first," said Stiffy, "I went out to see the visitors, every single day like I've done since they came, telling myself I should keep watch of them so that if anything happened, I could let that girl reporter know. But I don't think that's the reason anymore, not the main reason. I've got so I like to watch them for themselves. Once I told myself they were things from a long way off and that they really shouldn't be here, but it doesn't seem that way now. It's gotten so that they seem just like people to me. I used to be afraid of them, but now I'm not scared of them. I walk right up to them and put out my hand and lay it on their hides and they're not cold, but warm, just like a person's warm."

"If you're going to have breakfast," Norton said to him, "you better tell Sally what you want. I'm way ahead of you."

"You said that you were paying for my breakfast."

"That's what I said."

"Frank, how come that you . . ."

"Well, you might say that I had an impulse that I may be sorry for. If you don't hurry up . . ."

"Then," said Stiffy, "I'll have a stack of cakes with a couple of eggs, sunny side up, dumped on top of them. And if you have some sausages and maybe a piece or two of bacon and a couple of extra pats of butter . . ."

28. SOMEWHERE IN UTAH

The sergeant said to the colonel, "If these pissants of scientists don't get their cameras and them other damn fool instruments set up to their liking pretty soon, the sun will be down and we'll have to scrub this exercise."

"They want everything just right," the colonel told him. "It's got to be right the first time. We don't want to have to make a second try at it. You may not think so, sergeant, but this mission has the highest possible priority. It comes straight from Washington and we can't afford to goof."

"But, Christ, sir, they sight in those cameras and then look through them and then sight them again. They been doing that for hours. They're a pack of fumbling old maids, I tell you. They got that chalk mark on the visitor's tail side and the rifle's sighted in on it. I sighted it myself and I know where it is pointing. The visitor hasn't moved and it still is pointing at the chalk mark. And that's another thing, why for Christ's sake, a rifle? Why not something a little heavier? You're not going to tell much bouncing a .30-caliber bullet off that big a mass. It won't do more than tickle it."

"Frankly, sergeant," said the colonel, "I've wondered about that myself. But that's what the orders say. They are most specific—a .30 caliber from a hundred yards. That and nothing else. It's got to be a .30 caliber from a hundred yards and the cameras and the other instruments must be positioned to the satisfaction of these gentlemen . . ."

The colonel broke off what he was saying when he

154

saw that one of the scientists who had been fiddling with the cameras was walking toward them.

"Colonel," said the man, when he came up to them, "you may proceed with the firing. Before you fire, however, be sure that personnel is at a distance of at least two hundred yards. We suspect that there may be considerable back blast."

"I hope," the sergeant said, "that the electronic gadget you fixed up to fire the piece will work."

The man said, unperturbed, "I am sure it will."

"Now, sergeant," the colonel said, sharply, "if you will move the men out. We want to wrap this up as soon as possible."

The sergeant moved off, started shouting orders.

The scientist asked a technician, "The cameras are ready?"

"They'll start running with the signal that fires the rifle," said the technician. "There's so damn much film involved. Those cameras eat it up."

"Colonel," said the scientist, "it's time for us to move out with the rest of them."

The visitor stood as it had stood for hours, motionless in the midst of the sandy waste. The cross made in chalk shone dully against the blackness of its hide.

"What beats the hell out of me," said the colonel, "is how it has stood there all this time with us fooling around to set up the shoot. Doesn't it know we're here?"

"I'm sure it does," said the scientist. "My feeling is that it simply doesn't care. I would suspect it has some contempt of us."

Finally, the scientist halted his walking and turned about, the colonel turning with him.

"Sergeant," yelled the colonel, "is the area cleared?"

The sergeant bawled back. "It's all cleared, sir."

The sergeant nodded to the man from Washington, who raised the tiny instrument he had been carrying in his hand and made a pressing motion with his thumb.

The rifle spat and the visitor spat back with a flood

of raging energy that engulfed the mounted rifle. The colonel threw up an arm to shield his eyes against the brilliance of the flare. When he took it down, he saw that the rifle and the mount on which it had been positioned had turned into a shimmering whiteness from the heat. The whole assembly was slowly sagging to the ground. A clump of nearby sagebrush flared to floating ash.

The colonel glanced at the visitor. It was still where it had stood, as if nothing had happened, but the white chalk mark had vanished.

29. WASHINGTON, D.C.

Drink clutched in his hand, Senator Davenport paced up and down the room.

"Goddammit, Dave," he said to Porter, "you people down at 1600 have to take some action. You can't just let these things keep on taking over."

"But, Daddy," said Alice, "they're not taking over. They've not really done anything at all."

The senator paused in his striding, stood glaring at his daughter.

"Not done anything!" he brayed. "They are using up our forests, they're eating lumberyards. They made away with those cars . . ."

"Old cars," said Alice. "Second-hand cars that some dealer was waiting to foist on an unsuspecting public."

"The dealer paid good money for those cars," her father said. "He took them in on trade-ins. He gave them room on his parking lot. He probably fixed them up. He was entitled to his profit. He had earned a profit."

"You say the administration should be doing something," said Porter. "Just what kind of action do you think that we should take?"

"How the hell should I know?" roared the senator. "I'm not the President, I'm not an advisor of his. If I did have some advice, he wouldn't listen to me. I don't know what is going on. Neither does anyone else. You're the press secretary; why don't you tell me what is going on? How much information do you have that you are holding back?"

"Offhand," said Porter, "I'd say scarcely anything."

"That milksop of a scientific advisor you have down

there has been working on it," said Davenport. "He has a large force in the field, he's spending millions on his investigation. How come he's not come up with something? I heard today the army had made some sort of firing test against one of the visitors. Can you tell me what came out of it?"

"I don't know," said Porter.

"Dave, if you did know—let's just say you do know— would you tell me?"

"Probably not," said Porter.

The senator turned to Alice. "There you see," he said. "That's the kind of arrogance we can expect from the White House gang."

"Dave has said he doesn't know," said Alice.

"Also he said that if he did know he probably wouldn't tell me."

"You have to give him credit for being honest with you, Daddy."

"Honest, hell! It's arrogance, I tell you."

"Senator, I'm sorry if I seemed arrogant," said Porter. "Also, I am sorry there's nothing I can tell you. The fact is that you probably know as much as I do. And as for taking action of any kind at all, Alice is quite right. These things have done nothing that is actionable. Even if they had, what is there we could do about it. They're too big to hassle. I have a feeling it might be dangerous to try to push them around, even if we had reason to push."

"They're disrupting the country," said the senator. "The visitors are consuming some of our best timber stands and the building industry will suffer. A lot of lumberyards have been destroyed and the chances are that others will be. Lumber is already expensive and this will make it more expensive. New homes will cost more than they are costing now and the prices of new homes even now are so high that they are beyond the reach of most families.

"If the visitors don't cut out riding herd on planes, the airlines will cut back their schedules. Some of them already are talking about it. There's just too much chance of accidents and the insurance companies, realizing this, are about to boost their rates. The airlines already are screaming that insurance costs are prohibitive and that they can't stand another raise."

"More than likely," said Porter, "the entire situation is in a shakedown period. It may soon begin to straighten out. We are being hit right now with the worst of the impact. The public is a little nervous and upset and is inclined to exaggerate all consequences. Give it a little time . . ."

"I don't think the situation will improve with time," said the senator. "The public, you think, will settle down. I don't think it will. These goddamn cults and holy roller preachers are injecting a lot of emotionalism into the social structure. The cults are bad enough, but we can live with them. The people, in general, know that they are crackpot based and what to expect of them. The real danger is the outburst of evangelism, the rush to the brain of old time religion. History tells us that in the Middle Ages there were similar outbreaks of religious frenzy. The peasant walked away from his land, the artisans away from their shops, all of them going off on a spiritual binge. The same is beginning to happen now. Industry and business is suffering from increased absenteeism, costly errors are being made in the work that is done."

"It all comes down," said Alice, "finally, to the dollar. Our businessmen and industrialists are losing money, or afraid they will be losing money."

"And what's wrong with that?" asked the senator. "Money is the basis of our economic order. And while you may not think so, the basis of our social order as well. I tell you, the country is starting a long slide to collapse. And those ninnies down at the White House don't even recognize it."

"I think we do," said Porter, "although we're not as pessimistic in our assessment as you seem to be. There are other things that call for priority consideration."

"What other things?"

"Well, a wide variety of . . ."

"Stop there!" shouted the senator, triumphantly. "I knew it! I knew there was something that you weren't telling me. Something you were hiding."

"Senator, I assure you . . ."

"You are onto something, aren't you? You've found out something about the visitors that won't bear talking on."

"Not that I know of," said Porter.

The senator sat down in a chair, gulped the remainder of his drink.

"You don't need to tell me," he said. "I wouldn't want to know, not until it's time for me to know, for a lot of us to know. And you are sitting on it. That's good. Not broadcasting it. Protecting it. I know that fuzzy-minded Secretary of State wants to share what we find with everyone, including Ivan. We can't afford to share . . ."

"Senator, you are absolutely wrong. We don't know one single goddamned thing."

"Spoken like a gentleman," said the senator. "I knew you had it in you. I knew you could be counted on to keep your mouth shut."

He looked at the watch on his wrist. "It's getting late," he said. "I kept you longer than I should, ranting at you. You and Alice will be late for your dinner reservation."

30. LONE PINE

One of the visitors had fallen behind the others. It was standing still and was not cutting trees. On either side of it, the other visitors were continuing with their cutting, regularly spewing out the bales of cellulose behind them.

Stiffy Grant came to an abrupt halt as he came around the edge of the uncut forest and saw what had happened. He reached up a hand and tipped his hat back on his head, ran a hand across his brow to wipe it dry.

"Now what the hell?" he asked aloud. There seemed to be no answer. Studiously, he focused his eyes, but only with an effort. He reached for his back pocket and took out the bottle, uncapped it and put it to his lips, throwing back his head to drink. Finished with the drink, he eyed the level of the liquor in the bottle with some dismay. There weren't more than another two drinks left in it. It wasn't the best of liquor; in fact, it was the cheapest to be bought, but it was liquor and he mourned its disappearance. He recapped the bottle carefully and eased it into the back pocket, patting the pocket to make certain the bottle was secure.

Walking carefully so he would not fall (for if he fell, he might break the bottle), he set out to find what might be wrong. Maybe it got tired, he told himself, and had stopped to rest, although over all the time that he had kept tab on the visitors, not a one of them had ever stopped to rest or had given any sign of tiredness.

Norton had bought his breakfast for him and that

meant that he had enough money left to buy another bottle of the booze. It was good to feel, he told himself, that he had at least another bottle in his future. That Norton, say what you might of him, was a decent man.

The visitor that was standing still turned out to be a greater distance off than he had estimated, but he kept plodding doggedly up the swath that it had cut, warily avoiding the bales that it had dropped, and finally reached it.

"What's the matter, fellow?" he asked, walking up and putting out a hand to rest against its hide. Once he put it there, he leaned against it for a moment to get himself a little steadied.

And as he held his arm straight out against it to gain some steadiness, he knew there was something wrong, something not quite the way it had been before, although it took a little time for him to pinpoint the wrongness.

Then he knew. The visitor was cold. Gone was the pleasant, friendly warmth that he had always felt before when he had laid a hand upon one of them. He shook his head in amazement and took away his hand. He stumbled along beside it for a dozen feet or so and then laid his hand on it again. The hide was still cold, all the warmth was gone.

Fumbling his way along it, he laid his hand upon its hide time and time again. Always the side was cold, stone cold. He turned and leaned his back against the visitor and slid down, collapsing to a sitting position.

Cold and motionless. No longer floating a few inches off the ground, but resting on the ground.

Could this be death? he asked himself. Could the visitor be dead? Cold and still and that was the way of death. And if it had died, why had it died? What had happened to it? And another thing—if it now were dead, it once had been living, but that was no news to him. For a long time, it had seemed to him, without question, that the visitors were alive. Not only alive, but friends. He wondered about that as he thought it, for it had been a long time since he had

had a friend. It was strange, he thought, that he should have found a friend among people other than his own.

Huddled against the cold visitor, without even bothering to cover his face, letting the tears run unhindered down his stubbled cheeks, Stiffy Grant wept bitterly for a friend that he had lost.

31. MINNEAPOLIS

Al Lathrop, the managing editor, sat at the head of the conference table. He was idly tapping his pencil on the desk. Whatever are we here for? Kathy wondered. There were just the three of them, she and Jay and Johnny. Johnny could be expected to be here, of course, but not the others. Never before, in her time at the *Tribune*, had she ever been called into the conference room. Here it was that the various editors huddled, well before the first deadline, to discuss the stories they had, deciding what to do with them. Such news huddles, however, were held late in the day and this was only a little after lunch.

"I thought," said Lathrop, "that we should get together to talk about what long range plans we should be making in covering the story of the visitors. Since it started, it seems to me that we have done somewhat better than an adequate job. We have done it well—conscientiously and objectively. I think we will continue doing exactly that. But now it may be time to begin to think about possible new dimensions to the story. Johnny, you have been on top of it since the first of the visitors landed at Lone Pine. Would you have some thought about what we should be doing next?"

"Al, it's just possible that it's too early to try to do any more than continue to report the facts as we can determine them," said Garrison. "At first, we were dealing with a piece of news that had high shock value in itself. Our concern then, of course, was not to go beyond the most factual and objective reporting. The news itself, the bare recital of it, had sufficient impact. For my part, and I think in everyone else's opinion, it seemed important that we not engage in any kind of writing to increase the impact. In fact, there was no need to. Jay wrote a few general background articles, but he did not engage in any speculation beyond much that had previously been written before the visitors showed up. His articles were intended to do no more than inform our readers, as gently as possible, what concepts could be involved. Other than that, we stuck to straight news reporting."

"But, now," Lathrop said, "the public, in general, has accepted the situation. Many of them may not like it, may find it difficult to accept. But, by now, most everyone does realize that the visitors are here and may be staying for a while. My point is that now may be the time to embark on some background work, digging a bit more deeply into possible consequences . . ."

"Giving our readers something to think about," said Garrison.

"That's exactly it. Throw out a few questions they should be mulling over."

"Al, what you are saying is perfectly logical," said Garrison. "The time will come for that, but I still think it's too early. This kind of writing can only be done if a great deal of careful thought is put into it. We can't go off half-cocked. We have to have some information or at least some indication of some sort of information before we can begin writing that kind of articles. The information, I agree, need not be as solid as we'd want in writing factual news, but it would have to have some substance. Otherwise, we could be caught a long way off base. We could turn out awfully wrong."

"I didn't mean that we should immediately go into backgrounding. I didn't expect that we'd walk out the door and start writing think pieces. But it does seem we should be considering it, getting sorted out in our mind the kind of writing we'd like to see done. We have a lot of people out in the newsroom who have been spending a lot of time observing the visitors and writing about them. Some sort of consensus should be taking shape in the minds of some of these people. Kathy, you and Jay probably have been the most involved of all our staff. Have you any thoughts about the situation? For starters, Kathy, how do you feel about the visitors?"

"I like them," Kathy told him.

"Well, now," said Lathrop, "I hadn't quite expected that. But go ahead and tell us what you like about them."

"For one thing," she said, "they haven't jostled us. They have been nuisances now and then, but done us no actual harm."

"A man was killed at Lone Pine."

"The man was the aggressor. He fired at the visitor. Since then, there has been no one hurt. The visitors have been decent people."

"People, Kathy?"

"Sure, they're people. Different from us, but they still are people. They are intelligent. I'd suspect they have an ethical sense."

"That may all be true," said Jay, "but my impression is that they are arrogant. They pay no attention to us. They ignore us, not studiously, as if they were working at it, but as if they honestly feel that we are not worthy of attention. At times as if they didn't even see us."

Kathy started to speak, but caught herself in time. If she could only tell them, she thought, but she couldn't. Not about Jerry, not even about the handshake she had experienced, although thinking of it as a handshake fell short of what it really had been. It had been something more than a handshake; it had been more personal and understanding than a simple handshake.

"Were you about to say something?" Lathrop asked her.

She shook her head. "Only to say that I do think of them as people. I wish I could say why, but I can't. I can't manage to define what I really feel."

"One thing I've wondered about," said Jay. "These things must have come from somewhere deep in space.

It seems fairly apparent that they eat trees to provide cellulose as food for their young. They may even use some of the cellulose to feed themselves. That we cannot be sure about. But the point I want to make is that they probably are not from this solar system. On no other planet in the system would they find trees or anything else that would provide cellulose. Which would mean that they must come from some other solar system, probably from a planet that could produce cellulose. If this is so, then they must have crossed several light-years, perhaps a great many light-years, for it stands to reason that every solar system would not have a planet that could provide them with the cellulose they seek. Such a planet, with many differences, of course, would have to roughly approximate the Earth and . . ."

"Jay," asked Garrison, "just what the hell are you getting at?"

"There might be a number of considerations," Jay said, "but the one I'm most concerned about is that their trip must have taken a great deal of time. Physicists tell us that nothing can travel faster than the speed of light, probably not even close to the speed of light. This might mean that our visitors could have traveled for many thousands of years before they came to Earth."

"They must have been desperate," said Kathy, "to embark on such a journey. Something must have happened to drive them out into space to search for another planet, having no idea where they'd find such a planet, perhaps not even knowing they'd find one at all. But they needed cellulose to feed their babies. Until they found cellulose, they could have no young. They would have been facing racial extinction."

"You make quite a case for them," Lathrop said to Kathy.

"She may be right," said Jay. "The scenario she outlines could be close to truth. They may have had to look at a number of solar systems before they found one with a planet that fitted their needs. If that is the case, our visitors must be an extremely long-lived race."

"You're talking about some background articles," Garrison said to Lathrop. "Kathy and Jay have given you a hypothetical estimate that would make a dilly of a backgrounder. How would you feel about them going ahead and writing it?"

Lathrop shrugged. "I don't think so. It's just too theoretical. It has no solid basis. It would come out with a sensational sound to it."

"I agree," said Garrison. "The same objection could be made to almost anything else that might be written. It would all be based on supposition. We have nothing solid on which to base any background writing. The best we can do is stick to what can be seen. If we get into theorizing, we'll find that we have nothing on which to tie the theories. We can't pretend to understand what is going on because we are dealing with a life form so unlike us that there's no basis for understanding. Kathy's belief that these things had to find a place where they could raise their young makes sense so far as we are concerned, but does it make sense so far as the visitors are concerned? They may have few concepts that would match our concepts. Their intelligence and outlook, their life style, if you want to call it that, may be, probably is, in large part not understandable to us."

"Maybe you are right," said Lathrop. "One thing—I don't want any of us going off the deep end. In this matter, we simply can't afford to be sensational. By the way, Matthews, in our news bureau, told me this morning there was a rumor in Washington that some sort of weapon test was tried out on one of the visitors. Is there any news of that, any hint of it on the wires?"

Garrison shook his head. "Matthews filed just thirty minutes ago. The question was raised at the White House press briefing today and Porter, the press secretary, denied he knew anything about it."

"How much can you depend on what Porter says?"

"It's hard to tell. So far he seems to have been above board. The scuttlebutt is that there is a hell of a row going on inside the White House, Porter insisting on full disclosure of everything about the visitors and some of the White House people wanting to clam up. If there were a weapon test, I would suppose it might be military. The chances are the results would be classified. Porter might have to cave in on something like that."

"Anything else?"

"Well, not much. Nothing but the regular flow of visitor news. A few days ago, a visitor showed up at an eastern Iowa farm, took over a freshly plowed field, went sailing up and down it until it had covered the entire field, then squatted down in a pasture to watch. It runs off everyone who tries to approach the field. The visitor, it seems, is an old friend of ours."

"What the hell do you mean? An old friend?"

"It has the number 101 painted on it in green."

Kathy jerked upright. "That's the one that was the first to land at Lone Pine," she said. "One of the federal observers painted the number on it. She was the one who had the babies."

"She?"

"Well, it had babies, didn't it? That makes it a she in my book. How come I missed that story?"

"It never got in the paper," said Garrison. "Got crowded out. Showed up in the slop. I rescued it. We'll get it in tonight. I don't know how it happened."

"We have to watch things like that," said Lathrop. "That's a good story. We should have run it."

"Al, it happens now and then. Not often. But it does happen. It's just one of those things. I've been wondering if Kathy should go down to Iowa and look into the situation. The visitor might remember her."

"That's ridiculous," said Lathrop. "Not a single one of them has paid any attention to a human."

"How do we know?" asked Garrison. "Sure, none of them has wandered over and said hello, but that doesn't mean they don't notice people. Kathy was at Lone Pine for several days and . . ."

"What good would it do if old 101 did remember her? There's no way to interview one of them. No way at all to get any information out of them."

"I know all that," said the city editor. "I just have a hunch. I don't think it would be a bad idea."

"All right. Go ahead. You run the city room. If you have a hunch . . "

The door burst open and Jim Gold thrust through it.

"Johnny," he said, "Frank Norton's on the phone from Lone Pine. Stiffy Grant has just found a dead one."

"A dead what?"

"A dead visitor," said Gold.

32. WASHINGTON, D.C.

Porter picked up the phone. "Dave," said the President, "can you come in? There's something I want you to hear."

"Immediately, Mr. President," said Porter.

He put the phone back in the cradle and got out of his chair. From her desk in the corner, his assistant, Marcia Langley, looked inquiringly at him.

"I don't know," said Porter. "More than likely trouble of one sort or another."

As he came into the outer office he made a thumb at the door to the President's office and asked, "Who is in there with him?"

"General Whiteside," said Grace.

"Only Whiteside?"

"Only Whiteside. He arrived a couple of minutes ago."

Porter knocked on the door and opened it. The President was perched on one corner of his desk and Whiteside was sitting in a chair against the wall.

"Come in, Dave," said the President. "Pull up a chair. The general has something rather strange to tell us."

"Thank you, sir," said Porter.

The President went around his desk and sat behind it, facing the two of them.

"I hear you had a rough half-hour with the press this afternoon."

"They wanted to know about some weapon test. I told them I had not heard of it."

The President nodded. "That's good. How did that sort of little white lie go down with you?"

"Sir," said Porter, "most things can be talked about and should, but I assumed the test, if not a security matter, at least, was highly confidential."

"It's a good thing you assumed that," Whiteside said sourly.

"Which I take to mean that it might be a long time before anything at all can be said of it."

"That's why I asked you in," said the President. "I respect you and your viewpoint sufficiently that I don't want to leave you operating in a vacuum. When you hear what Henry has to say, I think you'll agree it should be kept under cover."

He nodded at Whiteside. "If you'll run through it again, Henry."

The general settled himself more firmly in his chair. "I think that both of you are familiar with the exercise. We mounted a .30 caliber and took movies of the bullet's path, thousands of frames a second."

The President nodded. "Yes, we know."

"It was incredible," said Whiteside.

"Okay, Henry. Go ahead and tell us."

"When the bullet struck the visitor," said the general, "the skin of the visitor indented. The bullet did not penetrate. It simply made a dimple in the thing's hide. Like pushing a fist into a feather pillow. Like pushing a finger into your cheek. Then, almost immediately, the dimple rebounded back to its original position and a flare of energy bounced back, striking the mounted rifle and melting it. The funny thing about it is that the bullet itself, the projectile, was not thrown back, not all the way, that is. It bounced back for a short distance, then fell. Later we found it on the ground, where it had fallen."

The general stopped talking for a moment, sucking in his breath.

"Our people tell us," he said, "that is, our scientists tell us, that the visitor converted the kinetic energy of the projectile into potential energy. Doing that, you see, so that the energy could be handled. It's not absolutely certain, but indications are that the visitor absorbed the potential energy, analyzed it, and tossed back an even bigger flare of raw energy that destroyed the weapon. It struck the weapon square, dead-on, and that, the scientists say, is because the indentation was a parabolic indentation, its axis along the line of the projectile's trajectory. The indentation bounced back to its original position, but the shape of it was so precise that it threw back the energy, in some new form, exactly to its source. The scientists talked about a wave pulse or a reflected wave, but they lost me on that one. The point is that the visitor flung back the energy of the projectile, or at least that much, straight into the weapon that fired it. Even if the shot had been a lobbing shot, say, from a mortar, the return blast of energy would have followed precisely the trajectory of the projectile."

He paused, sucking in his breath again, looking from one to the other.

"Do you realize what that means?" he asked.

"A perfect defense system," said the President. "You toss back to the other fellow whatever he throws at you."

Whiteside nodded. "And perhaps in different forms of energy. That's what the people at the lab think, anyhow. It wouldn't have to be a blast of heat. It might be radiation—say, a storm of gamma rays. The visitor can convert kinetic energy to potential energy and it may have a wide choice of energy conversions."

"How many people, besides the three of us, know of this?" asked the President.

"Quite a number of people, service technicians, troops and so forth, witnessed the exercise. If you mean what I've just told you, only three others than ourselves."

"They can be trusted?"

"They can be trusted. There'll be no talk."

"I think, to be on the safe side," said the President, "we must insist the firing test never happened. Would you go along with that, Dave? I know how you feel . . ."

"Much as it goes against my grain," said Porter, "I would agree I'd have to. But it will be difficult to keep the cover on. Some of the servicemen, possibly some of the technicians, will talk. Isn't there some other way it can be done? Say yes, there was a test, but there were no clear-cut results, that what little data we got was confusing and inconclusive."

"My advice," said Whiteside, "is that we stonewall it. That's the only safe way."

"Dave," said the President, "I've never asked you to cover up before. I'm asking you to cover up now. There was, of course, the matter of the object in orbit beginning to break up. I think I made a mistake on that one. You argued for full disclosure, but I weaseled on you. I made a mistake. I should have turned you loose rather than using the NASA announcement. But this is a different matter."

"This," said Whiteside, "could give us the edge we need. If we only can find out how it's done."

"We could call in Allen."

"Mr. President," said Whiteside, "I wish you wouldn't. Maybe eventually he can help with an answer, hopefully without actually knowing what he's doing. But he shouldn't be told about this. Six men know about it now; six men are too many, but there's nothing we can do about that. Let's keep it at the six. Allen is soft and a bit given to talk. He is somewhat bitten with the idea that scientific knowledge should be shared. The force that he has pulled together is working outside security and . . ."

"You don't need to belabor the point," said the President. "You are entirely right. We'll keep Allen out of it."

"My people think," said the general, "that with the visitors it is not a matter of defense at all. Not defense against an enemy, that is. They think the visitors absorb energy from any source that is available. Out in space, they'd absorb energy from all sorts of radiations or from small particles of matter, perhaps on occasion rather large particles of matter that might collide with them. In such an instance, they can convert the kinetic energy of such particles into potential energy, absorb what they can of it and reject that part they can't absorb. The ability is a sort of built-in safety valve against excess energy."

"You used a .30-caliber projectile," said the President. "Do your people have any estimate of how much larger projectiles the visitor could withstand?"

"I suppose a nuke might destroy them," said the general, "but the probability seems to be they could withstand anything short of that. The dimple made by the rifle bullet was small and shallow. The dimple would increase in size with anything heavier, but there is plenty of leeway. The visitor we used for the test didn't seem to notice. When the bullet struck, it never even flinched. It was standing, doing nothing, before the test. At least, nothing we could notice. It was still standing there, doing nothing, after the firing. What I'd like to do is try something a little heavier, progressively heavier firing tests."

"You can't do that," warned Porter. "You would blow your cover. Maybe we can get by, just barely get by, denying this one test. If you tried others, there wouldn't be a chance."

"That's right," said the President. "For the moment, we must be satisfied with what we have. What we must do now is find what the visitors are. How they are made. How they operate, if that's the word. Allen may be pulling something together soon that will help us."

"He hasn't much to work on," said Porter. "About all his people can do is stand to one side and observe."

The box on the President's desk beeped. Frowning, he reached out and punched a button.

"Grace, I thought I told you . . ."

"I'm terribly sorry, sir. I thought you'd want to know. Dr. Allen is here. He says he must see you immediately. It seems that someone out in Minnesota has found a dead visitor."

33. MINNEAPOLIS

The room was closing in on him and that was strange, for it had not closed in before. For the first time since he had lived there—a long two years—he became aware of the room's smallness, its cluttered bareness, its squalidness. He saw the grime upon the windows, the water streaks upon the wall.

He shoved the papers on the desk to one side and stood up, looking out the window to where kids were playing one of those nonsensical, running-and-yelling games that had no significance to anyone but themselves. An old woman, struggling with a grocery bag, was limping down the broken sidewalk. A dog sat lopsided before the stoop of a ramshackle house. The old wreck of a car, its battered fenders drooping disconsolately, stood in its accustomed place beside the curb.

What the hell is the matter with me? Jerry Conklin asked himself. And asking, knew.

It was this visitor business. It had preyed upon him ever since it had happened. He had not, since then, been himself. The worry of it had robbed him of his dedication as a student, had nagged at him almost every waking hour. It would not let him be. It had interfered with his work on his thesis and the thesis was important. He simply had to get the thesis written.

Would it have been better, he wondered, if he had come forward to tell the story of what had happened to the proper authorities? And having gotten rid of it by the telling of it, he might now be shut of it and able to get down to work. Yet, for some reason, he had not been able to do that. He had told himself that he balked against the ridicule and the hidden laughter the story would have brought, although that might not be the only reason. Although he could not imagine what other reason there might be. He had thought that telling it to Barr might be some help, but it hadn't been. The exobiologist, despite the fact that he had listened without laughter, had been no help at all. Nor had the telling of it, even under the circumstances, had the cleansing therapy of a confessional.

And, now, he simply could not tell it. Telling it now, so long after the fact, would lump it with the stories all the kooks were telling about being taken up by the visitors. Telling it now would do no more than link him with the lunatic fringe that had sprung up with the advent of the visitors. Difficult to tell his story before, it was now impossible.

Although, more than likely, he was not through with it yet. At some time, the investigators who had hauled his car away would find a license plate or a motor number and the car would be linked to him. Perhaps, he told himself, they already had found the evidence that would link him to the car. He had done nothing about the car and perhaps he should have, but had not been able to decide what to do. He should have reported its destruction to his insurance company, but what could he have told them? For a time, he had considered reporting it stolen, but had not acted on that impulse. If he had, he probably would find himself in more trouble than he was right now.

He moved away from the window and back to the desk. Sitting down, he pulled the papers in front of him. No matter what, he told himself, he had to get some work done that afternoon. Kathy would be picking him up at six or so and they'd go out to eat.

Kathy, he thought. What the hell would he have done without her? It had been her strength and steadiness, her loving solicitude that had carried him through the last few days.

The phone rang and he picked it up.

Kathy said, "Jerry, I'm so sorry. I can't see you to-night. I'm going out of town. Up to Lone Pine again."

"Oh, hell," Jerry said. "I had been sitting here, counting on seeing you. What is it this time?"

"They've found a dead visitor up there. Washington probably will be sending in investigators. We have to have someone up there and Johnny picked on me."

"A dead visitor? What happened?"

"No one knows. It was just found dead. Stiffy Grant found it. You remember Stiffy. I introduced you to him."

"Yeah, I remember him. Tell me, how would Stiffy know if it was dead or not?"

"It was cold," she said. "No longer warm, but cold. And it wasn't floating. It was resting on the ground."

"And now they're going to rush in and dissect it to find out how it works."

"I suppose that's the idea," Kathy said.

"It has a gruesome sound to me."

"To me, too, but it's logical."

"When will you be back?"

"I don't know. A day or two, I think. I will see you then."

"I was counting on seeing you tonight."

"So was I. Jerry, I'm awfully sorry. And so disappointed."

"Oh, well, you have a job to do. So have I—the thesis. I'll get some work done on it."

"And, Jerry, something else. Old 101 has been found."

"101?"

"Yes, don't you remember? I told you. How one of the men from Washington painted a green 101 on that first visitor to land."

"Yes, you did tell me. So it has been found. Where is it?"

"On a farm near a little place in Iowa. Davis Corners. The farmer thinks it planted something in the field and now is guarding it. When he approaches the field, it runs him off."

"What could it have planted?"

"Maybe nothing. That's only what the farmer thinks. Johnny was going to send me down there, then this Lone Pine business came up."

"Why should he have sent you down there? What could you have done?"

"It was just one of Johnny's hunches. He operates by hunch, runs the city desk by hunch. Some of the hunches are good, some of them pay off. Some people might call it a newspaperman's intuition. Actually, it's hunch. Now I have to go. The plane is waiting and Chet is standing here, first on one foot and then the other."

"I'll miss you, Kathy."

"So will I miss you. Get lots of work done while I'm gone."

"I'll try. Thanks for calling, Kathy."

He hung up the phone and sat idly at the desk. The room closed in on him again. He saw the grimy windows and the streaks upon the wall.

Old 101, he thought. Somewhere down in Iowa, guarding a field. And why should it be in Iowa? There were no trees in Iowa, or at the best, few trees. Nothing like the trees in Minnesota. The farmer thought it had planted or sowed his field. And what could it have planted? He shook his head, puzzled. The farmer, he told himself, must be mistaken.

He got up from the desk and walked up and down the room, remembering again, with a sharpness that terrified him, those few hours (or few minutes?) he had spent inside the thing that was 101. He saw the luminous disks again, the pale blueness of the light, the strange flickerings. There had been something there, he thought, that he should have understood, some fact or facts that, had he stayed a little longer, he might have been able to perceive.

If he could have stayed a little longer, if he could talk with it again—and stopped himself, damning himself for a fool. For he had never talked with it, never really talked with it. From it he had done no more than gain impressions, the sense of home and the sense of trees. And those impressions, he told himself, bitterly, might not have come from 101 at all. They might have come from some unexpected aberrations in his mind.

He went back to his desk and sat down again, pulling the papers in front of him, picking up his pen. But he could not work. The writing that he'd done no longer was writing, but strange, alien squiggles. He stared at the squiggles, trying to make them out, startled by his not being able to make them out, angry and confused, his mind churning.

Maybe, he told himself, the answer might be there, down on that farm in Iowa. And that, he thought, was sheer insanity. He could go to Iowa, out to the farm, and 101 would chase him off, even as it had chased the farmer. He was dealing in a fantasy and knew it, but knowing it did no good. The fantasy still hung on. The impulse became a certainty—he had to go to Iowa. Although what he'd do once he got there, he had no idea.

He rose from the desk and paced up and down the room, fighting it out with himself. One idea hammered at him, zeroing in on him. He needed an answer and this was the only way that he could think of that might provide an answer. It might turn out to be nothing, but he couldn't pass it up. He had to take a chance. He had to play his hunch. Johnny Garrison was a hunch player, Kathy had said, and at times, his hunches did pay off.

He fought it out half the afternoon and it would not go away. He had to go to Iowa. He had to go to Iowa and he didn't even have a car. But Charlie would let him use his car. If he asked, Charlie would loan the car to him.

Limp and sweating, he lifted the phone and dialed Charlie's number.

34. LONE PINE

Looking through binoculars, Kathy could see, across the river, the knot of men who were at work on the dead visitor. There was no way she could make out what they were doing. The only thing she could determine was that in some manner (using saws, she wondered?), they had cut sections out of the dead body, probably securing samples to be taken back to Washington, or perhaps elsewhere, for closer examination. They were busy with a number of pieces of equipment, but the distance was too great to make certain what they were doing. There had been no chance to talk with anyone who might answer her questions. Security was tight. The bridge the army engineers had thrown across the river was closed by national guardsmen and other guardsmen patrolled the river bank to stop anyone who might try to cross.

The other visitors paid no attention to what was going on around the dead body of their fellow. They continued cutting timber and spewing out the bales of cellulose. Some of them were budding and a dozen or so of their young were scurrying about, chomping at the bales of cellulose.

Kathy lowered the glasses, laid them in her lap.

"Anything to see over there?" asked Norton.

"Nothing I can make out," said Kathy. She handed the glasses to him. "You want to have a try?"

"Even if I saw something, I'd probably not recognize it," said Norton. "I thought maybe they would try to move the dead visitor somewhere. To the university down at Minneapolis, maybe. But I guess it's just too large. That thing must weigh tons."

"Maybe they will later on," said Kathy, "but as I understand it, it was important to get some tissue samples as soon as possible, if what they are getting can be called tissue."

Norton lifted the glasses to his face, stared through them for a long time, then took them down, handing them to Kathy.

"I've never seen such tight security," said Kathy. "Nor set up so fast. Chet and I got here only a few hours after you phoned us, but by that time, they had it buttoned up. Ordinarily, there would be some sort of public relations setup to give you some idea of what might be going on. But here there's nothing. Not even someone around to tell you there'll be no information. We're just locked out."

"Washington probably figures this is important. Top secret."

"Sure they do," said Kathy. "And more than that, they were caught flat-footed and had to move fast. Who would have expected that one of the visitors would die and they'd have a shot at it. When we write about how tight the security is, the government will complain. Claiming we are overemphasizing."

"In a little while," said Norton, "Lone Pine will be swarming with newsmen. Like it was before. Maybe then someone will be able to jar something loose."

"I tried," said Kathy, "but there's no one to jar. Just those silly, flat-faced guardsmen who won't let you through. Most of them won't even talk to you. Not even the officers. Usually officers will talk, at least a little, to show you how important they are, if for no other reason. I tell you, Frank, I don't even know why I'm here. I could just as well have stayed back in the newsroom. Here I'm not doing any good. I don't know what the hell I'll tell Johnny when I phone him. Maybe someone else could have done better. Maybe Jay . . ."

"I don't see how," said Norton "As you say, there's no one here to talk to."

"What beats me," said Kathy, "is that there aren't even any rumors. In a tight security situation such as this, there are always rumors. Someone had heard something and is embroidering on it. But here there isn't even that. Stiffy is just as empty as I am. You'd expect that by now Stiffy would have heard something that he could enlarge a bit and pass on. Nor Sally, either. If she'd heard something, I'm sure she'd tell me."

"You got to hang in there," said Norton. "If you hang in long enough . . ."

"Jerry and I were going to have dinner tonight," said Kathy. "Both of us were counting on it. It's been a long time since we've shared a dinner—a sit-down dinner, not just grabbing a hamburger at a fast-food joint. Poor Jerry, he's had a bleak time of it. Six years as a student, living hand to mouth, picking up odd jobs so he can get the little money that he needs, living in a tiny room. I thought we should get married. Then, at least, he'd have a decent place to live, but he would have none of that. He refused to let a woman support him. The man has pride and I respect him for it, but that doesn't keep me from feeling sorry for him, and he'd be sore if he knew I felt sorry for him. So I can't show it. We could have shacked up and that would have made it easier for the two of us, but neither of us wanted that. There's nothing really wrong with it; a lot of people do. But both of us shied away from it. I don't know. It seemed sort of cheap and both of us agreed . . ."

"It'll work out," said Norton, trying to comfort her. "He's only got a little while before he has his doctorate and then he'll get a job . . ."

"I don't know why I'm telling you this," she said. "I shouldn't, but it just came out of me. Frank, why should I be telling this to you?"

"I don't know," said Norton, "but I am glad you could. If it helped you any, I am glad you could."

They sat silent for a time in the autumn afternoon. Finally, Norton said, "In a day or two, before the end of the week, I'll be taking a few days off. I do it every fall. Usually earlier than this. This matter of the visitors makes me late this year. I'll drive up through the wilderness area, a canoe strapped to the top of the car. I'll park beside a little river that I know and will spend a few days canoeing. A sort of farewell to the autumn wilderness, a few days with it before bad weather closes in. I just paddle along and look, taking it easy, not pushing myself. I won't work at it. Maybe do a little fishing. Mostly looking, though."

"It sounds nice," said Kathy.

"I was thinking. Why don't you phone Jerry and ask him to come up here. Tell Johnny you're taking some vacation. The two of you join me on this little jaunt. You get away from your deadlines, Jerry from his classes. It would do the both of you a world of good."

"I think it would," said Kathy, "but we can't. I used up all my vacation time in June and Jerry's got his thesis."

"I'm sorry," Norton said. "It would have been nice to have had the two of you along."

"I'm sorry, too," said Kathy. "Thanks so much for asking."

35. WASHINGTON, D.C.

The President came into the press office as Porter was preparing to leave. The press secretary rose from his desk, surprised, and said, "You are working late, sir."

"And so are you," said the President. "I saw your light and decided to come in."

"Is there anything I can do for you?"

"Only listen to me," said the President. "I need someone I can sit down with and take off my shoes."

He walked to a sofa against the wall and dropped into it, slouching, stretching out his legs, locking his hands behind his head.

"Dave," he asked, "is all of this really happening or am I having a bad dream?"

"I fear," said Porter, "that it is happening. Although there are times when I ask myself the same question."

"Can you see an end to it? A logical end?"

Porter shook his head. "Not at this point, I can't. But I have a sort of ingrown faith that it will work out. Even the worst situations usually do."

"All day long," said the President, "I have people hammering at me. Things they want me to do. Actions they want me to take. Probably silly things, but to the people who advocate them, I don't suppose they're silly. I have a stack of letters asking me to designate a day of prayer. I have phone calls from men I have always regarded as reasonable suggesting a proclamation calling for a day of prayer. And I'll be goddamned if I'm going to call a day of prayer. Sure, presidents at various times have asked the people to observe a day of prayer, but only on occasions that patently call for prayer, and I don't think this situation does."

"It stems from all the religious fervor this business has stirred up," said Porter. "When people don't know what else to do, they suddenly turn to religion, or what for them may pass for religion. It constitutes a mystic retreat into unreality. It is a search for an understanding of forces that are beyond our capability to understand, a seeking for some symbol that will bridge the gap to understanding."

"Yes, I realize all that," said the President, "and, in a way, I can sympathize with it. But to call for prayer right now would overemphasize the problem that we face. What's happening baffles the hell out of me, but I feel no sense of panic. Maybe I'm wrong, Dave. Should I be feeling panic?"

"I don't think so," Porter said. "It's not a matter of panic. What is driving these people to urge a day of prayer is the obsessive urge of the suddenly devout to force everyone else into at least a simulation of their state of mind."

"I've tried over the last hour or so," said the President, "to sit quietly by myself and try, somehow, to get straight in my mind what we are really facing. Thinking, I suppose, that if I could get that straight in my mind, I might just possibly be able to figure what to do. The first thing I told myself was that, as of the moment, we are not facing any threat of violence or coercion. The visitors, as a matter of fact, have been quite well behaved. It looks to me as if they may be making an effort to understand the sort of society we have, although there must be some aspects of it that are hard for them to understand. And if they are doing this, I told myself, then they must intend to operate within the parameters of our society in the best way that they can. I can't be sure of this, of course, but that's the way it looks and I gain some measure of reassurance from it. Of course, at any time at all, something might happen that will change it. The police down in that Alabama town where the visitor sat down in the stadium arrested a bunch of dimwits trying to get into the stadium with a box of dynamite. I suspect they intended to blow up the visitor."

"Even had they succeeded," said Porter, "they probably would have failed. It would take more than a box of dynamite, most likely, to inconvenience one of the visitors."

"What you say is true, Dave, if the data from Whiteside's firing test is accurate and I assume it is. But it would have been a deliberate act of aggression that could change the attitude of the visitors toward us. Until we know a whole lot more than we know now, we can't afford to commit an act of violence, even an unintentional act of violence. I have a feeling that the visitors, if they put their minds to it, could outdo us in violence. I'd not like to come down to a shooting match with them."

"We do need to know a lot more about them," said Porter. "How is Allen making out with the dead visitor? Have you heard anything from him?"

"Only that the investigation is underway. He's doing the preliminary work on the spot. Once that is done, an effort might be made to move the body to some facility where the work can be carried out under more favorable circumstances."

"Moving it might be quite a chore."

"I am told there are ways it can be done. I understand the Army Corps of Engineers is working on the problem."

"Any indication of why the visitor might have died?"

"It's funny that you should have asked that, Dave. That is one of the first questions that popped into my mind. Seems to me that when something dies, the inclination always is to ask the cause of death. All of us are very much concerned with life and death. H. G. Wells popped into my mind immediately. His Martians died because they were defenseless against the diseases of the Earth. I wondered if some bacterium, some virus, some fungus might have done the visitor in. But the cause of its death apparently was a question that Allen never thought of. At least, he said nothing about it. He was just excited that one of them had been delivered into his hands. There is something about that guy that gives me the cold shivers every now and then. Dammit, there are times when he doesn't seem human. He's too much the scientist. To him the scientists are a brotherhood set apart from the rest of humanity. That attitude bothers us. The chances are that Allen and his men will learn something about the visitor that it might not be wise to advertise. I have tried to impress this on him and I think he understands, but I can't be sure. I know how you feel about this, Dave, but . . ."

"If there is information that shouldn't be made public in the interest of national security," said Porter, "then I'd go along with holding it back. What I object to is secrecy for the sake of secrecy. I am confident the findings from the dead visitor can be handled. Certainly, there will be something that can be safely announced. If there is enough of that sort of information, the media can be satisfied. Some of them may suspect the full story is not being told, but there's not too much for them to complain about. What worries me are the people who are doing the investigating. The press could get to some of them."

"I warned Allen on that. He is using only men in his own department—not the people he recruited from outside. He swears that he can trust them. It is unlikely that anyone can get to them, let alone talk to them. We've got a security net around Lone Pine a snake couldn't wriggle through."

The President hoisted himself to his feet and started for the door, then came back and sat down again.

"There's another thing I don't like," he said. "It's that goddamned U.N. There is a push to declare that the visitors are an international, not an internal, matter. You are aware of it, of course."

Porter nodded. "I had some rather sharp questions on it at today's briefing. For a while, the boys had me skating on thin ice."

"The resolution is going to be voted," said the President. "Sure as hell it will. There's no way we can stop it. Only half a dozen governments will stand with us. We've twisted all sorts of arms, but there is little we can do. All our little sanctimonious underprivileged brothers that we're breaking our ass to help will vote against us."

"They can pass the resolution. They'll play hell enforcing it."

"Sure, I know that, but we'll get a bloody nose for all the world to see. We'll drop a lot of prestige."

"Maybe it is time to let the prestige go. This is our show. We are the ones who have the visitors on our backs."

"Dave, you may be right. But there are other considerations. State is frantic at the prospect."

"State is always frantic."

"I know. But it's not only State and the U.N. resolution. There are others who are giving us heat. The environmentalists are up in arms because we are doing nothing to protect our wilderness areas against the visitors. The lumber interests are howling to high heaven. The farmers, seeing visitors come down and roost in the middle of their fields, are getting restless. The entire business world is in an uproar. The stock markets are reacting like a yo-yo. At times, I catch myself thinking and I know it's wrong to think it, but I can't help it—why did it have to be us? Why couldn't it have been Europe or South America, or even at times, God help me, the Soviet Union?"

"I can understand how you might feel that way," said Porter. "There is so damn much . . ."

"If only I could win once in a while," said the President. "If I didn't have to fight so hard for every inch of progress. Take the energy bill. It all makes sense, it is all possible within the state of the art. I could bring in hundreds of top notch engineers who would swear that the plan is practical. A solar energy farm in the deserts of the Southwest, a few more millions to nail down a cryogenic transmission and storage system. Another year is all it would take, the engineers tell me, a few more millions. Enough energy to power the entire country, a transmission system that could distribute or store the energy with virtually no loss of power. But does Congress see it that way? Hell, no, they don't see it that way. Half of them are in the clutches of the big energy corporations, the other half so stupid that it's a wonder they can find their way home when they leave the Capitol . . ."

"Some day," said Porter. "Some day they'll come around to it. Soon or late, they'll have to see . . ."

"Sure," said the President, "some day. I'll tell you when that some day will be. When gasoline costs five bucks a gallon and you have to wait in line for hours to get the three gallons your ration card allows you. When you go cold in the winter because you can't afford to use enough natural gas to keep warm. When you use 25-watt light bulbs to hold down the lighting bill . . ."

36. IOWA

The sun had set and the early evening dusk was settling in when Jerry Conklin turned into the gas station.

"Fill the tank and check the oil," Jerry told the attendant.

While the attendant was busy at the pump, Jerry walked to the edge of the road. The station was on the outskirts of one of the many small villages through which he'd driven; a quiet little trading center for the farming country that surrounded it. The town, the same as all the others, was made up of rows of small, neat houses and a tidy business district. Lights were coming on in some of the houses and there was little traffic on the road. An evening hush had fallen over the community, broken now and then by the yapping of a dog.

Jerry stood at the side of the road, looking up and down it. Within himself the ache still persisted. He had been stupid, he told himself, driven by an illogical need that he could not define. He should have known, he told himself, that the trip would come to nothing. It had been silly to think that 101 would recognize him—although, in a way, it might have recognized him. But if it had been recognition, he could find no comfort in it.

He had driven to the farmhouse late in the afternoon after several failures to find the place and having to stop along the way for further directions.

The farmer had been in the farmyard, puttering around with a hammer and nails, repairing a pigpen fence.

"Yeah, it's still sitting there, guarding the field," he

had said. "But it won't do you no good to go over there. You're welcome if you want to try, but I know what will happen. I'd go with you, but I got work to do. These hogs have been breaking out of here and I have to repair the fence so I can keep them in."

Jerry had walked to the field. Old 101 sat there, in a hay field off to one side of the plowed strip of land. It made no move to chase him off. It just kept sitting there. He had walked out to it and walked around it, staring up at it, trying to remember how it had looked when it had landed on the bridge. But while the memory of it straddling the river, with the bridge gone to kindling wood under its impact, still was sharp and clear, he found it difficult to equate it now with the way it had appeared the time he first had set eyes upon it. Somehow it seemed smaller now, although God knows, it was still big enough.

He had walked around it and moved up close against it, laying his hands upon it to feel the soft warmness of it. He had patted it gently and poked it with a playful fist. And it gave no sign.

"Tell me," he had said to it. "Tell me what I need to know."

It had told him nothing. It had paid no attention to him. But he was sure it knew that he was there. How he could be so sure of that, he did not know.

He had given it plenty of time. He talked to it. He laid his hands upon it and still it made no sign. So finally he had walked away, going slowly, turning back every now and then to look at it, but each time he turned to look, it still sat there as stolidly as it had been sitting all the time.

Although, he told himself, it had not chased him off. It had chased off everyone else who had approached it, but it had made no move against him. And that, in itself, he thought, might be a sign of recognition.

"Mister," said the station attendant, walking up to him and holding out the dipstick, "you need a quart of oil."

"All right, put it in," said Jerry. "This car always needs a quart of oil."

He paid the man and, getting into the car, drove out to the road and headed toward the town.

But when he reached the business district, he drove around a block and came out on the road again, heading back the way that he had come.

He was going back to that farm again and just why he was going back was not quite clear to him. An essential stubbornness, perhaps, he told himself, a desperate unwillingness to give up, a very stubborn faith in his silly conviction that there might be an answer he could get from 101. He didn't deliberately decide to go back, he didn't argue it out with himself, he didn't ponder it; he simply drove around the block and it was not until he was headed back down the road the way that he had come that he realized he was going back. Now that he had done it, he did not try to fight it.

He couldn't drive back to the farmyard again, he knew. While the farmer had been cordial, he had seemed a little nettled when he found that Jerry had not been chased by the visitor. Jerry had imagined that he detected in the farmer's face some trace of a dark suspicion.

Actually, he told himself, he did not need to go back to the farmyard. By walking half a mile or so, he could reach 101 by parking on a gravel township road. It would be dark by the time he got there and it was unlikely that anyone would spot him. The night was clear and in a little while, a near-full moon would be coming up and there'd be light enough to get where he was going.

He had a few bad moments when he got close to the farm, fearing that he would be unable to locate the place. But there were a few landmarks that he remembered—a rickety iron bridge spanning a small stream, a lone oak standing in a pasture close to an old haystack. Shortly aften ten o'clock, he found the gravel road, drove up it for a mile or so and parked. From there he calculated that he would be able to spot 101.

Either his navigating had been better than he'd known, or he was just plain lucky, for in a little time he did locate the farm and the dark bulk of 101 squatting in the hayfield. He was, however, farther from it than he had expected he would be. He began hiking across the fields, stumbling occasionally when a foot caught in furrowed stubble. He had to work his way through a couple of barb-wire fences and in the dark, that was a ticklish job to do. The night had turned chilly and he buttoned up his jacket, turning up the collar as protection from the wind. Down in a ravine off to his left, an owl was making tentative hoots every now and then, testing out its voice, and when the wind veered slightly, he could catch the baying of a distant dog.

He moved through a lonely emptiness and yet an emptiness that seemed to hold some threat within it. He had the feeling that at any moment, something could come welling up out of this land he crossed, although he never could quite determine what it might be that would come welling up.

The walk seemed to take forever. There were times when it seemed to him that he had not moved at all, that despite all his walking, he was only marking time in the self-same place. To make up for that, to overcome that terrible feeling of no progress, he drove himself without mercy, sometimes running. But he soon quit the running, for it brought too many stumbles. Then, suddenly, he was there. In front of him loomed the moon-limned bulk of 101.

He staggered across the last few yards and collapsed against the visitor, protected by its massiveness from the chill of the northwest wind. He had a strange compulsion to stay huddled there, as if he had reached some sort of refuge and must cling to it. But that was silliness, he knew, and staggered to his feet, leaning his head against it as he fought to regain his breath.

Leaning against the great black wall that rose above him, he tilted his head and saw the quiet sparkling of the stars that were cut off abruptly by the soaring blackness that was 101. The loneliness stayed on, the loneliness and lostness. He had thought that it perhaps would disappear when he reached the visitor.

But reaching the visitor, it seemed, had made no difference.

He had done it again, he thought. He'd come back again to repeat the folly that he had committed earlier in the day, the act of folly that had commenced that moment in his room when he had picked up the phone to ask Charlie if he could use the car.

Yet he had been so sure—not sure in any sense of logic, but sure in a way that was beyond all reason.

His breathing had grown even now. He stepped back from the visitor, slowly began to turn about to face the fields again, reluctant to turn around, reluctant to take that first step that would lead him back to the car parked on the gravel road.

And, in that instant that he took the step, a snake-like something came swishing down upon him and snapped like an iron band about his chest. In mid-air he caught a glimpse of the autumn-bare fields, lit weakly by the moon, a glimpse of a tree-bordered creek that angled down a valley, the sudden flash of light from a distant farmhouse.

Then he was in that strange darkness that was not dark, but blue, caught a whiff of the dank mustiness that lurked in the dry, hot air. There was once again the swiftness of the flaring and the flickering that revealed impossible shapes that would not stand still long enough to see. The rows of circular eyes still were staring at him. It was, he thought, as if he'd never left this place.

He had fallen to his knees and now he rose slowly to his feet and as he did, he reeled under a flood of hammering sensations that assailed him out of nowhere. He went to his knees again and stayed there, head bent, hands against the floor to keep from falling flat upon his face.

And all the while the sensations hammered at him, thundering in his brain, so many and so powerful that he could not shut them out, nor was he able to distinguish what might be the import of them.

"Take it easy," he gasped. "Let up. Let me have a chance."

The sensations went away and he swayed a little, as if he might have been leaning against something for support and it had been suddenly snatched away.

Then the sensations came again, but softer now, stealing up on him, as a cat might creep up on a bird.

37. WASHINGTON, D.C.

"Daddy," said Alice, "I don't like some of the things that I have been hearing."

Senator Davenport, slouched in his chair, looked at her over the rim of his glass of Scotch.

"And what might you have been hearing, my dear?" he rumbled.

"All this talk up on the Hill—not out-loud talk, just cloakroom talk—about developing some sneaky way to get rid of the visitors. Like spraying psychedelic drugs on the trees that they are eating, like spending millions to develop a bacterium or a fungus that might be fatal to them. Saying it is better to spend a few million to get rid of them and let things get back to normal than to spend the same few million to find out about them."

"I do believe," said the senator, in an unusually mellow mood, "that I have heard snitches of such talk. Pest control, it's called. Not waging war against them— just pest control."

The senator shifted in his chair to look at Porter.

"Maybe our White House friend might have some comment on this."

"I would think," said Porter, "that this is one I had better stand aside on."

"Some of the boys, you know," said the senator, "seem to be getting a bit wrought up about the situation. They're just talking among themselves so far, but, before too long, they may go beyond that."

"To even think, this early, about wiping out the visitors," said Porter, "seems somewhat premature. I've heard some loose talk about developing a selective disease that would zero in on them. To my mind, it's only talk. No one has the least idea of how to go about it. First, you'd have to know what the visitors are and how their life system functions. Only when you knew that would you have any clue as to how they might react to various agents. There's a trap in the matter of selectiveness as well. How can we be sure that what would be developed would be selective? We might wind up with something that would wipe out not only the visitors, but the human race as well."

"It's a monstrous idea in any case," said Alice. "We have no real grievance against the visitors."

"Oh, I don't know about that," said the senator. "Talk to a true blue environmentalist who has persuaded himself that unless some action is taken, these things will destroy the last remaining wilderness, and you might detect a grievance. Or the president of a lumber company who has just had a couple of lumberyards consumed as a quick lunch by one of our big black friends. Or an airline official who is turning gray over the possibility that one of his jets will collide with a friendly visitor-escort. Or a man in an airport control tower who has one less strip on which to bring down planes."

"It's a matter of minority interests again," said Alice. "Small cliques trying to push around the rest of us."

"I'm surprised to hear you say that, daughter," said the senator. "It has seemed to me that you have always been fairly well minority-oriented. The poor downtrodden blacks, the poor downtrodden Indians . . ."

"But this is different," said Alice. "My minorities are cultural minorities; yours are economic—poor downtrodden businessmen who suddenly feel a pinch."

"The environmentalists," said the senator, "aren't economic. They're emotion-oriented. And born troublemakers."

"I'm beginning to have a feeling," said Porter, "that the public attitude toward the visitors may be in the process of change. At first, they were novelties and an occasion for a great excitement. Now they seem to be becoming irritants. They now are just black lumps, perched around the landscape, or flying over it, and in a number of rather minor ways, they are interfering with the daily lives of some people. Given a few months, probably only a few weeks, the minor irritations may grow into dislikes, maybe even hatreds— not originating in the special interests that are most affected, but in that phenomenal area we call public opinion. It would be a pity if this should happen, for we simply have to have the kind of patience that will give us an opportunity to find out what they are and how we can get along with them."

"Allen is working on that one out in Minnesota," said the senator. "Is he finding anything at all?"

"Nothing that I know of, senator. Nothing definite. He's not made even a preliminary report, if that is what you mean. But there is some scuttlebutt floating around that they are plants—at least, that they belong to the plant kingdom."

"Plants? Christ, that doesn't make any sort of sense."

"No, of course, it doesn't. I've been trying to track down where the rumor came from, but have had no success."

"There's this business, too," said the senator, "that the visitors may know how to control gravity. That's the one I'm interested in. That's something we could put to use."

"Mostly it comes from the fact that they float a few inches above the ground and that when they move, they don't seem to make use of propulsive units," said Porter. "Or at least propulsive units as we think of them. No one really knows, of course. The idea is no more than someone grabbing for an explanation—any kind of explanation for a mode of operation that defies all the physical laws we know."

"You two talk only about what we can gain from the visitors," said Alice. "Doesn't it enter your thinking that they may be thinking along the same lines— what they can get from us?"

"Well, sure," her father said. "They are getting cellulose. And cellulose is cheap enough if we can get gravity control from them."

"They also got a few cars."

"Well, yes, a few of them. Just that one time. Not any more. They're not taking cars any more."

"I've wondered," said Alice, "what they wanted the cars for. And I can't understand you, Daddy. To start with, you were up in arms about them—destroying trees and lumberyards, upsetting the country's business."

"I rethought my position," said the senator. "I began to see some rather attractive possibilities, if we can play our cards right." He said to Porter, "I keep hearing about a weapons test conducted against the visitors. It's a story that keeps floating around, but I can't get a handle on it. What do you know about it?"

"The same as you," said Porter. "I keep hearing the story."

"Nothing positive? No details?"

"None at all," said Porter.

"These things must have some sort of defense worked out," said the senator. "Out in space, they must have been open to some sort of attacks, although I can't imagine what kind of attacks. It would be nice if we could find what they have."

38. MINNEAPOLIS

The editors sat at the news huddle in the conference room. The sound of clacking typewriters and the hum of conversation came through the halfway-open door.

"We have the Black Hills-Indian story that Jones wrote," said Garrison. "We should be getting that in the paper soon."

"I thought you were saving that for the Sunday edition," said Lathrop.

"So I was, but it kept getting crowded out. Keep it too long and it could get dated. There is, as well, a piece that Jamison has been working on for weeks, an analysis of what a real energy crunch could do to this area. It's a good job. He talked with a lot of people. He really dug into it. It's long, but it looks as if we have the space today. There isn't much other news. I'd say we could strip it across the top of the front page."

"Haven't we a good story on the visitors?"

Garrison looked at Gold. The assistant city editor shrugged. "Nothing to get excited about. It's beginning to level off."

"As a matter of fact," said Garrison, "I'm beginning to have the feeling that the visitors haven't as much impact as they had a week ago. The edge is beginning to wear off the story. The readers may be getting a little weary of it. We've played the story hard. That was fine so long as the readers were avid for it. But if we keep on cramming it down their throats . . ."

"How about Kathy? She's still up at Lone Pine, isn't she?"

"She is," said Gold, "for all the good it does. There's nothing coming out of there. No one's getting anything, either from there or Washington. I've never seen the lid clamped down so hard."

"It sounds," said Garrison, "as if something fairly big is going on. Otherwise, why all the secrecy? But, apparently, we aren't going to get anything until someone is willing to talk."

"What about the Washington bureau?"

Hal Russell, the wire editor, said, "They're not getting anything, either. I talked with Matthews just a couple of hours ago. Nothing, he said. Absolutely nothing. Either no one knows anything or they are clamming up. Some rumors, but nothing that can be pinned down. Chances are, if anyone knows anything, it's only a few. In Washington, if more than a dozen people know something, one of them is sure to be talking about it. The news leaks out."

"So why are we keeping Kathy up at Lone Pine?" asked Lathrop. "If Washington is tight-lipped, what chance does she have?"

"Kathy is one damn fine reporter," said Garrison. "She has as much chance to dig out something as the Washington bureau."

"I think we ought to get her back here," said Lathrop. "With vacations and one thing and another, we are running shorthanded. We could use her here."

"If you wish," said Garrison, grim with a sudden anger.

"If you're still looking for a backgrounder on the visitors," said Gold, "Jay has an idea. He was talking the other day with someone at the university, a man in the native American affairs department. This man was drawing a parallel between us and the visitors and the Indians and the white men when the whites first showed up in America. He said the reason the Indians finally lost out was that their technology was upset by the white man and that, as a result of this, they lost their culture. Their defeat dated from the day when an Indian wanted an iron hatchet, to replace his stone tomahawk, so badly that he was willing to sell his natural resources, to enter into trade arrangements that were unfair to him, to get it."

"A story like that would be oblique propaganda," said Lathrop, "and both Jay and you should know it."

"Jay wasn't about to write it from the Indian view alone," said Gold. "He was going to talk to economists and historians and a lot of other people . . ."

Lathrop shook his head. "With the Black Hills-Indian situation, I think we should keep away from it. No matter how well the story was written, no matter how objectively, we would be accused of bias."

"Oh, well," said Gold, "it was only an idea."

39. IOWA

The river gurgled and lapped against the shore. Dick's Landing, located on a shelf several feet above the river, was made up of several dilapidated buildings. Above the buildings reared the steep heights of the Iowa bluffs. Beyond the river's edge was an island that hemmed in the channel or, rather, one of many channels, for here the Mississippi, spreading out on a wide flood-plain, became a watery jungle. To the east loomed the blueness of the distant bluffs on the Wisconsin side.

Jerry stood on the river bank, watching the progress of the small rowboat powered by a small and sputtering motor. The boat made its doubtful, hesitating way up the channel, bouncing in the roughness of the current. In the back of it crouched a hunched-over man, nursing the balky motor.

Opposite the landing, the man angled the boat in toward shore, finally bringing it in against the shaky dock. When he clambered from the boat and tied it, Jerry saw that he was older than he first had thought. His hair was an unruly iron-gray and his shoulders slightly stooped, but when he moved it was with the sprightly spring of a man much younger.

He came along the walkway of the dock and up the bank. When he came close, Jerry asked, "Are you Jimmy Quinn?"

The man halted in his tracks and looked at him with clear blue eyes, the skin at the corners of them wrinkled and squeezed into intricate crows-feet.

"That I am," he said. "Who's asking?"

"The name is Jerry Conklin. I was told you'd be coming in soon. I understand you know these bottoms."

"Man and boy I've known the Winnishiek," said Quinn. "A river rat I'm called and I guess that's what I am. These bottoms I have known since the day that I could toddle and a tangled mess they are. Islands and sloughs and lakes and channels, and I know them all for miles up and down the river. I've hunted them and fished and trapped them and I've poked into every corner of them. And what can I do for you?"

"I understand that some of the visitors have landed somewhere in the area, somewhere in these river bottoms."

"Visitors? Visitors? Oh, yes, now I know. I've heard the name. You mean those big black boxes folks say came out of the sky."

"That's what I mean," said Jerry. "You sound as if you saw one."

"Over on Goose Island," said Quinn. "That's the big island, plumb in the center of the river valley, four or five miles downstream from here. Near as I could make out, there are three of them. I don't know if they are still there. Just saw the tops of them, sticking out above the trees. It was getting on toward evening and I didn't linger none. Maybe I wouldn't have even if it hadn't been getting on toward evening. Spooky things they were. Nothing that belonged there. Gives a man shivers up his spine. Didn't rightly know what they were first off. Figured it out later on that they must be these visitors. How come you know? I never told no one. People would have laughed at me. They think I'm crazy, anyhow. To tell the truth, perhaps I am. I've been too long on the river."

"Would you be willing to take me to them?"

"Not now," said Quinn. "Not today. It's getting on close to night. This river's not a place to be at night. With the kind of motor that I have, it's a long way down to Goose. Dark would catch us on the way."

"Tomorrow, then. Or the day after tomorrow, more than likely. There is someone else who will want to go along. It may take me a while to locate this other person and she'll have to drive down from Minneapolis."

"A woman?"

"Yes, a woman."

"What would a woman want with them visitors?"

"She just possibly may know more about them than anyone in the world today."

"I be damned," said Quinn. "These days you never know what to expect of a woman. Should I take you down there, would there be something in it for me?"

"We'd pay you."

"Cash money?"

"Cash money," Jerry told him.

"You expect to get up close to these things? If they still are there. They might have left, you know."

"We would want to get close to them," said Jerry.

"I tell you, mister, I'm not getting up close to them. I'll take you there and I'll wait to take you back. But I'm not getting close to them."

"You won't have to come along with us. You just point them out. That's all you'll have to do. And wait to take us back."

"You let me know when you need me. Generally, I'm on the river the most of the day. Come in along toward evening."

"I'll let you know," said Jerry.

40. WASHINGTON, D.C.

Allen, the presidential science advisor, said, "This is only a preliminary report. Later on, there'll be more."

"You've found something, then," said the President.

"Something," said Allen. "Yes, something. It's hard to believe. I have a hard time making myself believe it. But the analysis is there. The facts are undeniable. There is no ground to quarrel with them."

"Doctor," said Whiteside, "you look a little pale around the gills."

"I suspect I do," admitted Allen. "This goes against the grain, against all the knowledge that we have. Those damn things are made up of cellulose."

"Cellulose?" asked the President. "That white, fluffy stuff?"

"When the visitors get through with it, it's no longer white or fluffy." Allen looked around the room. "There are only the four of us. Will there be others arriving?"

"Not this time," said the President. "Later on, when we know more, there may be another briefing with other personnel. This time around, just the four of us. General Whiteside has a special interest and should know what you've found. Dave is here because, by and large, he knows everything I know. At the moment, everything you say here is confidential. I assume your staff is not doing any talking."

Allen stiffened. "Only four men are involved," he said. "They understand the need of confidentiality."

"But there are a lot more involved than four," said Whiteside.

"The others are field workers," said Allen. "Collecting samples and doing other basic work on the Minnesota visitor. Only four are involved in the lab work. They are the only ones who know what I'm about to tell you."

"O.K., Doctor," said the President. "So go ahead and tell us."

"The creature basically is made up of cellulose," said Allen. "But not cellulose in the form that we know it. To precisely describe the situation, we have had to make use of highly technical terminology."

"Which we wouldn't understand," said the President. "You'll have to simplify it for us, Doctor."

"I'll do what I can. What I tell you will have to be oversimplified. And because of the oversimplification, perhaps a little short of the exact truth, but it will give you an idea of what we have come up with.

"The inner part of the creature is closely packed cellulose, compressed to an unbelievable extent. So closely packed that it can withstand structural stresses of several tons per square inch. On the face of it, this would seem impossible, but the figures are there. How it can be managed we have no idea, no inkling as to the process involved."

"You talk about the inner part of the creature," said Whiteside. "Does that mean the outer part is different?"

Allen shuddered. "Yes, General, it is different. An entirely different story. It is what you might call a cellulose-silicon polymer involving in some manner that we're not sure we understand the use of silicon-oxide bonds and hydroxl bonds—that is, hydrogen-oxide bonds. There is a lot of oxygen in cellulose. In the silicon-oxygen bonding, there are a couple of different forms and, to make matters even more complicated, a mix of the two forms are employed. In some cases, it amounts to a tetrahedral structure, a silicate akin to rock—a structure similar to feldspar and quartz. It's hard to say exactly what we have. There are a number of various linkages to make up what we tentatively describe as a polymer."

"It seems to me you are talking about the thing having a rock-like skin," said Porter.

"In layman language, that is what I am talking about," said Allen. "Hard as rock, probably much harder, and yet the silicon provides it with some elasticity, some give. Rocks can't normally be dented. This stuff can. It can be dented and then bounces back. It has at once hardness and ductility and an incredible thermal stability.

"We have theorized the use to which these capabilities can be put. It is only a theory, of course, but it does make sense. If these things operate across vast extents of interstellar space, they would have to get energy from somewhere. Their high thermal stability means they could soak up all sorts of energy, a lot of it, perhaps, from the impact of interstellar dust. The dust particles, no matter how small, would carry some energy. But in the form of kinetic energy. We think the skins of these things can convert the kinetic energy to potential energy, possibly can change that energy to whatever form it needs. Occasionally, they might collide with larger pieces of matter. Such a strike would indent the skin, with the skin picking up as much energy as it could handle, deflecting what it can't use when the indentation in the skin bounces back, in effect rejecting that part of the energy it can't handle. The dent in the skin would produce a reflected wave of energy, getting rid of it as the surface of a mirror would reflect sunlight."

Porter sneaked a quick look at Whiteside. The general had stiffened in his chair and wore a slightly slack-jawed appearance.

Allen sighed. "We also have some reason to believe," he said, "and I can't go into this as closely as I would like, for it can't be explained in layman terms—but we have reason to believe that the skin's composition is such that it can change gravitational flux and thus points to the possibility that the creatures can manipulate gravitational forces, that they can either be attracted or repulsed by gravitation. Which would explain, if true, how they are able to float an inch or two off the ground. It might also mean that gravitational control may be, at least partially, an explanation of how they travel through space. Locked in on a gravitational source in the direction in which they want to travel, they would move toward the source. Locked into another behind them, they could utilize it as a repulsor to push them away from that source."

Allen ceased talking and looked at each of the three in turn.

"Well, that's it," he said. "It sounds insane and I keep telling myself it has to be insane. Aliens, we said. And these things are alien. What bothers me, what keeps me awake at night is this—if they are so alien in the physical sense, how alien are they mentally? What chance will we ever have of understanding them, what hope they will ever be able to understand us?"

"Perhaps the intellectual span is not as great as the physical span," said Porter. "They seem to have done a fairly good job so far in understanding us. Somehow they seem to have sensed a lot of things they should not do. They have fairly well kept within the basic rules of human conduct."

"I hope you're right," said Allen. "I sincerely hope you are."

He spoke to the President. "In a couple of weeks, we may know more. We may find that some of our present thinking is wrong. We may have to modify some of our theories. Or we may come across some new and significant data. For the present, I have told you basically all I know. Of course, it could be elaborated upon endlessly, but there's no point in doing that now."

He rose from his chair, hesitated for a moment.

"There is one other thing," he said. "Interesting, but probably not too significant. But it does throw some further light on the visitors. You have heard of 101, of course."

The President nodded. "The first of the visitors to land at Lone Pine. I understand it's down in Iowa now."

"That is right," said Allen. "It is guarding a field

the farmer had just finished plowing. The farmer claims that it passed back and forth over the field as if it were planting something. When anyone approaches, it drives them off. One of our observers, however, managed to sneak up to the edge of the field without being driven off. He found that the visitor had planted pine seeds. Earlier we had been somewhat puzzled by the fact that the debris which was rejected by the visitors after they cut the trees contained virtually no pine seeds. Now we know why. The visitors winnow out the seeds and intend to plant them."

"It will take a long time to grow a new crop of pines from scratch," said the President. "101 may have its work cut out for it guarding its planting."

"Perhaps not," said Allen. "Our observer found that a number of the seeds had sprouted. Forestry experts tell us that such sprouting could not be expected this quickly. Our guess is that 101 treated the seeds in some way to speed up the sprouting process, probably to speed up the growth once they have started."

"Which poses another problem for us," said Whiteside. "Hundreds, if not thousands, of visitors taking over fields, planting them and then driving off the rightful owners. The farmers will be up in arms about that."

"To start with," said the President, "I had a queasy feeling about the visitors, a sort of gone-in-the-gut reaction. I think part of this, maybe all of it, was due to the fact that essentially I am a pure and simple political animal. I have political nerve endings. I twitch at every threat. I still realize that this business of the visitors, if I make one wrong move, could kill me politically. But, gradually, I have come to the belief that the two of us, we and the visitors, can get along together. They seem to think very much like us. If we could only communicate with them, I'm sure a solid understanding could be reached. The fact that 101 planted pine seeds re-enforces my thinking. The planting of a crop attests to a feeling for agriculture and the conservation of resources. In this way, too, their thinking parallels ours."

Allen started to speak, then hesitated.

"You were about to say something," said the President.

"That's right," said Allen. "I wondered if I should, but I guess there's no reason that I shouldn't. Perhaps of little significance, but to me intriguing. You remember when that first visitor came down at Lone Pine it landed on a car and crushed it."

"Yes, I do remember. There was no one in it, luckily. We wondered what became of the owner, why he, or she, never came forward."

"Exactly," said Allen. "We hauled in the car, if you recall."

"Yes, I do," said the President.

"Well, now we know. From the license plate. The owner is a young forestry student at the University of Minnesota. His name is Jerry Conklin. A few days after the incident, he came back to Minneapolis. So far as we can learn, he never told anyone about his car being totalled. He has not filed an insurance claim for the loss of the car. For a time, apparently, he acted fairly normally, but now that we have learned who he is, he has disappeared. The FBI is looking for him."

"What do you expect to learn when you find him?" Whiteside asked.

"I don't really know. You have to admit, however, that his reaction has been strange. There must be some reason he told no one what happened. And it's strange that he has not filed an insurance claim. He has not even made an inquiry as to who hauled away his car. I can't get rid of the feeling that he may know something that could be helpful to us."

"When you find him," said the President, "and I suppose you will, go easy on him. From where I sit he's committed no crime except to keep his mouth shut."

41. MINNEAPOLIS

The phone was ringing when Kathy came into her apartment.

She answered it, and then, "Jerry, where are you? You sound excited—or upset. I can't tell which. What is going on?"

"I've been trying to reach you," he said. "I called your apartment and your office. The office told me you were at Lone Pine and I tried Lone Pine. You had already left."

"I just got back," she said. "Just this minute. From the airport. Are you in town? You don't sound as if you're in town. Your voice is faint and there is noise on the line."

"I'm in Iowa. At a place called Dick's Landing. It's on the Mississippi, opposite what is called the Winnishiek Bottoms. You ever heard of that?"

"Not Dick's Landing. The Winnishiek, vaguely. I have heard it mentioned. What in the world . . ."

"Kathy, I went to that farm in Iowa. I talked with 101. It took me in again . . ."

"It remembered you?"

"I think so. We didn't really talk. It told me, it showed me. I got the impression that what it told me is important. But whether it is important to us or to 101 and the other visitors, I can't be sure."

"But Dick's Landing? And the Winnishiek?"

"It told me a location. Showed me where to go. I don't know what's here. Well, actually, I do—I know at least part of it. There's a place called Goose Island. Three of the visitors are there. But I don't know why it's important. I only know it is. That is what 101 impressed upon me. That I must go there. I want you with me, Kathy. If there is something important, you should be in on it from the first. You've been with this visitor story from the first."

"O.K.," said Kathy, "as fast as I can. I'll start out right now. Give me directions. Tell me how to get to this Dick's Landing. I'll be there in a few hours."

42. MINNEAPOLIS

For days, they had kept their vigil, but now the vigil ended. The group of Lovers who, on the day the visitor had landed on the airstrip, had fought their way onto the field, stood in stricken silence and watched the visitor slowly lift off the runway and sail away into the sky.

"We failed," said one of them, a gaunt young man with stringy hair and an ascetic face.

"We did not fail," said the willowy girl who stood beside him. "It felt our love. I know it felt our love."

"But it made no sign. It did not take us up. It took others up . . ."

An airport guard, one of the many who manned the barricades that had been thrown around the visitor, said, to no one in particular, "Let's break it up. It's ended now. Why don't you all go home."

"Because we are already home," said the youth with the ascetic face. "The Earth is home. The universe is home."

"I can't understand these kids," said the guard to a fellow guard. "Can you understand them? Christ, they been here for days, just hunkering down with sappy expressions on their faces."

"No," said the other guard. "I don't understand them. I never even tried to."

"Now let's clear out," said the first guard to the band of Lovers. "The show is over, folks. There's nothing left for you."

The crowd began breaking up, slowly drifting off the field.

"They should never have let them in," said the

second guard. "It was against all rules. Someone could have gotten killed."

"There wasn't any danger," said the first guard. "The strip was closed. If they hadn't been let in, we'd have had a running fight that might have gone on for days to keep them out of here. The commission thought this was the better way. I'll say this much for the kids; once they were let out here, they behaved themselves. They never caused any trouble."

The second guard said, "They were loving it. They were showing it their love. Did you ever hear such goddamn foolishness?"

The other guard grunted in disgust.

By this time, the visitor was a small speck in the western sky.

In the *Tribune* newsroom, Gold put the phone back in the cradle. He said to Garrison, "The one on Highway 12 is gone, too. Lifted off and left about the same time as the one at the airport."

"Almost as if there were some sort of signal, telling them to go," said Garrison. "I wonder what they're up to."

"This is the second phase," said Gold.

"What do you mean—the second phase?"

"Well, the first phase was when they came and looked us over. They've finished with that. Now they're doing something else."

"How do you reach that conclusion?"

"I don't know, Johnny. I'm just guessing."

"Maybe they are finished with what they came to do. They may be going into space, forming up again, getting set to go off someplace else. This may be the last we will see of them."

Hal Russell, the wire editor, came shuffling up the room. He stopped at the city desk. "A story just came in on the wires," he said. "They're leaving everywhere. It's not only here."

Garrison said to Gold, "Why don't you phone Lone Pine. Find out what's happening there."

Gold picked up the phone and began dialing.

Garrison asked Russell, "Anything else? Any hints? Any speculation?"

"Nothing," said Russell. "Just that they are leaving. Those that have been around for days are leaving."

"Damn!" said Garrison. "How do you handle such a story? There's a story here. Someone has to dig it out and I'd like it to be us. I know there is a story, but how can it be gotten at?"

"Jay and Kathy," said Russell. "They're the ones who know the most about the visitors. They may have some suggestions."

"Kathy's not here," said Garrison. "She's off on some wild goose chase. Phoned me last night. Said she was onto something that might be big. Wouldn't tell me what it was. Said I'd have to trust her. Al will be pissed off. He practically ordered me to get her back from Lone Pine. And here she's gone again."

He looked around the city room. "Where the hell is Jay?" he asked. "He's not at his desk. Is there anyone who might know where he is? How about you, Annie?"

The city desk secretary shook her head. "He's not signed out. I don't know where he is."

"Maybe he's in the can," said Russell.

Gold hung up the phone and said, "The visitors at Lone Pine have disappeared, too. Some of the youngsters are still there, chomping at the bales."

"What does Norton think of it?" asked Garrison.

"I didn't talk with Norton. I talked with Stiffy. He's holding down the office. Norton is out of town. Took off this morning for a canoe trip into the primitive area."

43. WASHINGTON, D.C.

Porter waited for the members of the press to get comfortably settled, then he said, "I have no statement to make. I imagine that the most of you know that the visitors have disappeared. I would suspect that most of your questions will be aimed in that direction. I'll answer as I can, but I doubt I can be helpful."

"Mr. Porter," said the New York *Times*, "one possible answer that must have occurred to almost everyone is that our visitors have gone back into space, probably preparatory to proceeding somewhere else. Can you give us any indication if this might be true?"

"Mr. Smith, I can't," said Porter. "The same thought occurred to us. NASA is watching for any indication. Our space station is on the alert and so, I suppose, is the Soviet station. So far there is no word. But we must realize there is a large area up there to cover. The only possibility of seeing anything would be if the visitors formed into another mass, as was the case when they came to Earth."

"If the Soviet station saw something, would they communicate the information to us?"

"I can't be sure, of course. I rather think they would."

"Dave," said the Washington *Post*, "this may sound like a loaded question and I hope that you . . ."

"The *Post*," said Porter, "never asks a loaded question."

An outburst of laughter drowned out the *Post*. Porter lifted a hand for silence.

"Go ahead," he said. "I'll stipulate, in advance, that it is not a loaded question."

"What I wanted to ask," said the *Post*, "is this: I

think it is no secret that the appearance of the visitors posed some rather bothersome problems, political and otherwise, for the administration. Can you tell me if their disappearance might be of some relief to you?"

"I was wrong," said Porter. "This is a loaded question. However, I'll try to answer it with whatever honesty I can muster. It seems to me that we may be premature in assuming that the disappearance means we've seen the last of the visitors. There is a possibility they have only shifted their bases of operation to more remote areas. As to whether the administration would heave a sigh of relief at their going, the answer must be iffy. I can't deny the visitors gave us some occasion for worry. We had a problem dumped in our lap that no one had ever faced before. There was no precedent to serve as a guide for us in our dealing with them. We had some difficulty in assessing their impact on the various segments of the population. At times, I don't mind telling you, we were completely baffled. But I think that, over all, the situation was handled not too badly.

"This is one side of my two-part response. The second part is that after some days of dealing with the problem, we had fairly well come to the conclusion that our people could get along with the visitors and that there might be some benefit derived from them. I, personally, will feel rather strongly, if indeed the visitors are gone, that we are the poorer for their going. Perhaps there was much we might have learned from them."

"You say there was much we might have learned from them," said the Kansas City *Star*. "Would you care to amplify on that?"

"Only to point out," said Porter, "that in them we were in contact with an alien race from which we might have learned a new technology, might have gained some fresh perspective, might have learned of principles and ways of thought of which we, to this point, have been ignorant."

"Can you be more specific? Dr. Allen, for some days now, has been working on the dead visitor. Might not he have come up with some specific information that could be useful to us?"

"Nothing about which we can be certain," said Porter. "I told you a few days ago that the creature's structure is based on cellulose, but in a form with which we are unfamiliar, and with which, more than likely, we'll remain unfamiliar for some time. One possibility is that if we can learn the secret of this alien cellulose, the procedure by which the cellulose is changed into the bodies of the visitors, we may be able to utilize cellulose as a substitute for many of our decreasing non-renewable resources."

"Back there a ways," said the Chicago *Tribune*, "you suggested the visitors might be changing their bases to more remote areas. By that, do you mean they are hiding out?"

"I didn't say that, Harry, and you know I didn't."

"But the implication appeared to be there. Why would you think they might be hiding out?"

"First of all, I didn't say they were hiding out. If they should be, my answer is that I have no idea."

"Mr. Porter," said the New York *Times*, "it would seem, on the surface at least, that it would be reasonable to assume the visitors may be putting a second phase of their operation into effect. First they came and spent some time observing us. Now they have made another move, disappearing, perhaps as a prelude to launching another . . ."

"Mr. Smith, you are asking me to speculate upon a speculation," said Porter, "and the only answer I can have to that is that I have no reaction. It is true that your speculation does seem to have some validity—as you say, on the surface at least. But I have no kind of information that would justify an answer."

"Thank you, sir," said the *Times*. "I thought it was a question that should be asked."

"I am glad you asked it," Porter told him.

"Dave, I think we should proceed with this further," said the Milwaukee *Journal*. "I think the point raised by the *Times* is a good one. I was about to ask a similar question. These things have looked us over. They may have a much better idea of what makes us tick than we can know, perhaps enough information to determine what their next step should be."

"I did not question the validity of the query, as Mr. Smith well knows," said Porter. "I agree that it is a consideration we should hold in mind. But with no information that would justify a response to it, I don't think I should try to answer it. There is only one objection to the viewpoint that I can think of. It makes it seem that the visitors are plotting against us, that they may have some hostile motive and are developing strategy to carry it out. So far, they have not been hostile."

"But we can't know what their motives may be."

"That is right. We cannot know their motives."

"Your phrase 'more remote regions' intrigues me," said the Los Angeles Times. "Mr. Secretary, are there all that many remote regions left in the United States?"

"I'm sorry now that I employed that phraseology," said Porter. "I think all of you are making too much of it. What I had in mind was that the visitors have disappeared from the more densely populated areas. They may begin to appear elsewhere, but, if so, we have no word of it. As to your question about remote areas, I should say there are still a lot of them. Vast forest regions still exist in New England, in northern Minnesota, Wisconsin and Michigan. There are similar areas in other states as well. In mountainous regions, particularly in the Rockies, there are a number of remote areas, which also is true of the southwestern deserts."

"It seems to me that you are convinced they've not actually disappeared, that they've not gone back to space," said the Washington Post. "Why do you seem so convinced of this?"

"I wasn't aware that my personal reaction was showing through so clearly," said Porter. "This is not an official position and if you use it, I hope you will make it clear it is not. My own thinking is that the visitors would be unlikely this soon to leave a planet where they've found the natural resource they apparently were seeking. It is probable that not too many planets would be found where they could discover plant life that would produce as much cellulose as our forests do."

"So, having found it, you think they would stick around for a while."

"That is my thinking, not necessarily the administration's thinking."

"Throughout this entire visitor situation," said the INS, "the administration has maintained what I think can be described as a hopeful, perhaps even an optimistic, mood. There must have been many trying times for you, but still you always seem to have struck that note of optimism. Can you tell me if the thinking is as optimistic as it seems?"

"What you are trying to ask," said Porter, "is whether the optimism you say you detected was merely a political optimism or was it real?"

"Thank you, Dave, for completing my question for me."

"I think," said Porter, "that under any circumstance, the tendency might have been to remain optimistic for purely political reasons. But I can tell you, without quibble, that a true feeling of optimism has existed. The visitors did not act in a hostile manner. It appeared to us that they were trying to determine how they should act toward us. Almost never did they violate any of our basic rules of conduct. It seemed that they were trying to be decent. I think the feeling existed in the White House that they would not willingly do anything to harm us. It is possible, of course, that they might harm us unwittingly."

"You seem to be saying you think that would be unlikely."

"Yes," said Porter, "I do think it would be unlikely."

44. IOWA

For more than half an hour, they had fought their way through a water-logged jungle—trees, vines and brush. The ground was uneven and treacherous underfoot, mounds and ridges of semi-solid ground separating narrow tunnels of open water and small stretches of swamp. There was, as yet, no sign of the grassy prairie, slightly elevated above the outer rim of the island, that Jimmy Quinn had told them they would find once they had beat their way through the encircling timber area.

Occasionally, when the towering trees thinned out slightly, they caught a glimpse of one or two of the visitors that apparently were resting in the grassy interior. They had first seen them coming down the river, once Goose Island had come into view.

"They are still there," Quinn had said. "I thought they might have left. There was something on the radio this morning about the visitors all leaving."

Finally, they seemed to be traveling up a slight incline. The going became easier. There were no longer any of the swampy areas and the underbrush was thinning out, although the trees grew as heavily as ever.

"I think we're almost there," said Jerry.

And, finally, they were there. They came out of the trees and before them lay the vast extent of grassland. As they came out into the open, both of them stopped abruptly, staring in wonderment.

The three visitors sat in the clearing, at some distance from one another, but it was not the visitors that riveted their attention.

Interspersed between the visitors, standing in neat, straight rows, were cars, or what appeared to be cars. They were shaped like cars. They had doors and seats and steering wheels and in the front of each of them a single, flaring headlight. But they had no running gear.

"Cars," said Kathy. "Jerry, those are cars but they haven't any wheels."

"Whatever they are," said Jerry, "they are still making them, or building them, or budding them, or whatever you may call it."

The sight of the long straight rows of cars had so fastened Kathy's attention that she had paid but slight attention to the visitors. But now, when she looked, she saw that all three were in the process of budding, although the buds were not the shapes that they had been when the visitors had been producing young. Rather the buds were elongated and lumpy.

A bud burst open on the visitor that was nearest them and from it began to emerge one of the things that looked like a car. It gleamed wetly, but as she watched, the wetness dried, revealing a glossy yellow sheen.

"It's a yellow one," said Jerry. "Did you notice that the cars are of different colors. Reds and greens and grays—all the colors you could ask."

Slowly the yellow car emerged from the bud and finally dropped off. It came to rest, floating a few inches above the ground. Quickly, it swung about and scooted swiftly toward the nearest line of cars. It swung precisely into line and halted, stationing itself next to a green car. On the other side of the green car was a red one.

"How cute," said Kathy, delighted. "They come in every color."

"I was just telling you that," said Jerry, "but you didn't listen."

"Those can't be cars," said Kathy. "I know they look like cars, but they just can't be. What would the visitors want with cars?"

"I wouldn't know," said Jerry, "but they do look like

cars. Futuristic cars. Like the pipedream of a car designer who is intent on catching the public eye. They haven't any wheels, of course, but they don't need wheels; they float. These cars, if that is what they are, must operate on the same principle as the visitors themselves. They should because they are children of the visitors, but in a somewhat different shape."

"Why should they be budding children in the shape of cars? Why would they want youngsters in the shape of cars?"

"Maybe," said Jerry, "because they are really cars and are meant for us."

"For us?"

"Think, Kathy. Think about it. The visitors came here and found what they were looking for. They found trees from which they could process cellulose. It may be that these cars are payment for the trees."

"That's ridiculous," said Kathy. "Why pay us anything? They came and found the trees and took them. They could just keep on taking them. And for us, you said. We don't need this many cars. We couldn't use them in a lifetime. There must be a hundred of them, maybe more than that."

"Not just for us. Not just for you and me. For the people of the country."

"They couldn't make enough of them."

"I think they could. There are just three visitors here. They have been here for less than a week. In that time, they've budded more than a hundred cars. Take a thousand visitors, or ten thousand visitors, give them six months . . ."

"I suppose you're right," said Kathy. "They could make a lot of cars. Come to think of it, 101 told you to come here. She knew what you'd find. She wanted you to find them."

"Probably not 101 alone," said Jerry. "The visitors wanted us to find them. 101 was just the spokesman. Each one of these things, more than likely, knows what the rest of them are doing. A sort of hive communication. When 101 first landed, she sent out signals to the others. They can talk among themselves."

"You think the visitors want us to spread the word about the cars."

"We are being used," said Jerry. "That must be it, we are being used. We are the PR people for the visitors. We may be a test team as well. I don't know. Maybe they want us to see if the cars can be operated in a satisfactory way. They can't be sure, perhaps. They know a lot about us, but maybe they aren't sure that they know enough. When a car manufacturer designs a new model, the model must be tested . . ."

"And they picked you because you are a special person to them," Kathy said. "You were the first to be inside one of them, to communicate with them. Maybe the only person. These stories of other people taken up may be only . . ."

"101 shook hands with you. You're forgetting that."

"Yes, but how could 101 be sure I'd be here with you? How could she know you'd phone me?"

"Maybe she didn't. Maybe . . ."

"Maybe what?"

"Kathy, these things could be smarter than we possibly could guess. They could read us like a book."

"Suddenly," said Kathy, "I feel all shivery inside. I've never been afraid of them before, but now I am afraid. I have the feeling it could be a trap. Some sort of trap that we are falling into, not even knowing we are falling into it."

"A trap, perhaps," said Jerry, "and, yet, they are making cars for us. Cars that can float, that possibly can fly. No need of roads; they can go anywhere. They'll need no gasoline. They may last forever, never need repair. Giving them to us as payment for the trees. As payment for the cellulose that will allow them to have young again, averting racial death. If you were facing racial extinction, wouldn't you make cars—or anything they wanted—for the race that saved you?"

"You're way ahead of me," said Kathy. "I can't accept the thought that these are actually cars and that they are being made for us. You talk as if you're sure. How can you be so sure?"

"Maybe from something that was told me by 101.

Something I didn't know at the time, but am realizing now. It makes sense, I tell you. It is reasonable. They have had a look at us. They have seen what it is we want. They read us, Kathy. They know the kind of things we are. They know how to buy us. They know what we'll sell our souls for and . . ."

"You sound bitter, Jerry."

"Not bitter. Just realizing what is happening. And that we can't stop it. Even if we turned around and walked away, we couldn't stop it. Someone else would find the cars. And maybe it's right that the cars should be found. Maybe in the end it will work out right. But they're too smart for us. The human race is a Yankee trader and we have met our match."

"We have stood here, talking," Kathy said. "We've tried to talk ourselves into believing a sort of fairy tale. All we've done is talk. I still can't think that they are cars. I can't be sure they're cars."

"Let's go," said Jerry, "and see if they really are."

45. MINNEAPOLIS

It was Gold's day off and Jay, coming back to the newsroom from a late lunch, stopped by the city desk and sat down in Gold's chair. Garrison was hunched over his desk, idly making doodles on a sheet of copy paper. Annie sat in her corner. She had finished a sandwich she had brought as her lunch and now was peeling an orange, making an artistic job of it.

"Anything happening?" Jay asked the city editor.

Garrison shook his head. "Nothing here. Nothing anywhere else, I guess. Hal tells me the wires are coming up empty, so far as the visitors are concerned. There have been reported sightings in Texas and Montana, but they've not been confirmed."

"We wait," said Jay. "That is all we can do. We did all we could. We phoned dozens of people in the state. Please let us know if you hear anything. Editors of weekly papers, sheriffs, mayors, businessmen, friends of ours. If they hear anything, they will let us know."

"I'm trying to think," said Garrison. "There must have been more that we could have done."

"It's not your problem, Johnny. Not yours alone."

"I know, but dammit, I would like to be the one who found the answer. Some little clue as to where the visitors may have gone."

"And why they went."

"Yes, I know. But that can come later. First, we have to find them. Something to put out on page one. My guess would be northern Minnesota, up in the wilderness area. They may be hiding out there . . ."

"Or Canada. Or the Pacific Northwest," said Jay.

"There is a lot of wild country they could be holing up in."

The city desk phone rang. Annie put down the orange and picked up the receiver.

"It's for you, Johnny," she said. "It's Kathy. She's on three."

Garrison clawed for the phone, signaling Jay to pick up Gold's phone.

"Kathy, where the hell are you? What you got?"

"I'm in Iowa," Kathy said. "Place called Dick's Landing. On the Mississippi. I'm with Jerry."

"Jerry?"

"Yes, you remember. The big oaf I was going to go to the concert with. That time you bought the tickets."

"Yes, I remember. What's all this got to do with you being down in Iowa?"

"We found three of the visitors, Johnny. On Goose Island . . ."

"To hell with the rest of it. The visitors. What about the visitors? What are they doing?"

"They are making cars." ·

·"Kathy. Don't kid me. Don't make any jokes. I've — had a hell of a day so far. I can't stand any more."

"They are making cars. We have two of them. We flew them from the island. I have a yellow one and Jerry has a red one. They're easy to handle . . ."

"You said flew. You flew a car?"

"You can fly them. They haven't any wheels. They float, like the visitors float. They're not hard to operate, once you get the hang of it. It took the two of us no more than an hour or so to find out how to run them. There are things you push. Like having a plane. And there is no danger. If you're about to run into something, they veer off. Without you doing anything, they veer off . . ."

"Kathy," said Garrison, icily, "tell me the truth, for Christ's sake. You really have these cars?"

Jay spoke into the phone. "Kathy, this is Jay. I'm on the line with Johnny. This is no joke, is it? You really have the cars?"

"You're damned right we have them."

Garrison said, "Kathy, get hold of yourself. You're not making sense. What are they making cars for?"

"We don't really know," said Kathy. "We can't be sure, that is. We think they may be making them as payment for the trees they took. But we don't really know; it's only what we think. It seemed to be all right with them when we flew off with the two we have."

"And now that you have them . . ."

"We'll be coming back. Be there in three or four hours. Maybe faster. We don't know how fast these things can go. We'll fly them. Not bother with the roads. We'll follow the river north."

"Oh, Jesus, Kathy, this can't be right. Making cars, you say . . ."

"Well, I don't know if you can really call them cars . . ."

"Just a minute, Kathy," said Jay. "Hang on for a minute."

He took down the receiver and cupped the mouthpiece, looking across the desk at Garrison.

"Johnny," he said, "she's a good reporter. A damn fine reporter."

Garrison cupped his phone. "I know, but, Christ, I can't go along with this. What if it turned out wrong?"

"It's five hours to press time. She'll be here by then. She can write her story. We can get pictures of the cars. We can get it all nailed down."

Garrison nodded. He uncupped the phone and spoke into it. "All right, Kathy, we'll be waiting for you. We won't do a thing until you get here. We'll have photographers. Can you land those things on top of the building, on the roof?"

"I don't know. I would think we could. They handle easy."

Jay spoke into the phone. "Kathy, how are these cars powered? Do you need gasoline? What do you need?"

"Nothing," Kathy told him. "The visitors bud them. They are powered in the same way the visitors are powered, however that may be. Jerry thinks they are actually visitors, but in the shape of cars. There are a hundred of the cars, maybe more. We took only two. They bud them fast. The three visitors have been on the island only a week. Three of them made more than a hundred cars in only a week, probably less than a week."

"All right," said Garrison. "We'll sit on it. We'll keep it quiet. So far the story is ours exclusively. We'll see it stays that way. Be careful. Don't take any chances. We want you here in one piece."

"I'll be seeing you," said Kathy.

Garrison cradled the phone and looked at Jay.

"What do you think?" he asked.

"I think we've just bought the first iron hatchet to replace our stone tomahawk."

Garrison mumbled something under his breath, then said, "Yes, I remember you talking about that. We should have run the story when you brought it up."

"I can still write it."

"No," said Garrison. "Hell, no, everyone will be writing that story now. Now there is another story to write. What happens to the auto industry if the visitors keep on making their cars and giving them away in payment for the trees—enough of them for everyone in the country? What happens to all the people who lose their jobs in the Detroit factories and in other plants? What happens to the oil industry when no one needs to buy gasoline for their cars? What happens to the auto service and maintenance people, all the service stations and the people pumping gas? What happens when we don't need to build roads any more? What happens to the finance companies that live on car payment plans? And what happens when the visitors, once they have made enough cars to give everyone a car, turn to making refrigerators and stoves and furnaces and air conditioners? How will the states register the new cars, the free cars? How will they regulate them? How do they go about taxing them? And the hell of it is that the visitors are not doing this out of animosity. They have no animosity toward us. All they have is gratitude. If they had only worked with the government, gone through governmental channels . . ."

"More than likely," said Jay, "they don't even realize there are governments. They may not know what a government is. They probably have no political concept. They have looked us over and found out how best they can pay us for the trees. And they looked at people and not at governments. They probably are unaware of what they are doing to us, not knowing anything about the complex economic structure we have built. The only economic system they may know is simple barter. You give me something; I'll give you something in return. And the hell of it is that the people will buy it. Once the people know about the free cars, once they start getting their hands on them, no one, in government or out, will dare to lift a finger, say a word, against the visitors."

"And that's why they're hiding out," said Garrison. "So they can make cars without interference. Hiding themselves so hordes of people can't come charging in to pick out a car. Thousands of them out there making cars. How long do you think it will take them to make enough of them?"

"I wouldn't know," said Jay. "I'm not even sure you're right, but the guess is good. I hope to God it's only cars. We probably can weather the situation if cars is all they make."

46. WASHINGTON, D.C.

"Dave," asked the President, "can we be absolutely certain the news reports are right? It all sounds so fanciful. Almost beyond belief. What I mean . . . a few facts blown out of context."

"I had the same reservation," said Porter, "when the first report came on the wires. So I went to the source. Called the *Tribune* in Minneapolis and talked to the city editor. Man by the name of Garrison. I felt a little foolish doing that, almost as if I were questioning the integrity of the paper. But I felt I had to do it. Garrison was quite decent . . ."

"And the reports are correct?"

"Basically, yes. Garrison told me he couldn't believe it himself to start with. Not until the two cars landed. Said that after his reporter's phone call, he sat there in a daze, saying over and over to himself there was something wrong, that he had misunderstood what the reporter had said, that there had to be some foul-up."

"But now he knows. Now he's sure?"

"Now he knows. He has the cars. He has pictures of them."

"Have you seen the pictures?"

"It was less than half an hour ago the *Tribune* went to press. The story caught everyone, the news services included, by surprise. It would take a while to get the photos from the *Tribune*, a while longer to transmit them. They should be coming in soon."

"But cars," said the President. "Why, for Christ's sake, cars? Why not something really fanciful? Why

233

not diamond necklaces? cases of champagne? fur coats?"

"The visitors are good observers, sir. They have been watching us for days . . ."

"And they saw a lot of cars. Almost everyone has one. Those who don't have one want one. Those who have an old car want a new one. Old cars. Beaten-up cars. Wearing out cars. Accidents on the road. People killed and cars demolished. The visitors saw all this. So they gave us cars that never would wear out, that need no gasoline, that need no roads, that can never crash because they veer off when there is the danger of a crash, no maintenance, no repairs, no paint job . . ."

"We can't be sure of that, sir. That's a speculation."

"A car for everyone?"

"We can't be sure of that, either. That's what Garrison thinks. That's what his reporter thinks. As I understand, however, the *Tribune* story is very careful not to say that, although the implication's there."

"It can wreck us, Dave. Whether there is a car for everyone or not, it can blow the economy to hell. Because the implication, as you say, is there. I'm thinking of calling a moratorium, a financial holiday. Shutting down the stock market, the banks, all financial institutions, no financial transactions of any kind at all. What do you think?"

"It would give us time. That might be all it would give us. And a few days only. You couldn't make it stick for more than just a few days."

"If the market opens tomorrow morning . . ."

"You're right. Something has to be done. You'd better talk to the attorney general, the Federal Reserve. Probably some other people."

"Time might be all that it would give us," said the President. "I agree with that. But we need some time. We need some elbow room. Give people a chance to think things over. A chance for us to talk with people. I told you the other day I felt there was no reason for panic. Goddammit, Dave, I'm close to panic now."

"You don't look it."

"Panic is something we can't afford. Not visible panic. Politics give you a long training in the control of personal panic. Right now my gut is jumping, but I can't let it show. They'll be coming out of the woodwork to crucify us. Congress, the press, business interests, labor leaders, everyone. All of them claiming we should have foreseen this situation, should have been doing something to head it off."

"The country will live through it, sir."

"The country, but not me. It does beat hell how things turn out. Up until now, I figured I had it made for another term."

"You still may have."

"It would call for a miracle."

"All right. We'll carpenter up a miracle."

"I don't think so, Dave. Not that we won't try. We'll have to see what happens. Allen and Whiteside will be joining us. Grace is trying to locate Hammond. I want his input. A sound man, Hammond. He can handle the mechanics of the financial holiday. We'll have to have Marcus over later. There'll be others coming in. God knows, I need all the advice that I can get. I want you to hang in close."

"After a while, I'll have to have a briefing. The boys are already pounding on the door."

"Hold up for a while," said the President. "Maybe in a couple of hours, we'll have something to give them. Go out now, empty, and they'll maul you to death."

"They'll maul me, anyhow. But it's a good idea to wait a while. I'm not looking forward to it."

The box on the President's desk beeped. When he answered, Grace said, "General Whiteside and Dr. Allen are here."

"Show them in," said the President.

The two came into the room and were waved to chairs.

"You've heard?" asked the President. "It was too involved to try to tell you when I spoke to you."

They nodded.

"Car radio," said Allen.

"TV," said the general. "I turned it on after you phoned."

"Steve, what do you think of it?" asked the President. "There seems to be no question the visitors are making cars. What kind of cars would they be?"

"As I understand it," said the science advisor, "they are budding them. They bud their young, forming them in the images of themselves. I suppose there's nothing to stop them from budding in the image of cars."

"Some of them ate some cars," said Whiteside. "In St. Louis, I believe."

"I'm not too sure that has anything to do with it," said Allen. "Certainly, they probably could analyze the cars once they ingested them, but the cars they are budding apparently are similar only in external features to our manufactured cars."

"Then why did they snap up the cars in St. Louis?" asked the general.

"I wouldn't know," said Allen. "All I know is that the cars the visitors are budding are visitors. Not actually cars at all, but visitors in the shape of cars, apparently capable of being used as cars. They are biological, not mechanical vehicles."

"The reporter who found the cars," said the President, "seems to think, at least she suggests, the cars are being budded out of gratitude. A free-will offering to the people of the planet that supplies their cellulose."

"About that I wouldn't know," said Allen. "You are talking about how these damn things think. On that I couldn't ever hazard a guess. We've been studying the one that died for days and we have not even the slightest idea of its anatomy, of how it manages to live and function on the physical level, let alone the mental. The situation is analogous to a medieval man trying to understand how and why a sophisticated computer works. Not one single organ that can be compared to a human organ. We are completely baffled. I had hoped we might be able to determine what caused the creature's death. In this we have failed. Until we find how the organism functions, there's no chance of pinning down the cause of death, or of anything else, for that matter."

"You'd say, then," said the President, "there is no chance to communicate with them. If we could somehow talk with them, even in sign language or something, or . . ."

"Not a chance," said Allen. "No chance at all."

"What you are saying," said Whiteside, "is that we have to sit and take it. This car business. Detroit down the drain. Detroit and a lot of other places. The military has contracts . . ."

"If the visitors had only come to us," said the President. "If they only would have come and tried to let us know what they intended . . ."

"By us, you mean the government," said Allen.

The President nodded.

"What everyone fails to realize," said Allen, "is the true, utter alienness of these creatures. They are more alien than can possibly be conceived. I figure them for a hive organism, what one knows or sees or feels all the rest of them know as well. Such a society would have no need of a government. They would never have thought of it. They wouldn't know what a government was, because there never was a need for them to develop the governmental concept."

"We have to do something," said the general. "We have to protect ourselves. We need to take some action."

"Forget what you are thinking," said the President. "You told me, in this office, a few days ago, the visitors could withstand anything short of a nuclear blast. That was your calculation, you said. We can't use nukes . . ."

Allen straightened in his chair. "Then there was a weapons test," he said. "I kept hearing about it, rumors about it. But, surely, I thought, if there had been one, I would have been informed. Tell me, why wasn't I informed? Your findings might have thrown some light . . ."

"Because it was none of your damned business," said the general. "Because it's classified."

"Even so," said Allen, "it might have been important and you should have . . ."

"Gentlemen, please," said the President. "I apologize for the slip of the tongue. It's all my fault." He looked at Allen. "You never heard it, of course," he said.

"No, Mr. President," said Allen, "I never heard a word that was said."

"The fact remains," said the President, "that we can't use nukes . . ."

"If we could get all the visitors herded together," said the general, "then, maybe . . ."

"But we can't do that," said the President. "We don't even know where they are—or, at least, not the most of them. Probably scattered all over the country. Hiding, making cars . . ."

"Sir, you can't be sure of that."

"Well, it's a logical assumption," said the President. "It's understandable. They couldn't sit out in plain sight, making cars. The people, avid to get cars, would rush in and swamp them."

"Maybe," said Whiteside, grasping for hope, "they may run out of trees. They must have to eat a lot of trees to make cars."

"That would be unlikely," said Allen. "There are a lot of trees in North America. And should they begin running short of them, there still would be the rest of the world, including the equatorial jungles. And don't forget they'll be growing trees to replace those they eat. Number 101 planted the field in Iowa."

"That's another thing that worries me," said the President. "If they start using too much farmland to grow trees we might run into a food shortage. I know we have large amounts of wheat in storage, but that would be soon used up."

"The danger there would be," said Allen, "that if there were a food shortage, the visitors might start making food. Our people, in effect, would be placed on a dole system."

"While all this is interesting," said the President, "and perhaps even pertinent, it is getting us nowhere.

What we should be talking about is what we should be doing now."

"I just now thought of something," said Porter. "When I talked with Garrison, he mentioned a name. Jerry Conklin, I believe. Said Conklin was the one who really was the first to learn about the cars, but that he objected to being identified, so his name was not mentioned in the story. It seems to me I've heard that name before. It seems to ring a bell."

Allen came to rigid attention. "Of course, it does," he said. "That's the man whose car was crushed when the first visitor landed at Lone Pine. The one that disappeared when we tried to find him. And here he pops up again. This strikes me as rather strange."

"Perhaps we should bring him in and have a talk with him," said Whiteside. "It's just possible this young fellow knows some things he should be telling . . ."

"Wait a minute," said Allen. "We found out something else. Conklin is a friend, apparently a close friend, of a reporter for the *Tribune*. Kathy, I think was the first name."

"Kathy Foster," said Porter. "She was the one who found the cars, who wrote the story."

"Maybe we ought to have them both in," said Whiteside. "Ask the FBI to pick them up."

The President shook his head. "Not the FBI," he said. "We'll act civilized about it. We'll invite them as White House guests. We'll send a plane to pick them up."

"But, sir," the general protested, "this man has disappeared before; he could disappear again."

"We'll take our chances on that," said the President. "Dave, will you make the call?"

"Gladly," Porter said.

47. MINNEAPOLIS

A copy aide, bent sidewise under a heavy load of papers clutched beneath one arm, tossed a copy on Garrison's desk, then hurried on.

Garrison picked up the paper, unfolded it, glanced swiftly across the front page. It was not greatly changed over the first edition, except for the new article that had not been written when the first edition had gone to press. He laid the paper down on his desk and admired the new story. It had a two-column head and an artist's sketch of the control panel of the visitor-car. He read the first paragraph:

If you should become one of the lucky ones to get your hands on a visitor-car early, there need be no concern about its operation. Handling it is a simple matter, easily understood. To start it, you depress the first button on the panel to your right. (The button marked A on the artist's sketch.) To cause it to move forward, depress button B. Speed is controlled by rotating the dial above the control panel, to the right for higher speeds, to the left for slower. All the way to the left to stop. Elevation is controlled by the lever to right of the panel. To rise, push it up; to descend, push it down. The buttons, the dial and the elevator lever are unmarked, nor are they graduated. You must get clear in mind what each control will do. Since there are few of them, the operation is not difficult . . .

Garrison let his eyes go down to the final paragraph:

It might be a good idea to clip this story and the diagram, putting the clipping in your billfold or purse. So that if, some morning, you find one of the cars parked in your driveway . . .

Garrison said to Gold, "This was a good idea. It relates the reader directly to the cars. It's something everyone will read. I'm glad you thought of it."

"Well, hell," said Gold, "it's time I began to earn my salary."

Hal Russell came loping down the aisle. He stopped before the city desk and said to Garrison, "More of the visitors have been spotted. One bunch in Idaho. Another of them in Maine."

"All making cars," said Gold.

"All making cars," said Russell.

"They're beginning to surface," said Garrison. "By this time tomorrow, we'll have spotted a fair number of them."

"Thing is," said Russell, "people are out there looking for them."

"They have reason now to look," said Gold. "A new car in everyone's garage."

"The next big story," said Garrison, "will be the delivery of the cars. People waking up and finding them parked in their driveways."

Gold shook his head. "It might not happen that way. Maybe drawings will be held to see who gets the cars. A sort of nationwide lottery. Or maybe they'll just be dumped out in a field or in vacant city lots and let the people fight for them. A car to the fastest and the meanest."

"You have some damn strange ideas," Garrison told him.

"For myself," said Gold, "I want a robin's-egg-blue car. My wife never let me have one. We've always had red cars. She likes red."

"Maybe there'll be enough of them," said Russell, "that you both can get one—you a blue one and your wife a red."

"In that case," said Gold, "we'll have two reds. She'd never let me have a blue. She thinks blue is sissy."

"Have either of you figured out the mathematics on this?" Garrison asked. "Could the visitors really make that many cars? Have we ever had a solid figure on how many of them there are?"

"I don't think a solid figure," Russell said. "Several thousand, I would guess. According to Kathy, three of them made more than a hundred cars in less than a week. Say it was a week. That's more than thirty cars a visitor. Put five thousand of them at it and that's a hundred and fifty thousand cars a week. The figure could be higher, but, even so, that's more than a quarter million cars a month."

"Our population is two hundred fifty million," said Gold.

"You wouldn't be making cars for everyone. A lot of those two hundred fifty million are babies and kids underage. You wouldn't give them cars. And remember all those baby visitors who are growing up. In another year, maybe in another six months, they could be making cars. As I remember it, the babies were pupped in fairly large litters. Say an average of ten babies to every visitor. In a year's time, say, several million cars a month."

"All right," said Garrison. "All right. I guess it could be done."

"And then," said Gold, "they'll start making beer. They could make beer a lot faster than cars. Say a case a week for every male adult. A case a week would be about right, I'd judge."

"Hot dogs," said Russell. "And pretzels. They'd have to make hot dogs and pretzels to go along with beer."

The phone rang. Annie answered it. "It's for you," she said to Garrison. "On two."

Garrison stabbed a button and picked up his phone. "Garrison. City desk."

"This is Porter at the White House," said the voice on the other end. "I called you earlier."

"Yes, I remember. What can I do for you?"

"Does Miss Foster happen to be around?"

"I'll look and see."

He rose, with the phone in hand, located Kathy at her desk. He waved the phone above his head. "Kathy," he bawled. "A call for you on two."

48. WILDERNESS AREA

Norton steadied the canoe with choppy paddle strokes, staring at what the bend in the river had revealed. There, straight ahead of him, five masses of square blackness loomed above the deep green of the pines.

Visitors, he told himself. What would visitors be doing here, deep in the wilderness? Although, once he thought of it, he realized it might not be strange at all. More than likely many of the big black boxes had landed in areas where they would not readily be found.

He chuckled to himself and dipped the paddle deep, driving the canoe toward shore. The sun was dipping toward the western horizon and he'd been looking for a place to camp. This place, he told himself, would do as well as any. He'd beach the canoe and look over the visitors. After that, he'd build a fire and settle for the night. He was surprised to find that he was pleased at finding the visitors. There was, he thought, something companionable about them—as if unexpectedly he had come upon some neighbors whose existence he had not suspected.

He hauled the canoe up the shelving, pebbly beach and strode into the forest, heading for the visitors. There was, he thought, one strange thing about it—not the strangeness of finding the visitors here, but the fact that there was no racket. They were not sawing down or ingesting trees. More than likely they had processed all the cellulose they needed, had budded young and now were simply taking it easy, a time for resting once their chores were done.

He burst into the clearing they had made and skidded to a surprised halt. In front of him stood a house. It was a somewhat lopsided house, leaning drunkenly to one side, as if the builder had done a poor job of it and it had come unstuck. Just beyond it stood a second house. This one stood foursquare, but there was still a certain wrongness to it. It was a moment before he could make out what the wrongness was, and then he knew—it hadn't any windows.

Beyond the houses stood the visitors, so closely ranged together that they gave the impression of a group of great buildings clustered in a city's downtown district.

Norton stood undecided and confused. No one in their right mind, he told himself, would have come into this wilderness, built two houses, then gone away and left them. Nor would any builder construct a lopsided house and another without windows. And even if the hypothetical builder had wanted, for some unfathomable reason, to do so, he would have had no reasonable way in which to transport his materials to the building site.

The pines moaned softly as the wind blew through them. On the other side of the clearing in which the houses and the visitors stood, a small, bright bird flickered for a moment against the green wall of the encircling conifers. Other than the sound of the wind in the pines and the bright flash of the bird, the place stood unmoving and silent. The stillness and the brooding somberness of the primeval forest overshadowed all, serving to blot out and soak up even the wonder of the houses and the visitors.

With an effort, Norton uprooted himself and moved toward the first of the houses, the lopsided one. The front door was open, but it took him a moment to decide to enter. It was entirely possible, he thought, that the structure might collapse once he stepped inside of it. But he finally took the chance and went into the hall, which opened into a kitchen and what appeared to be a living room. He went into the kitchen, walking softly because he was afraid of jarring the house and hastening its collapse. Despite the house's structural oddity, the kitchen seemed quite normal.

An electric stove and refrigerator stood against one wall. Starting at the stove and running around another wall were cabinets, with counter top, drawers, dish cupboards and a sink.

Norton turned a dial on the stove and held a palm above the burner. The burner heated quickly and he turned it off. At the sink, he turned a faucet and a small trickle of water ran out of the tap, then stopped. He turned the faucet further and the tap sputtered. Water finally gushed out, but again it stopped. He turned off the faucet.

He went into the living room and everything seemed all right except that the windows were set into the wall at an unusual angle. Down the hall he found three bedrooms and they seemed to be all right, although there were certain small peculiarities in the dimensions of the rooms that puzzled him. Thinking about it, he found himself unable to say exactly what was wrong.

It was with a sense of relief that he stepped out the front door and headed for the second house—the one that had no windows. There was something—something rather startling—that puzzled him about the lopsided house and he wondered what it was. Not the canted windows in the living room or the odd dimensional qualities of the bedrooms, or even the faulty faucet in the kitchen. It had been something else and it was important. Walking toward the other house and thinking about it, he suddenly knew what it was that had bothered him so deeply—the lopsided house didn't have a bathroom. He stopped short and pondered it. Could he be wrong? It was incomprehensible that someone should build a house and not put in a bathroom. Carefully he ran through an inventory of the rooms and was sure that he was right. He could not have overlooked a bathroom; if one had been there, he'd have seen it.

The front door of the second house was closed, but it opened easily and smoothly when he turned the knob. Because of the lack of windows, the interior of the house was dark, but not so dark as to interfere with vision. Swiftly he checked the rooms. There were

four bedrooms and a den, a kitchen, a living room and
dining room—and two bathrooms, one off the master
bedroom. The floor in the first house had been of
wood; here all the floors were carpeted. Drapes hung
on the walls where windows should have been. He
tried the kitchen appliances. They worked. The stove
top heated when he turned on the burners, at the sink
the water ran; when he opened the door of the refrigerator a gush of cold hit him in the face. In the
bathrooms, the taps ran normally and the toilets
flushed.

Everything seemed perfect. But why should someone
build a perfect house and then forget the windows?

Or had someone built it?

Could the visitors . . .

He gulped at the idea and suddenly went cold.

If it were the visitors, then it did make sense. No
human would have built two houses in the middle of
a wilderness. To start with, it would have been all but
impossible to do it.

But the visitors? Why would the visitors be building
houses? Or practicing the art of building houses? For
it was quite apparent that these were practice houses,
constructed by someone who was not entirely clear on
the matter of how houses should be built. The lopsided house probably had been the first one to be tried.
The house in which he stood most likely was the
second, considerably improved over the first one, but
lacking windows.

He stood, shaken, in the middle of the kitchen, still
not certain, questioning himself. The only answer, reluctant as he might be to accept it, was that the two
houses had been fabricated by the visitors. But that
left a second, even more puzzling, less easily answered
question: Why should the visitors be building houses?

He groped his way out of the kitchen and across the
living room, went into the hall and let himself out the
door.

Long shadows had crept across the clearing. The
tops of the picket fence of pines to the west cut a saw-
toothed pattern into the reddening sun. A chill was

beginning to move in and Norton shivered at the touch of it.

He ran his hand over the siding exterior of the house and it had a strange feel to it. Peering closely at it in the deepening dusk, he saw that it was not siding, not separate lengths of lumber, but that the exterior seemed to be moulded in a single piece, like a preformed plastic.

Slowly he backed away from the house. Superficially, except for the lack of windows, there was nothing wrong with it. It was an almost exact copy of the kind of house that could be found in any suburb.

He ran his gaze from the rooftop down to the basement wall—and there was no basement wall. It was a detail that had escaped him—this lack of a basement wall. The house hovered half a foot or so above the ground, suspended in the air.

Suspended, Norton told himself, as the visitors were suspended. There was no question now—no question of how the houses had come into being.

He walked around the corner of the house and there they stood, the visitors, clumped together, like a massed group of darkened buildings standing in the center plaza of some futuristic city, the lower half of them blotted out in the forest dusk, the upper half highlighted by the dying rays of a setting sun.

From their direction came another house, floating along a foot or so above the ground, the whiteness of it ghostly in the twilight. As it approached, Norton backed away, apprehensively, ready to break and run. The house came up, then stopped, as if to determine its position. Then slowly, majestically, it wheeled into line with the other houses and came to a halt, the three of them standing in a row, somewhat closer together, it was true, than would be the ordinary case, but very much like three houses sitting on a street.

Norton took a slow step toward the third house and as he did, lights came on inside of it, with the windows gleaming. Inside it he saw a table in the dining room, set with glass and china and two candlesticks, with tall tapers in them waiting to be lighted. In the living room, the screen of a TV set glimmered and across from it stood a davenport and all about the room were chairs, with a curio cabinet, filled with dainty figurines, ranged against one wall.

Startled, he moved to turn away and as he did, he caught the hint of shadows, as if someone were moving in the kitchen, as if there was someone there taking up the dinner to be brought to the waiting table.

He cried out in terror and spun about, racing toward the river and the canoe that waited there.

49. WASHINGTON, D.C.

When Porter rang the bell, Alice came to the door. She seized him by the arm, hurried him inside and closed the door behind him.

"I know," he said. "It's an ungodly hour and I haven't got much time. But I wanted to see you and I must see the senator."

"Daddy has the drinks all poured," said Alice, "and is waiting for you. He's all a-twitter as to why you should come running out to see us in the middle of the night. You must be knee-deep in matters of importance."

"A lot of motion," Porter told her. "A lot of talk. I don't know if we're getting anywhere. You've heard about the business holiday?"

"A late bulletin on TV. Daddy is all upset about it."

But the senator, when they came into the room where he was waiting for them, was not visibly upset. He was quite the genial host. He handed Porter a drink and said, "See, young man, I didn't even have to ask. I have learned your drinking preference."

"Thank you, senator," said Porter, accepting the glass. "I stand in need of that."

"Did you take time to eat tonight?" asked Alice.

He stared at her, as if astonished by the question.

"Well, did you?"

"I'm afraid that I forgot," said Porter. "It did not occur to me. The kitchen did bring up something, but, at the time, I was with the press corps. It was all gone when I got back."

"I suspected it," said Alice. "Soon as you called, I made some sandwiches and started up the coffee. I'll bring in something for you."

"Sit down, Dave," said the senator, "and say what you have in mind. Is there some way I can help the White House?"

"I think there might be," said Porter, "but it's up to you. No one will twist your arm. What you might want to do about it is a matter for your conscience to decide."

"You must have had some rough hours down there," said the senator. "I suppose it is still rough. I'm not sure I agree with the President on his financial moratorium, but I do realize there was a need of some sort of action."

"We were afraid of what the snap reaction might be," said Porter. "The holiday will give some level headed men the time they'll need to head off total panic."

"The dollar is going to take a beating on the foreign exchanges," the senator told him. "No matter what we do, it will hit near bottom. By tomorrow afternoon, it might be damn near worthless."

"We can't do anything about that," Porter said. "Give us the chance to win a round or two back home and the dollar will climb back. The real danger that we face is right here—the Congress, the press, public opinion."

"You mean to fight it out," said the senator. "I think that's the only thing you can do. Not back down. Not give ground."

"We're hanging in there," said Porter, grimly. "We are not about to say that we were wrong in the handling of the visitor situation. We'll make no apologies."

"I like that," said the senator. "Much as I may disapprove of some of the things that have been going on down there, I do like this show of strength. The way things are tonight, we need strength at the core of government."

Alice brought in a plate of sandwiches and a cup of coffee, set them on a table beside Porter's chair.

"You go ahead and eat," she said. "Don't even try to talk. Daddy and I will do the talking. We are full of talk."

"Especially my daughter," said the senator. "She is fairly bursting with it. To her this business is not, as it may be to the rest of us, a great calamity. She sees it as a chance at a new beginning. I don't think I need to say I am not in agreement with her."

"You are wrong," she told her father. "And you," she said to Porter, "probably think the same as he. The both of you are wrong. This may be the best thing that ever happened to us. It may shake us up. It may shake some sense into our national consciousness. Shake us loose of the technological syndrome that has ruled our lives for the past hundred years or so. Show us that our economic system is too sensitive and shaky, built on a foundation that basically is treacherous. It may demonstrate to us that there are other values than the smooth operation of machines . . ."

"And if it did turn us around," the senator interrupted, "if we are freed from what you like to call the tyranny of technology, if you had a chance for a new beginning, what would you do with it?"

"We'd end the rat race," she said. "The social and economic rat race. We'd work together for mutual goals. We'd bring an end to the intensely personal competition that is killing us. Without the opportunities for the personal advancement that our technology and the economic system on which it is based encourages, there'd be slight incentive to cut the throat of another person to advance ourselves. That is what the President is doing, although he may not know he's doing it, by calling for the holiday for business. He'll give the business world and the public a breathing spell to grope their way back to sanity. Just a little way back to sanity. If they could have a longer time . . ."

"Let's not you and I argue about it now," said the senator. "At some later time, I will discuss it with you."

"With all your pompous smugness," said Alice. "With your ingrained conviction . . ."

"Dave must get back," said the senator. "He's needed at the White House. He has something weighing on his mind."

"I'm sorry, dear," she said to Porter. "I should not have intruded. Can I listen to what you have to say to the senator?"

"You never intrude," said Porter, finishing his second sandwich. "And, yes, I wish you would listen to what I have to say. Don't hate me too much for it. I might as well be frank. The White House wants to use the senator."

"I don't like the sound of it," said the senator. "I dislike being used, although I suppose it is a part of politics—to use and to be used. What is it, specifically?"

"We can survive," said Porter, "or we think we can, if we can keep the Hill off our backs for a little time. Time is all we ask. No great accomplishment. Just a few days' time."

"You have your own people up there," said the senator. "Why should you come to me? You know that it has been seldom I've played ball with you."

"Our people," said Porter, "will do what they can. But this particular piece of business would smell of dirty politics. With you handling it, it won't."

"And tell me why I should help you. I've fought you down the line on almost every piece of legislation that you have sent up. There have been times the White House has been moved to speak most harshly of me. I can't see how there can be any common interest."

"There is the interest of the nation to consider," Porter told him. "One of the outcomes of what has happened will be an increasing pressure on us to call for outside help. On the grounds that the situation is not solely national, but international, and that the rest of the world should be in there working with us. The U.N. has been screaming about this from the very start."

"Yes, I know," said the senator. "I disagree with the U.N. It's none of their damn business."

"We have too much at stake," said Porter, "to let that come about. I'd like to make an allusion to something that is confidential, top secret. Do you want to hear it?"

"I'm not sure I do. Why should you want to tell me?"

"We need a rumor started."

"I think that's despicable," said Alice.

"I wouldn't go quite as far in my reaction as does my daughter," said the senator, "but I feel somewhat the same. Although I do not in the slightest blame you personally. I take it you're not talking for yourself."

"You must know I'm not," said Porter. "Not exclusively for myself. Although I would take it kindly . . ."

"You want to feed me something so that I can leak it—a very careful leak in exactly the right places, knowing full well that I'm the one who'd know where such a leak would have maximum impact."

"That's a rather crude way of saying it," said Porter.

"Dave," said the senator, "this discussion essentially is crude."

"I have no objection to the words you use," said Porter. "I would not have you soften them. You can say no and I'll get up and leave. I'll not argue with you. On my part, there'll be no ill-will involved. I'm instructed specifically not to argue with you, not to urge you to any action. We have no pressure we can put on you. Even if we had it, it would not be used."

"Daddy," said Alice, "despicable as it all may be, he's being honest with you. He's playing dirty politics in a very forthright manner."

"We were talking a few nights ago," the senator said, "about the advantages we might glean from the visitors. I admitted to some enthusiasm over the possibilities of gravity control. I said if we could get that . . ."

Porter shook his head. "It's not that, senator. I don't want to mislead you. Nor to trap you. I've tried to be above board with you. I've confessed that we want to use you for a leak. A word from you to certain people on the Hill, just a casual word is all . . ."

"A casual word, you call it."

"That is all. To a couple of well-selected people. We won't name the people. You choose them for yourself."

"I think I know," said the senator. "You don't even need to tell me. Now, answer me one thing."

"Yes, of course," said Porter.

"Has there been a weapons test?"

"Yes, there has been. The results are classified."

"And in such a case we must hold tight control of the visitors."

"I would say so, sir."

"Well, now," said the senator, "on close examination it seems to me my conscience is quite clear. And my duty plain to see. You have told me nothing, naturally. Just a slight slip of the tongue, of which I took no notice."

"In that case," said Porter, "I shall be getting back." He said to Alice, "I thank you for the food."

"The both of you," said Alice, "are despicable."

50. THE UNITED STATES

There was talk at breakfast tables.

"Herb, I always told you. Some good, I said, would come of the visitors. I always told you that, but you didn't think so. And now they'll be giving us free cars."

"There ain't nothing free. Not in this world, there ain't nothing free. You pay, one way or another, for everything you get."

"But the paper says so."

"The paper doesn't know. That's just what the paper thinks. The piece in the paper says it might be so. I won't count on no free car until I see it standing in the driveway."

"And it doesn't need any gasoline. It doesn't even need a road. You can fly it if you want to."

"There'll be bugs in it. Just you wait and see. There's bugs in all new models. And this flying business. Just try to fly it and you'll break your neck."

"You never believe nothing. Nothing good, that is. You're just a cynic. All you believe is bad. The paper says the visitors are doing it out of gratitude."

"Just tell me, Liza, what I've ever done for a visitor. Why should they feel gratitude to me? I ain't turned a hand to help one."

"Not gratitude to you, Herb. Not to you personally. Anyone you ever helped would die of shock. No one expects you to be any help at all. They'd fall down dead if you were any help. The visitors feel grateful to all of us just because we're here, just because we live on this planet. They want to do something for us. Not just for you, but for everyone."

There was talk in the ghetto streets.

"Hey, man, you hear about them cars?"

"What cars?"

"Them cars the visitors are about to give us."

"There ain't nobody going to give us cars."

"It says so in the paper."

"Not us, man. Maybe some honkeys will get some cars. We won't get no cars. All we'll get is screwed."

"Maybe it'll be different this time. Them visitors are different kinds of folk. Maybe they won't screw us."

"Listen, man, get rid of that idea. Everybody screws us."

And in an assembly worker's home in a Detroit suburb:

"Joe, you think it's true about the cars?"

"I don't know. How should I know? It's just what the paper says. The paper could be wrong."

"But if it isn't wrong? What if it isn't wrong? What if there really will be cars?"

"Christ, Jane, how should I know?"

"You would lose your job. A lot of people would lose their jobs. Ford and Chrysler and all the other companies can't go on making cars if there are free cars being handed out."

"The visitor-cars might not be any good. Run for a while and stop and once they stop, what do you do for repairs? They're just some new-fangled idea. Maybe some new advertising gimmick. I don't think the visitors are making them. Someone else is making them and some PR jerk has cooked up this story to attract attention. Some day them PR people will carry things too far and maybe this is it."

"You can't lose your job, Joe. We can't afford to have you lose your job. There's the house payments and the car payments and the kids need winter clothes."

"Don't worry so much, Jane. There have been all these flashy foreign cars and the assembly line keeps running."

"But these aren't foreign cars, Joe. And they are free."

"There ain't nothing free," said Joe.

There was subdued panic in the banks, in the board

rooms, in the unmanned brokerage offices. In a surge of selling on foreign exchanges, the dollar dropped spectacularly. The British and French governments scheduled a hurried joint consultation. The West German government officially called for support of the United States by other nations of the world. Strange stirrings took place behind the Kremlin walls, but foreign correspondents, even the old Moscow hands, had only a confused idea of what might be going on.

On Capitol Hill, in Washington, out of a flurry of meaningless motion, some sentiment developed for the drafting of a bill that would make it illegal for citizens to accept any sort of gifts from aliens. And a rumor grew . . .

"What do you know about this report that there has been a weapons test?" Senator Knox asked Senator Davenport when the two met just outside the chamber.

"Very little," said Davenport. "I just now got wind of it."

"How it got out, I don't know," said Knox. "It's supposed to be top secret."

"There may be nothing to it," said Davenport.

"I can't believe that to be true," said Knox. "It seems to be authentic. I'm beginning to think we should back the administration on this visitor issue. No matter how we stand on other matters. If we've got something from the visitors . . ."

"I'm inclined to go along with you," said Davenport. "Seems to me we should stay hanging in there. Although, I still am not too sure how much credence to give the rumor."

"Just on the chance that it is true," said Knox, "I would favor doing what we can. In the area of national security, we can't let the country down."

On a small river in the wilds of Minnesota, Frank Norton bent to the paddle, heading for the bridge where he had parked his car.

51. WASHINGTON, D.C.

The science advisor said to Jerry Conklin, "You, Mr. Conklin, tell a fascinating story."

"I came here to tell it," said Jerry, "under protest. Had it not been for Kathy and Garrison at the *Tribune*, I would have refused to come. They persuaded me that by coming here I would be performing a public duty. So I came and now I've told what I have to tell and it's up to you. I don't give a damn if you believe it or not."

"Mr. Conklin," said the President, "no one here has indicated disbelief. For myself, at this point, I'm ready to believe almost anything."

"I'd like to point out," said Porter, "that the story is much more than fascinating. I think, Dr. Allen, that you made an extremely bad choice of words. What Mr. Conklin tells us does explain one thing—how he was able to go straight to the location where the cars were being made. No one else knew or could have told him. The old river rat knew the visitors had landed on Goose Island, but he didn't know what they were doing there. You couldn't have paid him enough to go and find out. He was scared spitless of them."

Allen said, "I did not mean to seem to doubt what he said."

"It sounded to me as if you did," said Jerry.

Whiteside rumbled at Jerry, "I would say, young man, that it took a fair amount of guts to sit down and tell us what you have. You had decided to keep quiet about it and I can understand why you did. I think I would have done the same."

"What he has told us, essentially, is that a sort of communication with the visitors is possible," said the President, "but a one-sided conversation and on the terms of the visitor. A visitor, when the necessity arises, can have some limited conversation with us, but we can't with them."

"I told 101 to tone down its communication," said Jerry, "and, apparently, it understood."

"Did you try to talk further with it?" asked the President.

"Certainly, sir. I asked it why it showed me where to go, what I would find there, why it wanted me to go."

"And it didn't answer you?"

"Not only didn't it answer; it also threw me out. But this time not as violently as was the case the first time when it heaved me out into a tree. This time it set me down, rather gently, on the ground."

"This time it apparently wanted to be sure you would be able to go where it wanted you to go."

"I would suppose so, Mr. President, but I don't think that's all of it. The first time, I was only an alien organism, along with other alien organisms, that it wanted to have a look at. The second time I was—I was about to say an old friend, and that's not it, of course. More like an acquaintance. Someone it knew. Someone it could use."

"Possibly one that it could use again."

"I'm not sure about that. I can tell you this; I'm not going to hunt down 101 again."

"If we asked you to?"

"What the hell would be the use of it?" asked Whiteside. "He has told us what the score is. We don't ask it; it tells us. As it stands, there'd be no possibility of establishing conversation. It talks to us, if you can call it talking, but we don't talk to it."

"There have been stories," said the President, "of other people being taken up."

"I think you can discount those stories," said Allen. "For years, people have been telling about being taken up by the UFOs. So far as can be determined, it has largely been cult stuff, all of it self-serving. What these people claim the UFOs have told them is so unimaginative, such fuzzy thinking and patently such human thinking that, instinctively, you know it's a fabricated human story. If you really communicated with an alien, the result would not come out uniquely human. The concepts of such a conversation probably would be mind-boggling, which perhaps is an understatement. A large part of what one heard would not be understood."

"So you think all the taken-up tales now are either cult imagining or downright lies?" asked Porter.

"Certainly," Allen told him. "I'm convinced that Mr. Conklin is the only one who has been taken up. What he tells us fits the pattern of alien communication." He said to Jerry, "There were no words. I think you said there were no words."

"That's right," said Jerry. "Only pictures in my mind. At times, thoughts in my mind, but I couldn't tell if they were my thoughts or were something else."

"Well, let's say you went back to 101 again. You say you won't and I don't suppose you will. But let us say you did. Do you think it would take you up again?"

"Only if it had something that it wanted to tell me," Jerry said. "Only if there were a chore it wanted me to do."

"You're convinced of that?"

"Utterly convinced. I feel very keenly that it used me."

"And, yet, Miss Foster tells us of the handshake she got from 101."

"It was more than a handshake," said Kathy. "More personal than a handshake. A kiss, perhaps. I didn't realize what it was at the time. I thought, first a handshake, for that was the easiest way to characterize it. A handshake of gratitude, of thanks, of recognition maybe. To let me know that it knew I existed and was there. But now I know it was more than that. It was, I am sure, a sign of real affection. I think that impression is re-enforced by their making of the cars. They're not just showing off. Not trying to awe us or impress us. Not threatening us with a demonstration of what they can do. Not even paying us for letting them eat our trees. It's a show of deep affection for us. Maybe like Santa Claus. Maybe like giving a special friend a birthday gift. Like a young man buying roses for his girl."

"You make a good case for them," said the President. "And yet, if this keeps on, it will ruin us."

"Let's say, Mr. President, that a fond parent buys candy for her child," said Kathy, "not knowing, never having been told, what candy may do to a child's teeth. It's the same with the visitors. It's not knowing, that is all. They're only trying to be nice, not aware of what their niceness does to us."

"Miss, that may all be true," said Whiteside, "but they got me scared. I still think that a few well-placed . . ."

"Henry," the President said, sharply, "not now. Later, if you insist on talking about it, but not now."

"Let's get back to this business of taking up," said Allen. "To talk with someone, it appears, they have to take a person up. Mr. Conklin, can you think of any way they might be persuaded to take up—say, myself, or the President?"

"They wouldn't take you up," said Jerry. "They simply would ignore you. No matter what you did, they'd pay no attention to you."

"I would think that you are right," said Allen. "They're good at doing that. They've ignored us ever since they came. I have found myself wondering just how they perceive us. I've rather thought at times that they might see us as charming pets or as pitiful forms of life they must be careful not to step on. But, actually, I sense it's neither one of these. Miss Foster seems to think they have affection for us. After all, we allowed them to land on the planet where there was cellulose to save them from racial extinction. The cellulose allowed them to have young and if there had been no young, I would suppose the race finally would have died. If we give them human emotions, which I doubt they have, they then would feel gratitude. With all due respect to Miss Foster's viewpoint, I can't feel they're all that thankful. The point is that there is no way we can stop them from chopping down our trees. I am inclined to believe they have, rather than gratitude, an irrepressible business ethic, although they would not think of it as that. I know I phrase this clumsily. I think they are obsessed with making full and honest payment for anything they take. I think that's what they are doing."

"To sum up," said the President, "there does seem to be an outside chance that given time, we might be able to talk with our visitors. But it will take time, apparently, an awful lot of time, and more patience than we have. The one thing we haven't got is time. Would the others of you say that is a fair assessment?"

"I subscribe to it," said Whiteside. "That's the whole thing, all wrapped up, and we haven't got the time. Our time is all run out."

"We can weather it," said the President, as if he might be talking to himself. "We've got to weather it. If nothing else happens, if it's no more than the cars, we can muddle through. I have had some encouraging phone calls from leaders in the business world and the Congress seems more inclined to go along with us than I had thought they would." He said to Porter, "I take it, from what I hear, that you talked with Davenport."

"Yes, I did," said Porter. "A friendly interchange."

"Well, then," said the President, "I think this does it. Unless," he said, looking at Kathy and Jerry, "you have something else to add."

They shook their heads.

"Nothing, Mr. President," said Jerry.

"We thank you for coming to see us," the President told them. "You have done us a very useful service. Now we can see more clearly the problems that we face. You may rest assured that nothing you have told us will go beyond this room."

"I'm grateful to you for that," said Jerry.

"The plane is waiting for you," said the President.

"We'll drive you to the field any time you wish. Should you wish to remain in Washington, however, for a day or two . . ."

"Mr. President," said Kathy, "we must be getting back. I have my job and Jerry has his thesis."

52. MINNEAPOLIS

"This place feels like a wake," said Gold. "We're hip deep in news of great significance. The whole damn world going down the drain. The dollar almost worthless. Foreign governments howling doom. All the diplomats tight-lipped. The business community whitefaced. The kind of stuff we thrive on. Yet where is all the joy of a newsroom bristling with news, where all the jubilation?"

"Oh, shut up," said Garrison.

"The White House expresses confidence," said Gold. "Says we will see it through. There's a prime example of whistling down a dark and lonely street."

Garrison said to Annie, "You have any idea when Kathy and Jerry will be getting in?"

"In another couple of hours," she told him. "They're probably taking off right now. But Kathy will have nothing for us. She told me when she called there'd not be any story."

"I expected that," said Garrison. "I had hoped, of course . . ."

"You're a blood sucker," Gold told him. "You suck your people dry. Not a drop left in them."

"It's not working out the way it should," said Annie.

"What's not working out?" asked Garrison.

"This business with the visitors. It's not the way it is in pictures."

"By pictures, I suppose you mean the movies."

"Yes. In them it works out right, but just in the nick of time. When everyone's given up every hope and there seems no chance at all. Do you suppose that now, just in the nick of time . . ."

"Don't count on it," said Gold.

"Look," said Garrison, "this is the real thing. This is really happening. This is no fantasy dreamed up by some jerk producer who knows, in his secret, stupid heart that happiness is holy."

"But if they'd just talk to us," said Annie.

"If they'd just go away," said Gold.

The phone rang.

Annie picked it up, listened for a moment and then took it down and looked at Garrison.

"It's Lone Pine," she said. "Mr. Norton. On line three. He sounds funny. There's something wrong up there."

Garrison grabbed his phone off the cradle. "Frank," he said, "is there something wrong? What is going on?"

Norton's words came tumbling along the line. "Johnny, I just got back from my trip. I looked at the papers on my desk. Can it be true? About the cars . . ."

"I'm afraid it is," said Garrison. "Take it easy, Frank. What has you so upset?"

"Johnny, it's not only cars."

"Not only cars? What do you mean, not only cars?"

"They're making houses, too. Trying to make houses. Practicing at making houses."

"You mean houses people could live in?"

"That's right. Like the kind of house you live in. The kind of houses a lot of people live in."

"Where are they doing this?"

"Up in the wilderness. Hid out in the wilderness. Practicing where they thought no one would see them."

"Take a deep breath, Frank, and tell me. Start at the beginning and tell me what you saw."

"Well," said Norton, "I was canoeing up the river . . ."

Garrison listened intently. Gold sat motionless, watching him closely. Annie picked a file out of a desk drawer and began buffing her nails.

"Just a minute, Frank," Garrison said, finally. "This is too good a story, too personal a story for someone else to write. What I'd like you to do is write it for us. From the personal angle, just as you told it to me. First person all the way. I saw this, I did that, I thought something else. Can you do it? Would you do it? How about your own paper?"

"My own paper won't be out for another three days," said Norton. "Hell, I may even skip a week. Gone like I've been, I have little advertising. I have a couple cans of beans stashed on the shelf. Even if I skip a week I still can eat . . ."

"Sit down, then," said Garrison, "and start writing it. Three or four columns. More if you think you need it. When you're done, pick up the phone and ask for the city desk. Dictate the story. We have people who can take it down almost as fast as you can read it. And, Frank . . ."

"Yes?"

"Frank, don't spare the horses. Spread your wings."

"But, Johnny, I didn't tell you everything. I was just getting to it. In that last house, the one that was lighted up and had furniture . . ."

"Yes, what about it?"

"The house had just floated in. The visitors had just finished making it. But when I looked at it, I saw shadows in the kitchen. Moving shadows. The kind of shadows someone would make as they moved about the kitchen, taking up the dinner. I swear—I tell you, Johnny, there were people in that kitchen! For the love of Christ, are they making people, too?"

53. DE SOTO, WISCONSIN

The South Dakotan who had nursed his dilapidated car for more than five hundred miles, the machine rattling and banging, coughing and gasping, every wheeze threatening to be its last, pulled into the small town of De Soto, a wide place in the road hemmed in between bluff and river. He tried to find a place to park, but there was no place left in the town to park. The one long street was jammed with cars and people, and there seemed to be much angry shouting and running about, and the frightening, sobering thought crossed his mind that possibly all the people here had also come for cars.

Finally, he was able to pull his car over to the side of an indifferent gravel road that ran eastward up a coulee out of town. Many other cars had been pulled off the same road. He did not find a place to park until he was a good half-mile beyond the last house in the village. He got out of the car and stretched in an attempt to ease his aching muscles. Not only did his muscles ache; he was tired to the very bone, almost to exhaustion. He was tired and hungry and he needed sleep and food, but not until he got his car. Once he got his car, he could take the time to sleep and eat.

Just how to go about getting a car he had no idea. All he knew was that there was an island across the river from this town and that the cars were on the island. Perhaps, he thought again, he should have driven to Dick's Landing in Iowa, but the map had shown what looked to be small secondary roads leading to the landing. He had decided that he could make better time if he drove to this Wisconsin town that lay opposite Dick's Landing. Somehow, he knew, he had to get across the river to reach the island. Perhaps he could rent a boat. He wondered how much the renting of a boat might cost and hoped it would not be too exorbitant. He was carrying little cash. Maybe, he thought, he could swim the river, although he was not too certain that he could. He was a fairly decent swimmer, but from what he had seen of the river on his long drive down the valley, the Mississippi was wide and the current was strong.

He plodded down the road, skirting potholes, the loose gravel sliding underneath his feet. Ahead of him, several men were walking down the road, but he made no attempt to catch up with them, for now that he was here, he found himself surprisingly abashed. Maybe he shouldn't have come, but, at the time, the idea had seemed simple and flawless. God knows, he needed a car and here was a way to get one. Not for a moment had it occurred to him that others would come up with the same idea. He could not know, of course, but he suspected that the others in the town had come on the self-same errand. There was one consolation, however: There should be plenty of cars to go around. The story he had heard on TV said that at the time the visitors on the island had been found, they had made more than a hundred cars. It was reasonable to suppose that since the report, they had kept on making them, so there would be more than the hundred now. Maybe a couple of hundred. Maybe more than that. There were a lot of people in town, but surely with more than two hundred cars sitting there and waiting, there'd be plenty to go around. The big problem would be to find how to cross the river, but he'd deal with that when the time came.

He came to the outskirts of the village and continued trudging toward the business district, which fronted on the river. Perhaps there, he could find someone who would tell him what to do. By this time, some sort of procedure might have been worked out for picking up a car.

A knot of people stood on the sidewalk in front of a

bar and he drifted over to them. Three highway patrol cars were standing across the street, but there was no sign of the troopers who had been in them. A line of men were standing on the far side of the railroad track that arrowed between the town and river. All their backs were turned toward the town, as if they were watching something on the river.

The South Dakota man plucked apologetically at the sleeve of a man standing on the sidewalk. "Has there been an accident?" he asked, motioning at the patrol cars.

"There ain't been no accident," said the man. "One earlier in the day, but not within the last few hours."

"Well, what are the troopers doing here?"

"You must have just pulled in," said the man.

"That's right. Drove all the way from South Dakota. Rapid City—well, not really Rapid City, but a little town just east of Rapid City. Made it all in one run; only stopped for gas."

"Sounds like you were in a hurry."

"Well, you see, I wanted to get here before all the cars were gone."

"There ain't none of them gone," said the man. "They're all over on the island."

"So I'm still in time."

"Still in time for what?"

"Still in time to pick up a car."

"You ain't going to pick up no car. There ain't no one going to pick up a car. State troopers, they got the river sealed off. Some word has it they may be sending in the guard. They're out in boats patrolling on the river so no traffic can come up or down the stream."

"But why? The TV said . . ."

"We all know what the TV said. And the papers, too. Free cars for everyone. But you can't get across the river to the island."

"That the island over there?"

"Somewhere over there. I don't know just where. There are a lot of islands over there."

"But what happened? Why did the troopers . . ."

"Bunch of damn fools piled into a boat. More of them than the boat would carry, but they kept on piling in. The boat swamped out in midstream. Most of the damn fools drowned."

"But someone could set up some kind of system, some safe way to get across and . . ."

"Sure, they could," said the other man, "but no matter what you did, it wouldn't work. No one here has got a lick of sense. Everyone has got his heart set on one of the cars. The police are right. They can't let no one near the river. If they did, more people would get killed."

"But don't you want a car?"

"Sure, I want a car. But there's no chance to get one now. Maybe, later on . . ."

"But I have to have a car right now," said the man from South Dakota. "I just got to have one. I don't think that heap of mine will last to get me home."

He ran across the street and up the embankment to the railroad track. He reached the line of men who stood on the far edge of the track, pushing his way through them, shoving them aside. One foot hit the downslope of the embankment. Skidding on sliding gravel, he lost his balance. He fell and rolled down the slope, stopping just short of the water's edge. Lying there, he saw a huge man in uniform towering over him.

The trooper asked, almost gently, "Where do you think you're going, son?"

"I got to have a car," said the man from South Dakota.

The officer shook his head.

"I can swim," said the South Dakotan. "I can swim it easy. Let me have a chance. Let me take a chance."

The officer reached down a hand, jerked him to his feet.

"Now, you listen to me," he said. "I'm giving you a break. Get your tail up over that track. If I so much as catch sight of you again, I'll toss you in the cage."

The South Dakotan hastily clambered up the embankment. The crowd jeered kindly at him.

54. MINNEAPOLIS

"How sure can we be of Norton?" Lathrop asked. "He's not one of our staff."

"I'd stake my reputation on him," said Garrison. "Frank and I go a long ways back. We went to school together, have been in touch ever since. He's a dedicated newspaperman. Just because he chose to hide away up at Lone Pine doesn't make him any less a newspaperman. We act as if we were specialists here—some of us write the news, others edit it, still others make up the pages, and there are a few who write editorials. Each one to his own task. Frank does the whole damn thing. He starts each week with nothing and he pulls the news and advertising together, he edits what he writes, he makes up the paper. If there is need for an editorial any particular week, he writes the editorial and not only that . . ."

"No need to go on, Johnny," Lathrop told him. "I just wanted to know how you felt about it."

"If Frank tells me he saw evidence the visitors are making houses," said Garrison, "then I'll believe they're making houses. His story hangs together, he had a lot of detail."

"It seems incredible to me," said Lathrop, "that we have this one exclusive. That makes two in a row. We had the cars and now we have the houses."

"There's something I want to talk with you about," said Garrison. "I think we should let the White House in on it before we go to press. I've talked to the press secretary there. He seems a decent man. I can get through to him."

"You mean you want to tip them off," said Lathrop,

somewhat horrified. "Tell them about the houses. Why, Johnny? Just why in hell . . ."

"My thinking may be wrong," said Garrison, "but it seems to me the administration is absorbing a lot of punishment and . . ."

"It's good for them," said Lathrop. "The bastards have it coming. Not on this visitor matter—they've done fairly well on it. But they've been willfully wrong and pig-headed on most other things. A good dose of humility won't do them any harm. I can't seem to summon up much sympathy."

Garrison was silent for a moment, considering, trying to put his thoughts together.

"It's not the administration so much," he finally said, "as it is the nation. The White House is being stiff-necked about it; they're determined to ride the crisis out. Maybe they can do it. Maybe they had a chance of doing it before the houses came up. But the houses will wreck them. The cars are bad enough, the houses . . ."

"Yes, I can see that," said Lathrop. "The implication is there. Houses as well as cars. First the automotive business, now the housing industry. The dollar will be worthless. Our credit will be gone. But still we have to run the story. Even if we wanted to, and we don't, it's something that can't be covered up."

"There's no question about publishing," said Garrison. "We have to do that. The question is: Do we give our own government a chance to react to it before we let them have it straight between the eyes? Maybe, if they knew, they would have the time to shift their stance, stand on more solid ground to deal with it when it broke."

"The whole idea," said Lathrop, "is that we should go international on it. I'm not sure that's the right thing to do. After all, we have taken the brunt of this alien invasion. If there are to be any benefits or advantages because of it, they should go to us. The visitors chose us; we didn't invite them in, we didn't lure them in. Why they chose us, I don't know. I don't know why they didn't land in Europe or in Africa. But the U.N. has been yelling ever since it happened . . ."

"I don't know about that, either," said Garrison. "It would gall me to see it go international, but international or not, however we may go, I think the administration should be given a few hours to reconsider on the basis of new developments. They'll handle it better if they have some advance warning. They may elect to stand pat, tough it out. I don't know. You and I don't have to decide that. Our problem is a different one. We talk about our responsibility in dealing with the news. We think of ourselves as a public service institution. We do nothing willingly to harm or debase our cultural system. We talk a lot about digging out the truth and reporting the truth and that's an easy one in those cases where we can determine truth. But there is something else that goes beyond mere truth. And that's the power we hold. We have to use that power as wisely as we can. If we keep this bottled up for the sake of another scoop . . ."

"Dammit, Johnny, I want another scoop," said Lathrop. "I love them. You can't get too many for me. I roll in them with great delight. How can we be sure the White House wouldn't leak it? There's no such thing as a secret in Washington unless someone has slapped a confidential stamp on it."

"They would be unlikely to leak it," said Garrison. "They'd want to keep it quiet until they could figure out what to do, what action they should take. As soon as it is known, there'll be hell let loose. They'll need all the time we can give them. They'll be no more anxious to leak it than we are."

"Well, I don't know," said Lathrop. "About letting Washington in on it, I don't really know. Let me think about it, talk with the publisher."

55. ABOARD PLANE APPROACHING MINNEAPOLIS

"Everyone is determined to make them ogres," Kathy said to Jerry. "Nasty little ogres that came down out of the sky to do mischief to us. But I know they aren't. I touched 101—I don't mean touched just her hide, but the inside of her, the living spirit of her. It wasn't just a touch; it was a contact. And when I told the President about this, he was interested—most interesting, he said. But he wasn't interested, nor were any of the others. All they can think of is their precious economy. Sure, they want to know if there is some way they can talk with the visitors. But the only reason they want to talk to them is to tell them to stop what they are doing."

"You have to understand the President's position," Jerry told her. "You have to realize what the administration is facing . . ."

"Has it ever occurred to you, or to anyone," she asked, "that the President could be wrong, that all of us are wrong. That the way we live is wrong and has been wrong for a long, long time."

"Well, certainly," said Jerry. "All of us, everyone. We all make mistakes."

"I don't mean that," said Kathy. "It's not being wrong right now, but wrong from a long way back. Maybe if we could go back far enough in time, we might be able to pinpoint where we started going wrong. I don't know enough history to even guess where that particular time of going wrong might be, but somewhere along the time track, we took the wrong turning, started going down the wrong road and there was no way of going back.

"Just a few weeks ago, I interviewed a bunch of crazy kids at the university, real far-out freaks who called themselves Lovers. They told me love was everything, the be-all and the end-all, that there was nothing else that counted. They looked at me out of wide, round, innocent eyes with their naked souls shining through their eyes and I felt sick inside. I felt as naked as their souls were naked. I felt pity for them and was enraged at them, both at the same time. I went back and wrote the story and I felt sicker and sicker all the time I was writing it, for they were wrong, disturbingly wrong. They were far off the beaten track, so far out there was a sense that they were forever lost. But, maybe, they are no more wrong than we are. The thing is that we've gotten so accustomed to our wrongness that we think it's right. All-love may be wrong, but so is all-money, all-greed wrong. I tell you, Jerry . . ."

"You think the visitors may be trying to kick us back on the right track?"

"No, I guess not. No, I never really thought that. They wouldn't know what is wrong with us. Maybe if they did know, they wouldn't care; maybe they'd think it was our business to be wrong. They themselves may be wrong in what they are doing. Most likely they are. But what they are doing, wrong or right, may be showing up our wrongness."

"I think," said Jerry, "that, in any case, under any circumstance, it might be impossible to say what is wrong and what is right. We and the visitors are far separated. They came from God knows where. Their standard of behavior—and surely they must have such a standard—would be different from ours. When two cultures with differing standards collide head-on, one of them, or perhaps the both of them, will get roughed up. With the best intentions on both their parts, there will be some roughing up."

"Poor things," said Kathy. "They came so far. They

faced so much. They dared so greatly. We should be friends of theirs but we'll end up hating them."

"I don't know about that," said Jerry. "Maybe some people. The men in power, in any sort of power, will hate them, for they'll take away the power. But with the new cars, and perhaps other things, the people, the great faceless mass of people, will be dancing in the streets for them."

"But not for long," said Kathy. "They'll finally hate them, too."

56. WASHINGTON, D.C.

"With this new information," said Marcus White, Secretary of State, "I think it might be time to realign our thinking."

John Hammond, White House chief of staff, asked Porter, "Just how solid is this information? Should we check further on it?"

"I would think we might be checking on it," said Porter.

The President stirred uneasily in his chair. "Dave is right," he said. "We are checking on it. We have men in Lone Pine. Norton will guide them in. The National Guard is flying in a helicopter to take the party in. Everything is being kept under cover. The guard doesn't even know why the copter's going in. We'll soon know if the information's right."

"I think you can count on it being right," said Porter. "I've had some previous contact with Garrison at Minneapolis. He's a solid citizen. Remember, the man didn't have to tip us off. He had an exclusive story; he could have stayed sitting on it."

"Then why didn't he stay sitting on it?" demanded General Whiteside.

"He was giving us a break. Said he felt it was only right that we should have some warning, thought we'd probably need some time to get our feet planted under us before he went to press."

"He pledged you to secrecy?" asked Whiteside.

"Not in so many words. He said he assumed we would protect him. I told him that we would. And I assume we will. It's in our interest as well as his. Once this thing breaks, we had better have some idea of what we should be saying and doing. We need the time he gave us."

"I don't like it," said Whiteside. "I don't like it one damn bit."

"You don't have to like it, Henry," said the President. "None of the rest of us likes it, either."

"That's not what I meant," said Whiteside.

"I know it isn't what you meant," said the President. "I was putting a charitable interpretation on what you said."

Allen, the science advisor, spoke up. "It is my opinion that we have to accept the Lone Pine report as true. It may seem, on the surface, somewhat far-fetched, but when you consider it, it's not. If the visitors can make cars, it seems entirely reasonable they also can make houses. A more difficult job, of course, but only in degree. I, personally, would say they are equal to it."

"But houses!" said Whiteside. "Cars are one thing; houses are another. They can distribute the cars, but how will they go about distributing houses? By setting up new housing tracts, perhaps, taking over valuable farm lands or industrial sites for the tracts? Or knocking down rows of substandard housing and placing the new houses in their stead?"

"It doesn't make a hell of a lot of difference how they go about it," Hammond said. "No matter what they do, whether they do anything or not, the threat is there. So far as this country is concerned, the housing industry is wiped out."

"I had said," the President told them, "that we could weather the elimination of the automotive industry. I don't know about this other. The thing about it is that it plants an over-riding fear, a cancer in the economic picture. If the auto industry and the housing industry are gone, is there anything that's safe?"

"How is the car situation going out on the Mississippi?" Hammond asked.

"It's ugly," Porter told him. "We have Goose Island cordoned off, but the crowds are building. Sooner or later, there is going to be an incident of some sort.

There are a dozen or more people dead that we know of. A boat swamped and went down when car-seekers overloaded it. There'll be more of it, I'm sure. You can't keep people from getting their hands on free cars. The greedy bastards are going to make a lot of trouble."

"That is a single situation," White pointed out. "We can't waste time on it. What we have to do is work out a policy. When the news breaks, we have to have at least the beginning of a policy. We have to give the nation and the world some indication of what we intend to do about it."

"It's going to go down hard," said the President. "Whatever we do, it will be hard to take. From our first beginnings, we have been a proud people. Standing on our own feet. It's not in us to cave in."

"Some damn fool," said Whiteside, "started a rumor on the Hill that there had been a weapons test and we're onto something. It won't take long for Ivan to pick that up. Get him upset enough and one touch of a button . . ."

"That rumor," said the President, "wherever it might have come from, has served to keep the Congress solidly behind us. If it hadn't been for the rumor, no one knows what they might have done."

"That is all behind us," urged White. "We should forget it now. What's done can't be helped. We have to live with it. As I've told you from the start, we can't work it out alone. If we act in a reasonable manner, we will have the rest of the world behind us. We've not gone so far that we've lost good will."

"Even Russia?" asked the President.

"I don't know what they'll do to help. Probably more than we would expect. But if we react reasonably, they'll keep their fiingers off the buttons Henry talks about."

"And what else? Just what do you have in mind? What do you see?"

"I am convinced we have to agree, in principle, that the visitors constitute an international problem, that we must consult with other states considering the situation that has been created here. I think that most of the major states realize that no one nation, us or any-one else, could contain such a situation, that eventually, it will spill over national boundaries, any national boundaries, and that it will become a world problem. I think the time has come to invite help and coopera-tion from the rest of the world, from anyone who might be willing to help and cooperate."

"Marcus, you have talked with some of these people?"

"Informally, yes. Unofficially. Mostly, they have done the talking and I have done the listening. Those I have talked with are convinced that whatever hap-pens to us now will happen to them later unless the problem, or problems, can be solved."

"What sort of cooperation can you detect? We have to know. If we go international, we have to know where we stand, what we can expect."

"France and Britain are ready to come in—in any way they can be of assistance. Do what they can to bolster the dollar, do whatever they can. Japan has the same willingness. The Scandinavians are waiting only for a word from us. The West Germans stand ready, if necessary, with monetary aid."

"You mean foreign aid? For us!"

"That's exactly what I mean," said White. "Why flinch away from it? We've carried half the world on our back for years. We rebuilt Western Europe after World War II. It would be no more than turn and turn about. It's their ass as well as ours and they know it. The rest of the world can't afford to let us collapse. Even the OPEC people would rally around."

The President looked around the table with a stricken face. "Oh, my God!" he said.

"It's not only the matter of keeping us from going under," said the Secretary of State. "It's a matter of working out a new system—a new political pattern, a new financial concept, perhaps a rehauling of the entire economic structure. Not for the United States alone, but for the world. The visitors not only have come close to ruining us, but they have changed the situation for the entire world and we have to find a way to live with it. Nothing will ever be the same again. I think the first job, and perhaps the hardest, will be to honestly analyze what has happened. We have to know that before we can assess its impact."

"You're very eloquent on the subject, Marcus," said Hammond. "Do the other nations, the men you have talked with so informally and so unofficially, recognize all the factors that you have outlined for us?"

"I would say they do," said State. "At least, their thinking runs in that direction."

"But the tests," cried Whiteside. "We are onto something. Do we have to give up everything? Can't we, somehow, hold back on what we found?"

The President said, quietly, "I don't think we can, Henry. You have heard what the man said—a new kind of world and a new way to live in it. It comes hard for old battle-scarred dogs such as you and I, but I can glimpse some of the logic in it. I suppose that some of us, maybe the most of us, have been thinking something like this all along, but couldn't bring ourselves to say so."

"How the hell we'll ever work it out," said Hammond, "I don't know."

"Not us alone," said State. "The world. It's not up to us alone; it's up to all the others. If the world doesn't pull together on this one, all of us are sunk."

57. MINNEAPOLIS

Gold was reading copy on the Norton story. He lifted his head and looked across the desk at Garrison.

"This last paragraph," he said.

"What about the last paragraph?"

"Where he tells about seeing shadows in the kitchen, as if there were people in the kitchen. And he thinks, 'My God, are they making people, too?'"

"There's nothing wrong with it. It's a honey of a line. It makes cold shivers up your spine."

"Did you tell Lathrop about this? Mention it particularly to him?"

"No, I guess I didn't. I forgot. There were a lot of other . . ."

"And Porter?"

"No, I didn't tell Porter. It would have scared the pants off him."

"It could have been Norton's imagination. He didn't see any people. All he saw, or thought he saw, were shadows. Maybe he imagined shadows."

"Let me see it," said Garrison, holding out his hand. Gold handed him the sheet.

Garrison read the paragraph carefully, read it through again. Then he picked up a heavy, black editorial pencil and methodically crossed out the paragraph.

ABOUT THE AUTHOR

Clifford D. Simak is a newspaperman, only recently retired. Over the years he has written more than 25 books and some 200 short stories. In 1977 he received the Nebula Grand Master award of the Science Fiction Writers of America and has won several other awards for his writing.

Perhaps the best known of his works is *City*, which has become a science-fiction classic.

He was born and raised in southwestern Wisconsin, a land of wooded hills and deep ravines, and often uses this locale for his stories. A number of critics have cited him as the pastoralist of science fiction.

He and his wife Kay have been happily married for almost 50 years. They have two children—a daughter, Shelley Ellen, a magazine editor, and Richard Scott, a chemical engineer.